A Brother's Touch

A Brother's Touch

Owen Levy

AN AUTHORS GUILD BACKINPRINT.COM EDITION

A Brother's Touch

AN AUTHORS GUILD BACKINPRINT.COM EDITION

Published by iUniverse, Inc.

For information address:
iUniverse, Inc.
5220 S. 16th St., Suite 200
Lincoln, NE 68512
www.iuniverse.com

Originally published by Pinnacle Books

A Brother's Touch was originally published in 1982 by Pinnacle Books New York. Patrick O'Connor was the
acquiring editor and Karen Meehan provided copyediting services.

Special thanks to Owen Dodson and Janet Reed, both since deceased, who contributed to making the first
edition possible.

Cover Image: Fredrik Broden

20th Anniversary printing: June 2002

ISBN: 0-595-22674-4

Printed in the United States of America

Dedicated to the memory of
Timothy Quinn
Artist and Poet
1952–1975

And
to all the friends and colleagues
who did not survive the dark years of crisis
that followed.

The voice of my brother's blood crieth unto me from the ground.
GENESIS 4:10

It seemed that from all over the country the homosexuals had come to New York as to a center; a new Sodom; for here, among the millions, they could be unnoticed by the enemy and yet known to one another.
THE CITY AND THE PILLAR, Gore Vidal (1948)

A

BROTHER'S
TOUCH

CHICKEN'S DIARY

saturday. last night i made more money than i ever did before. 235 bucks! got two 50s right off. then some guy gave me 100 for the night but he changed his mind cause he told me to beat it after about an hour.

sunday. got myself a room in a house on 55th street. the rent lady says long as i pay on time she won't hassle me. i got a window that looks out over some nice back yards. the bath down the hall is a drag. i share it with some old guy who lives in the front. he looks pretty out of it to me. there's a bed and a table and a hot plate on the fridge. sure beats a bench in the port authority.

monday. panda sent one of the boys from the loft out on the street to find me. i told him to tell panda i wasn't coming back until i was ready. the hell with all those plastic people hanging out and chit chatting. chitchatchitchatchitchat-shitshat. and he must take a million pictures. snapsnapsnapsnapcrap!

wednesday. this john wanted to buy my pants. said he'd give me 10 bucks for them. i thought he was putting me on but the dude was serious. now why in the hell did he want my dirty torn-up blue jeans. guess he was going to smell them or wear them himself. he really wanted them bad. he offered me 20. i told him if i had another pair handy i'd sure let him buy them. he offered to drive me to his house in queens to pick up a pair of his to trade. he seemed real disappointed when i told him we'd have to do it some other time.

friday. the night was almost a complete bummer till i bumped into this dude snicker i see around once in awhile. he's always got a snort of something good. we went back to his place and got off. he says he can get more. enough so we can deal some. pretty good cat. never tries to come on like some of the others. plays it nice and cool. he told me his father used to hit on him all the time when he was a kid. weird.

sunday. called ma she was about the same. wish pa wasn't uptight all the time. he started yelling cause i called collect. ma was crying. she said she wasn't but i could tell. what a bummer.

monday. boy am i glad i found this old notebook. writing things down is going to help me keep track. otherwise the days just pass and i don't know where the hell they go.

wednesday. snicker came around. we did up all our bread on some dynamite dope and now i can't pay the rent. out on the street again. hung out in the port authority most of the night. then he took me around to this storefront in the village where the gays hang out. the dudes around there are all right. there's one real nice older guy. some of the others hassle me about marching with them but i'm keeping cool. any way we can stay at the storefront all day. its warm and there's coffee and we all chipped in to get some pizza and ice cream.

saturday. this old super that snicker knows is letting us sleep at his place. he's got this really great cat that likes to sleep up between my legs.

sunday. snicker and i were both on the street last night. he scored with one john and i turned three. that gave us enough for a hotel room and some dope. turns out snicker used to be one of cookie's boys too. what a laugh.

tuesday. snicker's in the hospital with hepatitis. the doctor checked me out and i'm okay. he gave me a shot of something. just to be on the safe side. boy I'd sure hate to be laid up in a hospital. poor snicker. he's not too happy.

thursday. spent the whole day in the museum on fifth avenue. never thought there were so many different artists. and painting's sure not easy. one covered a whole wall. there must've been a hundred people in it. and some of the statues were so real i thought they were people just covered with plaster. some kid shared his lunch with me in the park. i was going to walk through the zoo but it was too late.

tuesday. snicker' s out of the hospital. he says they released him but i think he just split when nobody was looking. marlowe's letting him sleep back by the furnace cause he thinks snicker's going to give him hep. but the old man's sure is nice to me. lets me drink all the beer i want.

saturday. i went out wednesday to try and make some money but ended up walking in this park uptown. this guy in a long black cape starts talking to me and he turns out to be a bishop. he lives in a real mansion with a big garden and servants. i thought it was some kind of a dream like when i was a kid and i wanted to be rich. anyway i hung out for a couple of days and he really got off dressing me up in his fancy robes and parading up and down the stairs. but it was starting to get too heavy for me. i had to split. he gave me a gold ring. i wonder how much its worth.

sunday. I ran into silkie on the street this morning and he sure did bring back memories. haven't seen him since san francisco when we lived in that commune on divisadero. what a freak! said he got busted for shoplifting and was in the city trying to hook up with people looking for good pot cause he had a big connection on the coast and he figured he could make some bread dealing. silkie doesn't know where most of the people we lived with are. a lot of them moved to oregon and a lot more just disappeared. he said he got off speed when he was in jail which is a good laugh because i remember old silkie when he used to zoom up and down haight street speeding his brains out. sure hope i get to see SF again. that sure was a good winter.

wednesday. went by the loft to see panda and the gang. he took some more pictures, gave me some bread and then turned me on to some really good smoke. just wish he didn't come on so heavy.

friday. this john in a T-bird let me drive for a while before we went back to his place. it handled real nice.

sunday. i passed out and i don't know for how long. i did up a hit of incredible stuff. will definitely get some more.

monday. i almost got busted. i knew there was something funny about the guy. he kept asking questions trying to get me to say things. the minute i caught on i got the hell out of there.

tuesday. tequila is such a scream. she tells people i'm her dresser. tonight we went into the club and the whole back room applauded her outfit. they must've seen that write-up in the paper. she loved it. took a bow at every table. the owner sent a bottle of champagne over. some chick from new jersey asked me to sign her napkin. she said i looked like a rock star. weird.

thursday. snicker' s got his own place in a hotel over on the west side. he's making money running for some big dealer on the east side. he says i can stay there when i want.

saturday. it was raining hard and i had to spend most of my time in doorways and around grand central station. not too many johns cruising around. i scrounged up carfare down to marlowe's. and we're just sitting around talking.

tuesday. my birthday. this lawyer took me out to the beach for a couple of days. it was pretty but real cold at night. i stayed in the sun mostly. he didn't hassle me too much and gave me 50 besides. he says maybe he'll take me out with him again.

PROLOGUE

THEY STUFFED THE BOY'S BODY INTO A rusty oil drum lying discarded in a storeroom on the abandoned pier. Later that night two leather-clad lovers rolled the barrel against the door to keep out intruders and delivered the corpse from its slimy womb. Oblivious to death's presence, the two men made violent love. When their passion subsided, one partner noticed the form sprawled nearby. He reached over and casually touched the body. His fingertips grazed the rigored flesh and pulled back in revulsion.

When the police emergency switchboard received the anonymous tip, two patrol cars from the Sixth Precinct station house were dispatched to investigate. Pier 48 at the foot of West 11th Street was a well-known rendezvous for homosexuals, one of the most notorious in an area dubbed "the gay ghetto"—an irregular slice of Manhattan roughly bounded by the Hudson River, West 14th, Greenwich Avenue, and Christopher Street.

The patrol cars arrived to find the area unusually quiet for a clear June night. Late traffic hummed by on the elevated highway that ribbons the waterfront. While two officers waited outside, the other pair, wielding enormous flashlights, slipped under the vandalized loading door that gave access to the derelict pier. On the opposite curb curious passersby began to cluster.

The officers cautiously explored the gutted loading docks and storage sheds on the main floor and found nothing. They gingerly made their way up rotting stairs to the second level, where they discovered a series of deteriorating offices and storerooms. It was eerily quiet; only distant harbor sounds and the occasional honk of a car horn broke the stillness. After methodically scanning each successive cubicle with their dazzling beam of light, they came to a door that was slightly ajar.

The first officer gave the door a push. It resisted. He stuck his flashlight through the opening and passed the light over the dingy interior. He threw his full weight against the door which gave just enough for him to maneuver the light awkwardly around. Directly against the door was a crimson oil barrel. Wedged under the barrel was what at first appeared to be a cast-off cowboy boot. Then the light froze on the remains of a young Caucasian male lying askew on the splintered planking.

By the time the wagon from the Medical Examiner's arrived, it was well past midnight. Word of police activity had spread to nearby bars and the crowd swelled. Some of the men crossed the street to get a better look, carefully maintaining a distinct perimeter between themselves and the police. Other patrol cars and several unmarked vehicles converged on the area. Suddenly the precinct captain's car pulled up. Several plainclothes detectives rushed over to greet him.

A ruddy-faced rookie in police blues chauffeured the spotless patrol car. He jumped out to open the rear door. The captain, a graying, evenly featured man, leaned out to confer briefly with several detectives and then left as abruptly as he had arrived. As the vehicle made a smooth U-turn beneath the highway, two white-suited attendants wheeled a shrouded stretcher from the pier out into the yellowish glare of streetlights and lifted it into the wagon. Excited whispers of speculations erupted among the spectators. Several patrolmen moved toward the gays.

One cop clapped his hands. "Show's over, *ladies*," he smirked. "Let's keep moving."

They were mostly youngish men in tight-fitting clothes that ranged from bleached denims with bright tops to leather to billowy beach styles. A few timid ones quickly moved on, while most held their ground. Among those leaving were the two men who had discovered the body. The shorter gave the taller a nod and they departed.

"The streets belong to the people!" someone shouted. It was a wild-eyed youth with flaxen hair who made the challenge. He folded his arms defiantly, and the night was filled with "All right!" and "Right on!" The blond boy ate it up.

In the old days this smart-ass would have gotten the taste of a nightstick and a ride in a police car, but relations between the so-called "gay community" and the local precinct had grown sensitive. And there had been unfavorable press coverage. The officer made no visible response and eased off.

"What happened?" demanded a small redheaded latecomer to no one in particular. The question helped break the tension.

"A body found on the pier," somebody offered.

"A-ha!" chirped the interrogator knowingly. "If you don't let them pick your pockets—they kill you!"

Few missed this reference to a ghoulish spate of brutal muggings that had been all the talk lately.

"Some sissies just love violence," the redhead added with a certain relish.

Gradually the crowd dispersed, and news of the fatal mugging spread through the neighborhood. By "last call," bar patrons were being duly warned to "stay away from the piers!" All along Christopher Street casual acquaintances stopped each other to talk about "the murder."

"Pretty soon the only safe place is going to be my apartment," purred one rouged and powdered youth loitering in the doorway of a tea store. His equally painted companion indicated agreement with pursed lips, raised eyebrows, and a sharp nod of his head.

By dawn an assorted gang of all-night stragglers congregated in Sheridan Square opposite the site of the Stonewall Inn, the seamy dance-bar whose closing by the police a few years earlier had spawned the modern gay rights movement. Among them were the talkative latecomer and the young blond political activist, the latter urging them all to put their words into deeds by turning out for meetings of the Gay Liberation Party. "We've got to fight back!" he exhorted.

Sometime around 7 a.m., after spending the night in cooler drawer No. 78 in the basement of the City Medical Examiner's building, the boy's body, draped with a white plastic sheet, is wheeled into the main autopsy room, a fluorescent-lit laboratory with yellow-tiled walls and a row of eight gleaming stainless steel autopsy tables. The attendant removes the cadaver's clothes and drops them into a tagged plastic bag. A police technician photographs front and side views of the head and torso, and takes a complete set of fingerprints.

A deputy medical examiner, gowned and gloved, enters the laboratory. Nodding graciously to his colleagues, he takes his place at the glistening station. Scanning the police report, the doctor activates the dictaphone. In a low monotone he recites the case number and describes the condition of the subject. He notes several tracks, or needle scars, on the calves of both legs and along the inside fold of either arm. On the right forearm is the most recent and apparently fatal puncture encrusted with dried blood. He also indicates, "There's a crudely cut tattoo on the left bicep, most likely self-inflicted, which reads 'Chicken,' probably a nickname."

He studies the tray of surgical tools and selects a scalpel. Making a straight incision from the pubic hairs to the top of the stomach, he then cuts a fork to either armpit, thereby inscribing a long-tailed Y over the chest and abdomen. Satisfied with the proportions of his handiwork, he runs the blade back over the imprint, cutting deeper this time and peeling the skin back as he works. The flaps of skin peel easily to expose the rib cage and related skeletal structures. There is very little bleeding because much of the blood has settled into the backside giving the buttocks a purplish tinge.

The attendant hands the doctor the "branch cutters," an electrical surgical saw. When switched on, the round blade moves back and forth from left to right in steady strokes. The doctor uses it to remove several ribs that are obstructing vital organs. After access is gained, he removes each organ, weighs it, and slices off tissue samples with a knife. Some tests he runs immediately; others will be made later. The remainder of each organ is deposited in a chrome receptacle lined with a white plastic bag.

Meanwhile the attendant has propped up the cadaver's head and shoulders with an oblong block of hardwood. He uses a scalpel to make an incision along the hairline at the base of the neck and after cutting from ear to ear peels the scalp back to expose the skull and sutures of the cranium. The attendant steps aside and the doctor takes the branch cutter, carves a notch to one side of the crown, and cuts out a circle in the bone around the top of the head. There are audible tearing sounds as he chisels away the connective tissue holding the disc; and when the disc is free, the brain tissue dangles out. With the scalpel the examiner severs the remaining connections and the jello-like mass plops out into his gloved hand. It is weighed, and its abnormal heaviness confirmed the diagnosis that was obvious from the beginning: narcotic overdose.

The doctor lops off a sample from the brain and tosses the remainder in with the other organs. The bag is secured, removed from the receptacle, and arranged in the stomach cavity. The surgeon realigns the flaps of skin and sutures the Y incision close. He gives the attendant a friendly nod to indicate he's through and steps out into the corridor to smoke a cigarette.

The attendant uses surgical toweling to replace the brain mass, slips the cranium bone into place, pulls the scalp back, and sews it shut. He hoses down the bloodstained flesh and absently watches the red fluid dilute as it dissolves into the water flowing beneath the grate. He sponges the corpse with a mild detergent solution, and when he sees no one is looking carefully arranges the tangled ringlets of golden hair. He swings the body onto a waiting gurney and wheels it back to cooler drawer No. 78. The spring lock's click punctuates the dull whirr of the refrigeration motors.

MONDAY

NEW YORK CITY APPROACHED FROM THE north is one of the most spectacular sights of modern times. On a bright clear day the skyscraper clusters on Manhattan Island seem majestically etched into the heavens—the glass and steel towers of a new Ilium. Indeed, when the elements of sky and sea conspire, New York seems a supernatural kingdom adrift on the horizon.

One motorist, however, had too much on his mind to be able to enjoy the vista. Preoccupied with the bad news that brought him wheeling southward, Angus Rivers paid little attention to the skyline. Briefly, when traffic on the Henry Hudson Parkway crawled to a halt near the Boat Basin, he absently studied the New Jersey shoreline to the West and the wall of ornate high rises flanking the Drive on the east. It was uncomfortably hot, and the strong glare caused by the sun reflecting on the river made him squint. He turned away his eyes and then closed them, intending to do so for only a second. Once again the circumstances leading to his trip played back in his mind.

The phone call came a little after midnight. Weathering a trial separation from his wife Sally, Angus had returned to live in the only other home he knew, his parents' house. The elder Rivers had long retired to bed, and Angus stayed up late, sitting on the front porch, gazing dreamily into the night-blackened countryside. The swirl of his thoughts broken by the shrill ring of the telephone, he loped quickly into the front hall to answer before the bell woke his parents. He assumed it was Sally: apologetic, yielding, a little horny.

Instead it was a call from the local state troopers. A message had just come in over the teletype. His baby brother Earl was a statistic: a drug overdose

1

casualty. One member of the family would have to report to the Office of the New York City Medical Examiner to identify and claim the remains. Angus jotted down the address and thanked the trooper for calling. His mother, suddenly awake, was at the upstairs railing.

"It's Earl," she said with a mother's sure instinct. "He's in trouble."

Angus went up the stairs to the old woman. Sitting together on the top step, his hand in hers, he delicately broke the news.

Throughout the night she wept and spoke of her dead offspring, mingling real memories and dreams of a son who had never existed. She sat rigid at the kitchen table, hands folded neatly in her lap. Her eyes, two red and swollen pools, stared into the distance. Angus and the old man sat by, lending wordless support. Angus, because he didn't have anything to say; and the old man, because he didn't give a damn, though he respected his wife's grief. After a while the old man went back to bed; she cursed him under her breath. Before dawn Angus stole a couple of hours of intermittent sleep on the living room sofa.

Around 7 a.m. he rang up the garage and told his boss Brody he needed a couple of days off to take care of family business. Brody was sympathetic, and after hearing the details told Angus: "Take as much time as you need. Your job will be here when you get back."

Then he called Sally, not that she'd care, but more in case one of the kids needed him. She was noncommittal and cool. He could hear it in the slight plaintive edge of her voice and in the awkward silences that punctuated their exchanges. She promised to keep in touch with his mother, and then she put the boys on to say goodbye. "Wait!" he wanted to say to her but couldn't. So he told the oldest, "Take care of Mommy," and hung up.

He visualized the faces of his two sons, the confusion and apprehension they felt over the separation, and it made him feel even more desperate for the reconciliation Sally refused to discuss. "I need more time alone," was all she would say, and the words stung each time....

The thunderous blast of an automobile horn jarred Angus awake with a start. Traffic ahead was moving, and he was now causing a tie-up. With excellent reflexes he shifted into gear and accelerated, and the '65 Impala soon held its own in the flow of downtown traffic. Angus exited the highway at 56th Street and weaved his way across town.

The city streets seemed even more crowded and littered than he remembered. In the West 30's he got stuck behind a garment truck that had thrown an axle. While waiting, he glimpsed a bewildering array of humanity stream pass. When he finally made it to First Avenue, he couldn't find a parking space. He circled the block several times looking for an empty spot.

Francis Henderson Shriner noticed Angus drive by a couple of times and then watched him park. The recently promoted metropolitan desk reporter had stepped outside to grab a smoke. This was the third week he'd been assigned to cover the morgue, and he still hadn't broken any major space. Nobody around the office had said anything directly; still, there had been veiled references to his predecessor's enviable record of piecing together big stories with only the slightest threads of factual information to go on. Once Shriner had gone back to the office and found a thick folder of previous morgue stories placed prominently on his desk. He recalled this embarrassment with about as much relish as his first trip down to the autopsy room to watch a procedure.

Now he watched Angus cross the street and climb up the steps. Since one of the assistant medical examiners had let Shriner look over the current cases, he was immediately able to match Angus to the Earl Rivers case. Actually it wasn't too hard to figure out. If there was one thing he'd learned in three weeks covering the morgue it was the disproportionately high number of blacks and Hispanics who ended up on those slabs in the basement. The occasional whites were most often elderly, brought in from run-down hotels and flophouses; sometimes they were homicides, but usually the deaths were of natural causes.

Of the weekend reports Shriner had looked over, he found the greatest story potential in the Earl Rivers file: 17, Caucasian, all-American good looks, minor police record, and found in a well-known homosexual haunt dead from a drug overdose. All he needed was the family angle, and the story would write itself. Shriner stubbed out his cigarette and followed his hunch inside.

The faint odor of formaldehyde wafted through the lobby. Angus recognized the smell all too well. It took him back to Nam and the G.R. point detail he'd pulled one long merciless summer in the jungle. The fetid scent of death had seemed to cling to his clothes and skin for weeks afterward.

A heavy-set black woman in a stained nurse's uniform presided at the reception desk. She looked him dead in the eye and growled, "Name?"

"Rivers. Angus Rivers," he managed. "It's my brother Earl. The troopers called last night."

The nurse made a notation on the log in front of her. "Take a seat, honey," she said. "One of the detectives will call you."

Angus did as he was told. He was thankful for the air conditioning after the blistering heat outside. The waiting room—actually a corridor partitioned off the lobby—consisted of two facing rows of alternating orange and turquoise plastic scoop-chairs. The walls were dingy institutional-beige tiles, and the space was dimly lit.

Two Latin women sat directly across from Angus. They were obviously mother and daughter. Drawn to the physical beauty of the younger woman, he found himself staring at her, although she paid no attention to him.

A small brown child played on the floor. Nearby, his mother wept quietly as a man stroked her hair. Further down a frail yellow-skinned woman in a heavy gray overcoat sat trance-like. A young black man laughed and talked animatedly to himself.

Angus sensed that someone was sitting down next to him, and he turned. It was the guy he'd noticed on the steps when he came in. Their eyes met, and they nodded. It was a camaraderie born of being the only two white men in the room.

"Cigarette?" Shriner offered a crushed soft pack. Angus hesitated, and then took one of the cigarettes. "Hey, you got another one, man?" yelled the black dude from across the way.

"Sure," Shriner said, getting up to meet him halfway. He pulled the cigarette out of the pack and handed it to him.

The man took the smoke and said, "Hope I can do the same for you some day."

Shriner gestured to light it, but he said, "That's okay. I'm going to smoke it later," and stuck it behind his ear.

Shriner sat back down. He lit his own, then Angus's.

"Thanks." Angus inhaled.

The two men fell quiet. Shriner found the silence excruciatingly long.

"I heard you tell the desk you were here about your brother?" the reporter ventured.

"That's right," Angus said calmly.

"Travel far?" Shriner pressed.

"About four hours. Of course it took almost that long to get across town!" They both cracked a smile.

"Where'd ya drive in from?" Shriner asked.

"Upstate. West of Glens Falls."

"You don't say. My folks had a place in Lake George. Spectacular country up there."

"You probably know more about that than I do," Angus snapped. He knew the types: tight-assed summer people. "I'm a native, not a tourist."

The summers he had worked busing tables and carrying bags in the resort hotels still got to him. Nothing was ever right as far as "the guests" were concerned.

Shriner was put off by Angus's tone and uncertain of the reason for it. He said no more. The two men became absorbed in the rituals of the waiting room.

The two Latin women were called. Angus watched them get up and disappear through a door marked MISSING PERSONS. He found the daughter's compact build even more enticing as she walked away.

"You like that, do you?" Shriner remarked. He couldn't help but notice Angus's look of appreciation.

"Very nice," Angus said and closed the subject.

Shriner coughed nervously.

"You work around here or what?" Angus asked. He had sensed all along this guy was up to something, and now he wanted to know what it was.

"You might say that," Shriner allowed. "I work for *The Record.*" He extended his hand. "My name's Frank Shriner."

Angus shook automatically. "What's that—a newspaper?"

"Yeah!" Shriner was a bit indignant. "Just the largest circulation daily in the country!"

"So that's what you're up to? Looking for a story." Angus laughed. Just the other day he was saying somebody ought to ask him what he thinks. "I had a drinking buddy in the press corps in Nam," Angus bragged. "We used to hit all the places. Maybe you know him Tony Destonado?"

"Whom did he work for?" Shriner asked drily. He was trying to be as unimpressed as possible.

"Tony's with one of the news services. A.P., I think."

"Never heard of him. But that don't mean nothing. There are plenty of guys I don't know. I'm going for coffee," Shriner suddenly announced. "You want some?"

"Sure," Angus said. "I take mine black."

The reporter walked over to a bank of vending machines down the corridor and got two steaming cups of coffee. He handed Angus one. Angus nodded appreciatively and took a sip.

"I knew you were up to something," Angus chuckled. "For a while there I thought you were just lonely."

"Cheers," Shriner said to Angus. They raised their styrofoam cups in a mock toast. He felt slightly foolish.

Angus looked quizzically at the reporter. "All right, hot shot, what do you want to know? Isn't that what you're here for—to get a story?"

Shriner didn't skip a beat. "O.K.," he said. "When was the last time you saw your brother?" He pulled out a note pad and pen.

"Haven't the foggiest," Angus answered. "Last summer maybe. Don't keep track of things like I used to."

"He a runaway?"

"Not really. The state called him a 'liberated minor.' That means the old man didn't give a damn and Ma, well, Ma—she's never been too well."

"How long was he living here in the city?"

"Let's see, I'm back about a year and a half. And I know he'd been living on his own a good time before that, 'cause Ma mentioned it in her letters for a while. Funny the things she used to write me about."

Shriner wrote greedily, much more than he could possibly use, but he was an elaborate note-taker.

"You see any action in Nam?"

"That's a dumb question!" Angus sneered, mock-defensively. Then, seriously, he said, "Three hundred and eighty-eight days in the jungle. Mostly in Plai Coo. I think it rotted my brain."

Angus made some strange animal sounds that drew the attention of those sitting around. He looked up and threw them his best Jack Nicholson smirk.

Shriner shot a nervous look around and huddled in closer.

"Would you say your brother was one of those Village types?" he asked cautiously.

"What's that supposed to mean?" Angus snapped.

"You know, long hair, drugs, that whole crazy sex scene they got going down there?"

"As a matter of fact, the last time I saw Earl his hair was shorter than mine." Angus emphasized the point by running his fingers through his own thick, dark mane. "Drugs? Well, I guess so. That's why I'm here."

"What kind of business are you in, Mr...." Shriner pretended to grope for the name. "What's your name anyway?"

"Angus Rivers."

Shriner licked the point of his pencil and jotted the name down.

"Look, Frank," Angus said. "How about you answering a question for me now."

"Shoot."

"You been around here a while. How much longer do you think I'm going to have to wait?"

"It depends," Shriner stalled.

"On what?"

"On whether you're next!" he said lamely.

Angus threw him a dirty look and got up to look for the john.

2

STAN FREED HAD AN UGLY HANGOVER. AT his age—approaching 50—and with his record capacity for imbibing, he thought such maladies were well behind him. Apparently not. He downed several aspirin and a couple of beers. The bit of shrapnel in his knee was acting up, and no matter how much he jerked his leg he couldn't seem to get the kink out. Limping awkwardly, certain his irregular gait was drawing the stares of passersby, he stumbled over to Party headquarters, a rented storefront off Sixth Avenue.

The property had previously housed a head shop and before that a coffee house. Prior to Stan's negotiating the lease for the Party's use, a fire had swept through the interior. Rather than take on the expense of a major renovation, the landlord made cosmetic repairs, slapped on a few coats of fresh paint, and lowered the rent. The prime Village location made it a good choice for the Party, even though telltale bits of10 charred metal and blackened brick were still evident.

Stan opened the two sets of locks and let himself in. A pile of mail scattered across the threshold. He scooped it up without bothering to examine any individual envelopes. As he switched on the lights, two lines of fluorescent tubes blinked intermittently until they were all more or less lit. Stan closed the door behind him and locked it. He felt a little uncomfortable. Then his eyes scanned the debris-strewn ruin that confronted him, and he regained his resolve.

Derelicts and street queens had turned the place into a round-the-clock hangout, and yesterday matters had come to a head. It hadn't taken much discussion among Party officers and regulars before it was decided to discontinue letting the premises be used for a 24hour "drop-in center." Though they were all brothers in the Cause, there was the matter of incompatible life styles to reconcile.

Of course he had felt some guilt when he locked the door last night after asking everybody to leave, but since he was paying many of the important bills from his own resources, Stan grew more confident. He told himself that there were always those who were willing to hang out but not a one who was willing to lend a hand. With no "volunteers" to keep the place clean, most of the routine maintenance chores had fallen on Stan's shoulders. So besides having a stack of clerical work to do, he had to get the place cleaned up for the evening meeting.

He went into the office cubicle and flipped on the fan. He turned off the telephone answering machine, and rewound the tape. As the messages played back, he sorted and opened the mail.

"Hello, hello?" cried an uncertain, high-pitched voice. "I'm calling for Rudy. Is Rudy there? It's one of those damn answering machines!" The voice trailed off as the connection was cut.

He opened the hand-addressed envelopes first. A schoolteacher from western Pennsylvania had visited the GLP center on his vacation and was so impressed with it that he had sent along a money order for 25 dollars.

"Faggots! Dirty faggots!" screamed a tense, hate tainted man's voice on the tape. "I'll blow your frigging heads off I catch one of you looking at me again." There was a loud click.

Stan barely paid attention. He was artfully maneuvering a shut-off notice from the electric company into the Bills Payable drawer. He simply could not sink any more of his funds into operating costs. All the income he really had left was his disability insurance. He had long ago spent the principal of a small family inheritance.

"Stan? Stan, this is Tyler," continued the tape. "Call me before noon. I know I said I'd be there early to help—but, let's just say I got tied up." A smothered guffaw, and he hung up.

"You're already an hour and forty minutes late," Stan reprimanded the machine. A whirr signaled the end of the messages.

Stan clicked off the answering machine and finished going through the mail. There was a request for literature from a university homophile organization and the first issue of a newsletter from a gay commune in San Francisco. "What this office needs is a full-time secretary," Stan roared.

Putting off a little longer the cleaning job that awaited him, he dialed his apartment.

A dozen rings later a sleepy-voiced Joey answered. "Hello," he sighed.

"Rise and shine!" Stan feigned cheer.

"Sure," Joey said softly. He wasn't quite over the edge yet; sleep's hold was strong.

"I need ya down here," Stan pleaded.

"Whadd'ya want? I'm sleeping."

"No one else is here yet, the place is a mess and I need help," Stan said in one long breath.

"What else is new?" Joey purred. He was awake for sure now. "Make me an offer I can't refuse."

"You got it!" Stan said, and they shared a good laugh. Stan found Joey's affection exhilarating.

"Okay. See you in an hour," Joey relented.

"Sooner," Stan insisted, mock macho.

"I'll try," Joey cooed, and hung up.

Stan basked in the warm glow he got from the short talk with his young lover. He was luckier than he had ever dreamed he could be. It was funny how he'd met Joey long after he had given up the romantic fantasies that had dominated his teens and twenties. In his thirties he'd become resigned to the idea that it would always be one-night stands—but now with Joey all that had changed.

He replaced the phone and thought about going out for coffee. But no, he'd better get started. His head had stopped throbbing and the pain in his leg had eased up. He moved into the main room and started collecting the assortment of dog-eared newspapers and magazines that were scattered everywhere and piled them neatly on the Literature shelf. He pushed the sofa and overstuffed chairs against the wall and got the broom. Beginning in a far corner, he methodically swept up the bits of paper and cigarette butts that littered the vinyl flooring.

The more he worked, the more discouraged his thoughts became. What a shambles the place had turned into! It seemed like only yesterday that they were looking the space over and visualizing its potential. He remembered the good vibrations of the first few meetings: the massive turnout of men and women eager to gain political and social status without compromise. Now it all seemed to be coming apart around him. The original loose coalition of activists had splintered into several stubborn factions. Stan blamed the break on a hysterical sect of "crazies" who advocated gay power with a relentless disregard for any sort of procedure. Somehow their most vocal member, Derek Wiggins, had managed to get elected Party chairman. Many found him too flamboyant and dictatorial, and attendance was dropping off. More and more Stan felt like a custodian. He was counting on tonight's meeting, and the other events of the week to bring back some focus, and some of the spirit of those first heady days.

There was a determined banging at the door. Stan checked his watch. It was too soon for Joey. He ignored the banging even as it grew louder. Then he remembered the message on the machine and realized it could be Tyler. He undid the two locks and swung open the door. Sure enough it was.

"For a hot moment I thought you weren't here yet!" Tyler chided devilishly. He pushed away the shaggy blond hair from his face.

Stan stood to one side and gestured for Tyler to enter. Tyler nodded graciously as he crossed the threshold. Stan locked the door.

"Rough night?" he inquired with a wink.

"Nothing I couldn't handle," Tyler parried,

"Good. Now handle this!" and he pushed the broom at Tyler who managed to catch it with a certain amount of grace. Then without missing a beat he boarded it witch-style and galloped around the room.

Stan broke up.

"Hey, what do you need me for?" Tyler asked as he looked around. "You're doing fabulous."

"Thanks! Do I get the job?" Stan snapped. He had suddenly stopped smiling. "One of these days ole Stan's not going to be around to keep things together."

Tyler had never realized how sensitive Stan felt about this. He quickly changed the subject.

"Say, where did you guys end up last night anyway? I thought you were going to meet us at Julius's. We saved you your favorite corner of the bar."

"Sorry about that. Joey and I never got out of the house last night."

"Well, you certainly don't look like you went wanting for a good time," Tyler said diplomatically. He thought that Stan looked terrible. His skin was the color of an old sponge, and purplish rings framed his eyes, bloodshot and watery.

"Damn." Tyler snapped his fingers. "I forgot to get the paper. You hear anything about that body they found on the pier the other night?"

"Vaguely," Stan said squeamishly. "It's much too early to talk about 'dead bodies.' Anyway, what's the death of one faggot more or less?"

Even Stan was startled by the cavalier manner with which he had tossed off the remark.

"You said it." Tyler agreed with Stan's sardonic comment. "We have got to make them care."

"'Them?'" Stan queried.

"The media, the government. The more visible we are, the less people can ignore us."

"Wait a minute. Don't you think there's a limit? Why read about another gory faggot murder. That's not very positive."

"Coverage is coverage. At least it'll let them know we need police protection—not harassment—like everybody else."

Stan nodded indifferently. He liked Tyler and was glad he came around to help. But sometimes he found Tyler's ideas a bit extreme.

"Give me a hand with these chairs," Stan directed. He led the way to a pile of folding chairs in a rear storage area.

Tyler knew the older man didn't always see things the way he did, but he never doubted that Stan would eventually come around to seeing his point. Tyler saw Stan as a staunch ally; all he had to do was lose some of his uptightness.

"I think it's time to form a media committee," Tyler went on, as they each took an armful of chairs. "Let the press know what we're doing in advance. Send out press releases! What do you think?"

"What do I know?" Stan shrugged.

"Press coverage even if it means exposing ourselves!" he said. He underlined his point by crashing one of the metal chairs into place.

Stan flinched. "If you say so," he said and forced a smile. He wasn't ready to "come out" quite *that* far. Organizing meetings and keeping books was one thing; becoming a spokesman was another. He had carefully avoided having his name mentioned in any of the literature that was handed out at demonstrations, although somebody had photographed a close-up of the back of his head in a crowd. The photo ended up on page three of one of the dailies. He probably would not have recognized himself if the camera had not captured the exotic pattern of his sport shirt.

"I haven't heard any more from Councilman Rhodes' office about tonight," Stan said to change the subject.

"You mean he might not be coming?" Tyler was perspiring so he took off his shirt.

"Well, the aide from his office said Friday that he would definitely be here tonight." Stan shot an admiring glance at Tyler's smooth bare torso. "He said somebody would call if he couldn't make it. Nobody's called…so I guess he's coming."

"Now take Rhodes, for instance," Tyler pounced. "Instead of leaving it up to his people to alert the press, we should be making our own calls."

"His office said they would issue an advance copy of his statement to the press. I figure, let them handle it. Personally, I think its not so much the gay rights per se that's attracting his endorsement. He's looking to pick up votes wherever he can get them."

"Well, we should be getting more mileage out of this 'endorsement' for ourselves," Tyler insisted.

"In the long run we will," Stan countered.

"Let's just hope he remembers us when he gets to Congress."

"Yeah, but first he has to get there."

The chairs were pretty much set up, and the place looked better.

"By the way," Stan remembered. "Weren't you supposed to pick up Reverend Tunney-Brown?"

"No. Remember, we changed that. The Dyke borrowed my pick-up last night, and she said she'd take care of it."

"The Dyke?" Stan frowned. "You mean June?"

"Oh, come on. Get off the can. She thinks it's funny too."

Three sharp taps at the plate glass window suddenly distracted the two men from a real fight. Stan recognized his lover's knock.

"Saved by the bell," he said to Tyler as he crossed the room to open the door.

A rumpled flower child dragged him self in from the street. He surveyed the orderly arrangement of chairs and moaned, "Whadd'ya need me for?"

"Immoral support," Stan offered as he embraced the boy. "Aren't you glad you came anyway," he murmured.

The display of affection made Tyler feel awkward. After a "hi" to Joey, Tyler withdrew into the office and made himself busy. He started jotting down notes of his thoughts, things he could bring up for discussion at the meeting later.

3

MONDAY WAS NOT MISSING PERSONS' DEtective Al Finnelli's favorite day. After a cozy weekend with his wife and kids at the rented summer place, who wanted to catch up on the morgue IDs that invariably accumulated while he was away? He and his partner, Special Detective Sid Brooke, had been going non-stop since 8 a.m. and, frankly, Finnelli needed a break. He couldn't speak for Brooke, though, because at the moment Brooke seemed to be thoroughly enjoying his job, thanks to the lovely senorita hanging on his every word.

All right, one more, Finnelli told himself and pulled the next file out of the basket. It was the minor who'd been found on the pier in the Village.

Finnelli had more style than to just stay at his desk and call the next case in. No, he liked to go out into the waiting area and take care of people properly. It was the way he did things: right.

"Rivers, Mr. Rivers," he announced to the expectant faces in the waiting area.

"Right here!" Angus stood up and crossed to meet the detective. "I'm Angus Rivers."

Shriner was hard on Rivers' heels. Finnelli spotted the newspaper reporter immediately.

"This guy giving you a hard time, Mr. Rivers? You know you don't have to answer his questions if you don't want to." There was no mistaking the detective's hostility.

"He's O.K.," Angus said defensively. "Just helped me pass the time."

"Well, he's not coming in here. You know better than that, Shriner." He threw the reporter a dirty look. Shriner slunk out of sight.

"I'm Detective Finnelli," he introduced himself to Angus as if nothing had happened. And as far as Finnelli was concerned, nothing had. He had had enough press coverage to last him the rest of his life. And especially, he blamed a distorted series of stories written by Shriner's predecessor for the failure of the Department to give him a long overdue promotion.

The two men shook hands, and the detective ushered Angus into his office. He motioned Angus into a wooden chair next to his desk. "Make yourself comfortable."

Finnelli no sooner sat down then the phone rang. "Excuse me," he said. Soon he was barking the details of a previous case to the caller.

Angus was drawn to the two Hispanic women being interviewed at the next desk. The older woman was hesitant as she spoke to her daughter in Spanish. The younger woman translated. In even English she explained that her mother's husband—she made it clear he was *not* her father—had been missing since Friday. "We call his job and the boss no see him since Thursday. My mother, she was worried all weekend."

Sunday night they visited the local precinct and the desk sergeant referred them to Missing Persons. The young woman described her stepfather, what he was wearing, and the route he took to work. As she spoke, the mother's expression changed from hesitant to uncomfortable to almost serene. Her relaxed features offered a startling glimpse of the great physical beauty she had surely possessed as a girl and young woman.

The young detective shuffled nervously through the papers of a file folder. What he was about to say was written all over his face. "There is one man," he inflected carefully. "He came in on Friday. A Spanish man, early 40's, he was hit on the head by some loose masonry falling from the roof of an office building in midtown. He probably never knew what hit him."

The daughter delicately translated the officer's words into Spanish, but that was not necessary since the old woman's face indicated that she already understood. Her eyes glistened. She spoke a firm command to her daughter. "My mother wishes to see the body," the girl said and blushed.

Angus was completely absorbed by this little vignette. He didn't notice Finnelli finish his call. The detective literally had to grab the man's shoulder to get his attention.

Angus swung back around. "I'm sorry."

"Nothing wrong with appreciating a pretty lady," the detective winked. Then it was back to business.

"Look, Mr. Rivers, I'm going to have to ask you a few questions before we go downstairs."

"Shoot," Angus said.

"When was the last time your brother contacted you?" Finnelli asked.

"I got a postcard. Last March."

"What did he write?"

"Nothing I can remember offhand."

"We found your brother in the Village on one of the abandoned piers that juts out onto the waterfront. We don't think he got there by himself. Do you know any of his friends…people he hung out with…any names?"

Angus shook his head. "I wish I could help you, sir. But we were out of touch. You know how it is."

"How old was your brother, Mr. Rivers?"

"Sixteen-I mean, seventeen. He had a birthday last month. My mother gave me his birth certificate if you want to look at it."

"Seventeen? That's pretty young to be out on his own, wouldn't you say?" Actually, Finnelli had seen them out and dead a lot younger, but he felt a moral responsibility to take that tone.

"Earl didn't think so," Angus countered with just a trace of cockiness. "He was always pretty independent. My folks are retired. Earl's what they call a 'late child.' There was no way the old folks could control him. He had a mind of his own."

"Do you know where your brother was living?"

"The 'Y,' I guess. At least that's where he said he was living last time I heard."

"When was that?"

"He called us up last Christmas. We talked a bit. You know how that is." Angus shrugged. He wasn't going to let this cop make him feel guilty.

"Did you know your brother had an arrest record?"

"Sure!" Angus replied with bravado. "There was some talk about it when I got back. I never paid much attention. Remember: I'd just come back from making the world safe for democracy!" There was no mistaking the mockery in his tone.

Finnelli bristled, but let it pass. What the hell did he care? "Your brother pleaded guilty to a misdemeanor: vagrancy, one count. And the only reason he wasn't turned over to the juvenile authorities right away was because he was carrying phony ID."

"Don't sound too serious to me," Angus muttered.

"Let me finish," the detective snapped. "He was picked up walking Third Avenue. In the East 50's. You know anything about that area?"

"What about it?" Angus shrugged.

"It's a well-known hangout for male prostitutes. Did you know your brother was hustling, probably selling his body for drugs?"

Angus focused in on the detective's words. "You mean my brother was going with old broads for money?" he laughed.

"No. I mean he was going with old johns for money and probably whatever else he could get."

It suddenly seemed very quiet in the small office. Angus noticed that the two Hispanic women and the other detective had left the room. Finnelli's stomach grumbled angrily.

"Excuse me," he burped. "The original charge was loitering for purposes of prostitution," Finnelli continued unfazed. "His court-appointed lawyer routinely plea-bargained it down to a lesser charge to get a quick guilty plea…"

Angus wasn't really listening very closely. He was trying to take in the latest revelation about his brother. Sure, he knew about faggots. He knew how they fed on young boys. But it was something he never thought about much. Now he had just received information that painted a scary picture of his own brother's life.

"What I'm getting at," the officer said, sensing the need to spell everything out for Angus. "Your brother was quite a character. Anybody could've dropped him off at that pier. A john. One of his junkie friends. A dealer. Right now we've got very little to go on."

Finnelli could see he was starting to lose Angus so he decided to get moving.

"All right, let's go downstairs for a look."

News hound Shriner scampered away from the open door. The last thing he wanted was another confrontation with Finnelli. After eavesdropping on the two men he was more than sure that he had finally stumbled on 'the Story.' He called the picture desk and haggled with the assignment editor until she agreed to send a photographer. He jotted down several more thoughts and soon wrote the sentence that would become his lead. The words flowed as the story practically wrote itself.

Finnelli led Angus out the door and down some steps. They entered a small tiled reception area in the basement. At one end was a desk and sitting behind it a morgue attendant flipping through a girlie magazine.

"Hey, Ferguson," the detective addressed the black man. "Let's have a look at 78." The attendant gave the detective a wink and a big grin. He picked up a ring of keys off the desk and disappeared behind a nearby door.

The detective touched Angus's shoulder. "If you wait over by the glass in the door, he'll bring your brother out in a few seconds."

Angus did as he was told. The whole place was starting to give him a very bad feeling. "Say," he asked, "don't working here ever get to you?"

Finnelli broke into a broad smile; probably the first genuine one since he'd first met Angus.

"Yeah," he agreed. "It gets hairy—but what doesn't?"

Ferguson wheeled the shrouded body into view behind the glass.

"Can you see all right, Mr. Rivers? If you prefer we can go inside for a better look."

"This is fine," Angus said as he stared intently through the window. The attendant lowered the white plastic cover and draped it across the cadaver's chest. Angus recognized his brother immediately, although the hair was much longer and blonder than he remembered. There was a curious expression on the face, not quite a smile, but definitely at peace. Finally Angus couldn't look anymore, and he turned away. He bowed his head and closed his eyes, squeezing the lids tight to hold back the tears he was surprised to feel coming.

The detective motioned the attendant to take the body away. "You better have a seat," he said gently.

"No. I'm all right." Angus wiped his eyes with the back of his hand.

Back upstairs Finnelli and Angus were greeted by the pop of a flashbulb. Finnelli hustled Angus into his office calling back to Shriner, "You think you got ya story, smart-ass!" The photographer managed another snap before the two men were out of view. "Sometimes I'd like to shove that guy's press card you know where."

Finnelli readied some release forms for Angus to sign and instructed him on procedures. The family would have to make arrangements with their local operator about shipping the body.

"Oh, and before I forget." He opened a locker and took out a bundle. He handed it to Angus. "Not much in there," the detective observed. "Just the clothes he had on when they found him. Whoever dumped him must have emptied his pockets first."

"Hey," Angus snapped. "That was my brother, not a sack of potatoes."

"Sorry I didn't mean anything by it." Experience had taught Finnelli to back off quickly before he became the focus of the bereaved's grief and anger.

"Earl was still just a baby," Angus found himself saying. "It's not fair!" He banged his fist hard against his thigh.

Finnelli could have told him his brother was not unlike a hundred other cases he'd worked on in the past couple of years: nice kids, mostly runaways or kids just having problems at home, getting involved with the scum of the city, falling into drugs and prostitution, and dead before they hit twenty. But there was no use for him to say anything. He kept to business.

"Have you got a local address in case we have to reach you?"

Angus hadn't thought about where he'd stay. "Try the Westside Motor Inn," he said after a moment. He'd stayed there once with some Army buddies on a two day pass before shipping out. The detective noted the address inside the case folder. "What are the chances of finding out who did this to my brother?" Angus asked, very deliberately. No matter how hard he tried, he couldn't release the final image of Earl on that slab downstairs.

"Did what? Technically the only crime is transporting your brother's body to the pier. The lab tests indicate the overdose was self-inflicted. He could've got the drugs on any street corner."

"Hey, what are you talking about? You trying to tell me that nothing is going to be done to solve this case!"

"Let me explain something to you," Finnelli began, hoping to defuse the man's obvious anger. "We're going to do our best, but without some sort of a solid lead or break we haven't got a helluva of a chance of finding out who was with your brother last Friday. From here the case is turned back to the P.I.U. unit at the Village precinct for further investigation. If anything turns up they'll be in touch."

Angus realized he was close to getting out of control. He thanked the detective and they parted amicably. As he was leaving, Shriner and the photographer mobbed him.

"Just one more question," the reporter urged.

Angus shook his head and pushed on by. He had lost interest in Shriner. He just wanted to get off by himself to sort things out. The reporter pursued him to the car, followed by the photographer snapping pictures furiously.

"Where are you going?" Shriner demanded.

"Get out of my way," Angus growled. He was sorry now that he had been on such an ego trip earlier and had talked to the reporter so freely in the first place.

"I'm at *The Record*. Ask for the City Room. Don't forget: the name's Shriner, if you got anything else to tell me."

The reporter dodged as the car pulled abruptly away from the curb. Angus found that traffic on the avenue was congested. He was tired and wanted to sleep. He remembered the motor inn and, headed there.

4

THE OLD CHEVY PICK-UP SPUTTERED TO A halt outside the GLP storefront. A ruddy-complexioned man of about 35, dressed in vaguely clerical garb, jumped from the truck on the passenger side. The tomboyish driver came around to join him. The Reverend reached round into the bed of the truck and retrieved his satchels, one bursting with books and papers. He paused, grips in hand, biceps bulging beneath his tight-fitting seersucker jacket, and studied the facade of the storefront. The expanse of window on both sides of the door was a poster collage of Movement figures and movie stars: Dietrich flirted with Che; Garbo ignored Mao. An unflattering caricature of a prone Richard M. Nixon was plastered over the glass in the door. The wood trim was painted a garish electric blue. Nowhere was there a picture of Jesus. The Reverend glanced up and down the street; if he had any impression of the character of the neighborhood, he refrained from registering any visible sign.

The driver was nervously watching him. "I'm from Brooklyn," she shrugged. "It all looks the same to me." The Reverend smiled benignly, but there was a far-off look in his eye. June tried the door. It was locked. She pounded loudly, assuring the Reverend with a big smile that somebody must be there to let them in.

The door opened a peek, then wider, and Stan flew out with a big greeting for the visitor. "Reverend Tunney-Brown!" he gushed, eagerly reaching for the larger of the two suitcases. "Let me take that," he insisted. No sooner had he taken the bag than the handle snapped. The bag went crashing to the pavement and barely missing the Reverend's big toe, which was prominently displayed in a Mexican sandal of recycled tire rubber.

"Safe trip?" Stan managed.

Reverend Tunney-Brown could not stifle a great throaty laugh. "You ever ride Greyhound L.A. to New York!" he boomed good-humoredly. "An experience not soon forgotten." He mimed rubbing the seat of his trousers. Stan introduced Tyler who gave him a hand with the suitcase as June showed the guest in. The Reverend delicately sniffed the air but abruptly stopped when he realized he was being observed.

"You'll be staying with me and my lover Joey," Stan rattled off nervously. "Joey," he shouted toward the back, "say hello to Reverend Tunney-Brown!" Joey waved shyly and went back to straightening out the rows of folding chairs. "We've got a brand new Castro convertible. You'll be as snug as a bug."

"Sounds heavenly to me," the Reverend resonated. "When do we get there?" adding none too subtly. Once more he sniffed the air.

"While you're here, there are a couple of things we should run over, then June or Tyler can drive you home."

"Well, if that's all right…"

"Don't worry about a thing, Rev, I'm your wheels for the rest of the week," Tyler chimed.

The Reverend seemed pleased. "Well, if you insist," he murmured. "But I would like a couple of hits off whatever your friend over there is smoking," he added sheepishly.

Stan guffawed then quickly tried to conceal it with a cough. "Joey, get over here and let the Rev have a toke."

Joey wasted no time getting the joint to the Reverend, who demonstrated his deep appreciation for the herb by alternately inhaling through his mouth and nose.

"I never travel with the stuff," he managed between hits. "I'm too well-known. Wouldn't help the Cause much if I got busted." He offered the joint to Stan.

"I better pass. Maybe later. That stuff knocks me right out."

Tyler had wandered off after June.

"You keep it, Rev," Joey said. "There's plenty more back at the apartment." He went back to lining up the rows.

"Why don't you have a seat on the couch there and I'll get the schedule." Stan took his arm and ushered him over.

"I hope you haven't set anything for before noon. I give my best interviews over a nice leisurely lunch." Before sitting down the Reverend removed his jacket. Beneath his clerical collar and bib he wore a black T-shirt.

Returning with some papers, Stan noted to himself that the Reverend might be putting on a little weight but he was still quite a hunk. Stan sat down beside him.

"Tonight," Stan began drily, "is our regular Monday night organization meeting. Councilman Porter Rhodes is expected to drop in. He's probably our strongest supporter on the City Council."

He would have added, "The cutest, too!" But somehow it didn't seem appropriate. "Right now Intro 77 is in a sub-committee made up of some pretty vocal opposition."

The Reverend was settled deep in the chair and seemed about to drift off.

"Of course we'll want you to lead those of us gathered in short opening and closing prayers."

"Wait, wait," the Reverend snapped to. "Let's not keep it too rigid. Here's how I usually work. You have the emcee give me a brief intro, I come out, make my remarks, then, depending on what kind of response I'm getting, I do a short prayer. You see the difference?"

"However you want it, Rev. No problem."

"Fine, fine. Now what about the interviews?" the Rev backtracked.

Tyler was back within earshot. "I'd like to hear this too," he said smugly.

Stan wasn't the least perturbed by the Reverend's casual assumption. "Nothing definite has been set yet," he said with great diplomacy. "You know how picky the straight media can be?"

"But you did send out a release on my coming to New York for your rally and a request for coverage?" the Rev pressed. "It was all in that kit of materials I sent you."

"I got your press kit all right," Stan began slowly. "But we usually telephone for coverage the day before an event. We'll let them all know you're in town. And that you're going to address the rally on Thursday."

The good Reverend concealed his disappointment. He had been spoiled by the coverage he received during appearances in San Francisco, New Orleans, and Boston. New York would be the culmination of his crusade and he had hoped to be featured in one of the major dailies or on a national TV talk show. New York's lack of organization disturbed him. In the excitement of the Reverend's arrival, Stan had forgotten to lock the front door, and a noisy group of street queens drifted in. Stan walked right over to them. He was not going to let them hang out unless they were willing to lend a hand. He raised his voice to make a general announcement. "Unless you're here to help us get ready for the meeting tonight and the rest of the week's activity, I'm afraid the storefront will not be open as usual."

There was silence. Then as the message sank in, there were boos, catcalls, and a large scream of indignation from one great muscular queen who looked like a quarterback in semi-drag. "Oh, shit," she boomed. "Where's Derek? He said he'd meet me here. What time is it?"

"Derek's not here yet," Stan held his ground. "You can help clean up and arrange chairs, or you can go out and come back later for the meeting."

"Humpf!" the big queen grunted. She took a sip from a bottle wrapped in the brown paper bag she was holding. She gave Stan a cold, hard eye, and then shifted the weight of the huge dance bag she was carrying from one shoulder to the other. "Let's go down to the pier," she told the ragged bunch that flanked her. "Guess we know where we're not wanted."

Then to Stan she said, "You tell Derek I was here. The name is Loooordes," letting the long syllable roll off her tongue as if to emphasize her grandness. She moved regally to the door, her motley crew in step, and out into the street without looking back.

Stan locked the door. He was embarrassed that the Reverend had witnessed such a scene.

"Hell," Tyler said, sensing his friend's nervousness. "You were right, Stan. No work, no privileges."

"Members of your organization?" Reverend Tunney-Brown inquired.

"The GLP doesn't have members as such. We are an umbrella group for a loose coalition of the gay community. Anyone attending for two or more consecutive meetings is entitled to vote or run for office," Stan explained.

"Is that so," the Reverend said. And perhaps for the first time he took a good look at his new associates and their surroundings.

Joey came out of the bathroom, the toilet flushing loudly behind him. "What was all the rumble?" he asked, buckling his belt.

"Just some queens looking for Derek," Tyler shrugged.

"Sounded like fifty people galloped in and out of here."

"More," June confided. She'd been wandering purposefully around, looking at the changes in the room. They seemed to meet with her approval. "I gotta go. See you fellows later." She started toward the door.

"What about my truck keys?" Tyler called.

"Oh, that's right," June stopped short. "You're taking the Rev over to Stan's."

Tyler had a change of mind. "Why don't you give the Rev a lift now," he said. "And I'll get the truck from you later—if that's all right with you, Rev?"

"Well, I would like to take a nap before the meeting tonight," he admitted.

"And Joey will go along to show you where everything is," Stan told him.

Joey seemed to like the idea. "I'll put the bags back in the truck," he volunteered.

"Here, let me give you a hand with the broken one," the Reverend offered. "See you folks later."

"Yeah, later," June echoed and ran ahead to get the door.

Stan went over to lock the door as soon as they were gone. When he got back Tyler was waiting for him. "See what I was saying?" Tyler couldn't help gloating now that they were alone.

"What?" Stan snapped defensively.

"About contacting the press more efficiently. You'd have to be blind not to see how upset the Rev was when he found out Barbara Walters wasn't panting to interview him. At tonight's meeting I'm going to propose we form some sort of media cell. Pronto!"

5

THE WESTSIDE MOTOR INN SEEMED MORE plastic and run-down than Angus remembered. He had no trouble getting a room and making arrangements to have the car parked.

The room was dark, the window shaded; it all seemed so tranquil he didn't bother to turn the light on. He put his bag down on a chair and the bundle with Earl's belongings on the bureau; and stretched out on the bed. He was glad he finally had the quiet and privacy to indulge his thoughts. Once more he went over what the cop at the city morgue had told him. What stuck out repeatedly was the news that Earl was queer—that was bad enough; but that he'd sold his body as well. It just didn't make sense. There had never been any indication that Earl was effeminate. Wouldn't that have been a sure sign? As far as Angus had ever known, Earl was just a normal kid. This revelation hit him hard. His own brother a faggot; to his way of thinking, that was worse than death.

He tried to imagine what two men would do together, and one of the figures became Earl. The image was disturbing enough to make him puke if there had been anything in his stomach to bring up. Over and over he reviewed Earl's growing-up years trying to pinpoint some sign or tendency of his turning out this way, but he couldn't come up with anything.

Now he was starting to feel guilty, almost as if he himself had been responsible, as if somewhere along the way he should have taken notice of his brother's development and somehow could have put him on the right course. Even in Nam there were guys that the others joked about, guys they said would give you a blowjob in the trenches if you wanted one. Angus heard about it secondhand.

He didn't know anybody directly; at least nobody had ever come right out and propositioned him or admitted they had let it be done.

His eyes were drawn to the green parcel sitting on the mirrored bureau. The strong sunlight seeping through the edges of the shaded window made the package appear crowned by a golden halo. On an impulse Angus retrieved it, opened it, and arranged the contents on the bed: a cheap ski-style sweater, badly stained; grimy Levi's; frayed jockey shorts, and a beat up pair of cowboy boots. That was all. Angus rummaged through the pockets of the blue jeans. The pants were brand new—just never washed; the pockets, empty. He examined one of the boots. The toe was pointy, and there was fancy stitching around the calf. They were once high-gloss black but now the leather was badly nicked and gouged. The heel was worn down to a wedge and the soles were almost through.

Angus stared in anger and disbelief at the pile of tattered rags. Could this be everything, the total of Earl's possessions? Angus threw the boot to the floor and, sweeping the clothes into a heap, fell into bed.

He studied the textures in the ceiling for a long time before he thought about calling his mother. The hotel switchboard put the call through. After less than a ring his mother answered. Her tiny voice responded affirmatively to the operator's request to accept the charges. "Hey, Ma," Angus said, giving his voice more hope than he really felt. "You all right?"

"Earl," she said. "Is it Earl?" She had started believing there might be some mistake.

"Yeah, Ma. It's Earl," he said quietly.

Her bubble burst; she began sobbing.

"Ma," he said firmly. "Before you start crying you gotta listen. Call over to Linden's funeral parlor. Tell Mr. Linden we want him to make the arrangements. He'll know what to do. You hear me?"

"Yes, son," she said, her tears momentarily silenced. "I'll call and tell him." Then she began to ask a mother's questions. Angus answered what he could, glossing over the uglier details.

After hanging up, he had a sudden urge to call Sally. He needed emotional support, and she was the only one he could turn to even though everything was supposed to be over between them. Hadn't Sally understood as well as she could for the first couple of years? She stayed with him and prayed for things to get better. Then one day she told Angus point-blank that she felt a whole part of her life had prematurely ended; that if he didn't want to try, at least she would rather live alone. A few days later he moved out, wondering if there was maybe another guy waiting in the wings.

Actually, Angus hadn't been completely' truthful with Sally to begin with. It was true that he was impotent with her, but what she never suspected was that other women did turn him on. He had frequently visited brothels in Nam, but so far he had yet to cheat on his wife stateside. Sex didn't seem to matter so much any more. There was a time when he prided himself on his prowess and his equipment. But that seemed a long time ago.

But then nothing was the same since Vietnam. He felt like a ghost moving across the landscape observing but unobserved. Some essence of his being had been irrevocably altered. He had lost the ability to relate to the world around him, and with it perhaps his essential humanity. The carnage in which he had casually participated and survived with no physical wound had left invisible scars.

The rhythm of his life was now punctuated by his Nam experience. His mind frequently flashed back to one moment or another in the 13 months he'd spent in the jungle, part of it on the front lines serving in the Medical Corps. Vividly he recalled the mounds of ruptured flesh, ragged and bleeding, that they rolled onto stretchers and then, dodging mortars and bullets, transported back to the Medivac choppers. So many times the helicopter became a flying hearse.

In the jungle he had had lots of good buddies, but he hadn't seen one of them since. They had been friendships made out of necessity and proximity. All that really mattered was keeping the beer cooler full, and the weed was always good and plentiful. In Nam he was always high on grass, but when he got back stateside, he found he didn't like turning on as much. Because maybe coming home was the biggest down of all. He half-expected to be treated like a returning hero, but he discovered instead that he was a national embarrassment. He was angry, but there was no place to direct his anger, and he was too tired to continue fighting at home. Gradually he slipped into the grind of prosaic existence, eking out a living for the wife and sons he had known only briefly before the war.

Angus awakened with a start. There were voices in the hall outside his door. He had dozed off. As he came around to full consciousness, the voices subsided.

He sprung out of bed and clicked on the light. He wondered what time it was. The bed was a mess; he had fallen asleep amidst his brother's effects. Some had fallen to the floor. Methodically he gathered them up.

He reached for one of the cowboy boots, raising it heel first. A ball of crumpled paper rolled out onto the carpet. Angus put the boot aside and picked up the paper. Smoothing the creases, he unfurled the scrap carefully. It was a piece of lined notebook paper torn from a larger sheet with writing on it. He recognized the childish round hand of his brother. It was some kind of a list. Angus held the paper under the lamp and studied it.

Beginning on the top line of the page Earl had neatly written out the first name and telephone number of a half dozen people he apparently kept in touch with. Angus slowly read the list over a couple of times. He didn't recognize any of the names, but he guessed all the numbers were local. He wondered how the piece of paper had gotten inside Earl's boot in the first place. Then he thought that maybe Earl had hidden it in his shoe for safekeeping. Why had the police missed it? Then he remembered that the paper had been tightly balled up. He stuck his hand inside the boot and could barely work his forefinger into the narrow toe. The paper had to be forced up there when Earl put the boot on in a hurry, Angus figured. But wouldn't the pressure of the balled-up paper have been uncomfortable, especially against his big toe like that?

Then Angus had a disquieting thought: maybe Earl hadn't put the boot on at all. Someone else had pulled the boot on and most likely *after* Earl had overdosed. He conjured a chilling tableau: a grinning, emaciated drug fiend forcing the boots on a prostrate, defenseless Earl. The image made him shudder, and he had an impulse to strike out, to subdue this grotesque culprit of his imagination, and somehow revive his dying brother. But no matter how he tried, nothing could bring Earl back. Angus looked on helplessly as his brother lie dying just beyond his reach. His frustration changed to anger, and filled him with a determination to find out who was responsible for this evil deed. He had to get to the bottom of Earl's death because he couldn't live with himself until he did.

6

A BIG BLACK LIMOUSINE PULLED UP TO THE curb. The rear door swung open; two men in dark business suits and a smartly coiffed woman stepped out. The taller man instructed the driver to drive around the block and wait. He was City Councilman Porter Rhodes. Accompanied by his wife Alice and an aide, Rhodes walked briskly to the GLP storefront. The aide got the door.

The meeting was already in progress. The long, narrow interior was not as crowded as the Councilman had hoped. There were several empty rows of seats. He recognized Stan Freed on the podium. Stan had made several visits to his office.

Stan saw the Councilman's party enter. "…Before we take a vote on this financial report, I would like to call your attention to the arrival of some very special visitors." He was beaming like a proud papa. "City Councilman Porter Rhodes and Mrs. Rhodes have joined us!" With a flourish of his hand he indicated the back of the room. All eyes and heads turned toward the door. The Councilman's imposing height and apple-pie good looks set a few hearts fluttering.

"Please, Councilman," Stan insisted, "Come right up here. You too, Mrs. Rhodes." There was scattered applause.

The Councilman made his way to the front. He seemed genuinely surprised by the recognition he was getting. He showed his big perfect teeth in a winning grin and raised his hands in acknowledgment. Alice Rhodes, dressed in a white linen summer suit, followed close by her husband and smiled pleasantly. She might have been on automatic pilot.

"Councilman, I know how busy your schedule must be," Stan fawned shamelessly. "Thank you for taking the time to be with us tonight."

Porter reached the podium and shook hands all around. GLP Chairperson Derek Wiggins appeared somewhat strained by the gesture; Reverend Tunney-Brown, enthusiastic. Stan turned and addressed the crowd: "Councilman Porter Rhodes—in case there's somebody out there who doesn't know—has been very outspoken in support of the Gay Rights Amendment." He turned to the Councilman. "Please, say a few words." There was more applause. The Councilman hesitated. Then, giving the impression that "duty must be done," he stepped up to, the lectern. Alice Rhodes took a seat vacated for her in the first row and looked adoringly up at her husband.

"First, let me thank you for the invitation to come here tonight," Porter began. "And I would like to say that I am glad to lend my support to the Gay Rights Amendment currently before the City Council. I have always made it my business to support responsible causes. Job and housing discrimination is a responsible cause." There were cheers and applause. "I voted for antipollution legislation to clean up the air we breathe," Porter continued. "I worked closely with the elderly to fight the closing of senior citizen centers. I sponsored the controversial Drug Addiction Services bill. I even voted to fund a Harlem restoration project. The rights of minorities in this city are the rights of all people. At this Thursday's Council meeting I will voice my belief in the basic civil rights of this city's gay citizens by voting 'Yes' on Intro 77."

Alice Rhodes sat perfectly erect with her hands folded neatly on her lap. At first she dared not look in any direction but straight ahead. She tried to listen to her husband, but after hearing him speak so often she knew pretty well what he was going to say. She began to covertly examine the unfamiliar surroundings. The storefront certainly needed major renovation, she thought. And the furnishings, well, they looked like trash dragged in off the street (which in fact they were). Her tight little smile never once eased up.

Stan was determinedly attentive as the Councilman spoke. Reverend Tunney-Brown cocked an ear so as not to miss a word. Derek absently picked his nose. Alice could tell from her husband's tone when Porter was winding down. She waited a beat then joined in the general applause.

The Councilman thanked everyone for the enthusiastic reception and explained he had to go on to another engagement. Alice rose to meet her husband as he stepped down from the stage. They made their way to the back, the Councilman shaking outstretched hands. The aide got the door, and the Councilman waved a final adieu as he stepped aside to let his wife out first. As Alice Rhodes stepped into the street her tight little smile evaporated.

There was a burst of chatter and laughter in the vacuum left by the Councilman's departure. Stan called the meeting to order and turned it over to GLP president Derek Wiggins.

"Quite an honor," Derek deadpanned in his gravelly voice, throwing a sultry glance toward the door. Each gesture Derek made was calculated for maximum effect. And each time he was rewarded with laughter. Derek conducted meetings as if he were a stand-up comic doing a nightclub routine. He would do anything to stay the center of attention.

"Now, let's see, where were we?" There was something about his tone, the way he folded his arms, cleared his throat, and showed his best profile that was reminiscent of the comedian Jack Benny.

"We were about to vote on the financial report," Stan prompted.

"Yeah, yeah, that's right," Derek agreed. "Let's vote."

A hand shot up. "Point of information." A pasty-skinned young man in thick frameless glasses rose.

"Yes!" Derek snapped. He was getting a little tired of these interruptions.

"My question is for the treasurer. Stan, is there a deficit or a surplus? It wasn't quite clear from your report. You only mentioned expenditures. Don't we have any income?"

Stan eyed the speaker coolly. He had been vague on purpose. "There is a deficit of several hundred dollars." He was too proud to mention how much money he had taken out of his own pocket to help meet expenses.

"Wow!" somebody piped. "We better raise some bucks quick, or our next meeting's going to be on the curb."

"Let's throw a rent party," Derek suggested. "I've got all the latest records."

"I like that; I like that," Lourdes agreed. "Charge three dollars and give 'em all the beer they can drink."

"I'm for T-shirts," another suggested. "Lavender ones with the words GAY & PROUD silk-screened across the front."

"Too obvious," objected Derek. "How about the word LOVE instead? Or better: something phallic!"

The last suggestion elicited squeals of approval from the audience. "Wait a minute. Let's take a vote on the report, please." It was practical Stan. "One of you can raise the motion when we introduce new business."

A vote was called, and the treasurer's report was accepted. The next order of business was committee reports. Joey, Stan's cherubic lover, was the only committee chairman ready to report. He headed the team organizing maneuvers for Thursday's march and rally. Stan watched Joey stride briskly to the podium. He was wearing a starched sailor blouse, and his face had a fresh-scrubbed rosy glow. His rich black hair was pulled tightly behind in a luxuriant ponytail. Stan found his serious manner exceedingly seductive.

After a careful and thoughtful recitation of Thursday's game plan, he asked for volunteers. "We're going to need about 30 people to act as parade marshals. You'll have to show up here Wednesday night for a briefing at eight o'clock. Bring your sleeping bags, and we'll get an early start from here in the morning."

Stan had a hand in writing his lover's impressive presentation but one would never guess to look at him. He was raptly hanging on every word as if he was hearing it all for the first time.

"We are also planning to make the march up Broadway to the park by candlelight. So please bring all your extra candles so that every marcher will be sure to have one." Joey concluded his report with the militant chant: "Gay Power to Gay People."

There was a huge roar of solidarity with several men responding in a quick staccato chant: "GayPower GayPower GayPower GayPower…Finally the roar dissolved into general applause. With a signal from Stan, Derek announced: "The chair is open for new business."

A hand shot up in front.

"What is it, Tyler?" There was no mistaking the irritation in Derek's tone. He thought Tyler too smart to trust and a little too pushy: traits that displeased him in anyone else but himself.

Tyler stood up. He swept the pale blond hair out of his eyes; although his features were pleasant, they would never be described as handsome. "As many of you probably know," he began easily, "there have been several mugging incidents down around the pier in the last few months. The police don't give a damn one way or another, and most victims never report it anyway. I think it's time that 'we'—the gay community—do something about the situation on the water-front." There were murmurs of agreement.

"It seems to me that people who want to hang out at the pier get what they deserve," Derek disagreed. "I ain't making no judgments or casting any aspersions."

"What've you got in mind, Tyler?" Stan asked over scattered giggles.

"I think we should form a Pier Committee," Tyler continued. "Do everything from publishing reports of muggings to looking into the feasibility of the city converting that incredible space into a recreation facility, say." He was talking off the top of his head, but he thought it sounded wonderful.

Derek started laughing, letting it vibrate deep in his throat. Then in his best Bette Davis delivery: "This is New York—*not* Peoria. We are homosexuals—not Girl Scouts. Let's worry about passing the gay rights bill *first.*"

"Hold on a minute, Derek," Stan said firmly. "Maybe Tyler's got something there. It's certainly worth looking into. At least I think so."

"You would!" Derek pouted and mentally stomped out of the room.

"Go on, Tyler. You had the floor."

Tyler nodded graciously. "First thing: a release ought to go out to the media. Hand-delivered. A history of the pier with as many facts about incidents down there as we can put together."

"Wait a minute!" Derek was sputtering. "What is this? Don't we have rules around here? Rules of procedure! Let's open discussion of this pier business to the floor." Derek was determined to have his way.

"It was never *closed,*" Stan observed under his breath.

Of the assorted men and sprinkling of women gathered, those who spoke up readily agreed that the muggings at the pier were a serious problem. "Yeah there was a murder there the other night," somebody commented, mainly to get his two cents in.

"No, that was an overdose," somebody else corrected. "I got the whole story from a morgue attendant I tricked with yesterday." The contributor winked, and there was no missing the implication: Wanna hear more? Come talk to me later.

A vote was taken to form a pier committee. It passed without difficulty. Tyler asked all interested persons to catch up with him, later. "Finally," Derek declared, "the floor is open to further new business. Now isn't anybody interested in a little party to raise some funds and FUN!" he stressed.

"I got a question." It was a woman sitting in a row of chairs along the back wall. She wore a simple cotton shift and sandals and was flanked by two unfriendly looking butches in men's sport clothes. She stood up. "It's about my boy," she said and hesitated a moment. "He's only eight years old," she continued, "but I think he's going to have problems." She paused to collect her thoughts. "He's always around women," she confessed. "All my friends are women, and I was wondering if that was good or not, you know, for his self-image?" She looked shyly around the room.

Though everyone listened attentively, no one seemed to know what to say. Naturally, Stan spoke up: "Let me see if I understand you. Your son's not getting a proper self-image because there's no man around to set an example for him?"

She shook her head violently. "That's it! An older guy to take him out sometimes, show him the kinds of things that guys should know about."

"But does he have to necessarily be gay?" chirped a black dude in striped bell-bottoms and a big bushy Afro. His name was Seedy. "You gotta give the kid some options."

"You think I want some straight creep poisoning my kid's mind!" she spat. "I could send him to his father for that."

"Why don't you bring him around," Stan suggested gently.

The woman shot a glance at her two companions. "Maybe I will," she said. "Or maybe a couple of you guys can drop by for coffee sometime."

"I still think the kid should have a choice," Seedy spoke up again. "You should get some straight guys to hang out with him too."

"What are you talking about?" she exploded. "You think I want him exposed to their sexist bullshit?"

"You bring him here, or I'll pick him up at your place," Stan said to defuse the situation. "I'll show him how to operate the mimeograph, take him for ice cream."

"Yeah, that's what you do," said Derek, who didn't want to devote any more time to this discussion. "Bring the kid around. Stan's the perfect father image. Right, Joey?"

What did Derek care if his remark was interpreted unkindly especially when he had hit upon a stunning theme for the fundraiser. "Let's give a costume ball," he panted. "And are you ready for this? We'll all come *as straight people!*"

He was dead serious, and no one dared laugh out loud.

7

ANGUS WAS PACING THE TINY HOTEL ROOM. He had stuck Earl's list to the mirror with a piece of chewing gum and had read it over so many times that he practically memorized all the names and numbers. He wondered whom these people were—friends, customers, maybe both? For several minutes he had been toying with the idea of calling someone on the list. What would he say? "Hello, this is Earl's big brother. How're you tonight?"

No, no, that wasn't the way. He'd tell them he called because he wanted some information. He wanted to know about his brother—the side of his life he had never even suspected. He snatched the scrap of paper from the mirror and crossed to the phone. By rights he should turn it over to the cops, but as Finnelli so savagely implied, kids like Earl were found in the gutter all the time. Well, Earl wasn't just *another* kid. He was my brother, Angus said to himself, and I loved him. And it took something like this to make him realize how much.

Angus got a line and dialed the first number on the list. The name next to it was "Fritz Hilton." First ring. No answer. Second ring. Third ring. Maybe this guy isn't home. Fourth ring. He let it ring a couple of more times to be sure then hung up. He looked over the list. He decided to try the second number. The name written next to it looked like "Tequila."

The first ring was barely completed when an impatient voice answered, "Hello!"

"Hello," Angus said.

"Eddie? Is that you again, Eddie?" she demanded.

"No, no," Angus muttered apologetically.

"Oh!" A pause. "You sure sound like Eddie." Then as an afterthought, she asked, "Who is this anyway?"

"Is this Tequila?"

"The one and only Tequila Sunrise at your service."

"Tequila Sunrise?" he repeated. "Like the drink?"

"Oh come on, honey, get it out. Who is this? I ain't got all night to screw around on the phone!"

"My name's Angus. Angus Rivers."

"That's nice. What can I do for you?"

"You knew my brother Earl."

"Sure."

"Well, I was wondering if I could come over and talk to you about him."

"Look," she began, lowering her voice and smoothing out the abrasive tone. "I'm busy at the moment." Pause. "This Earl—where did ya say I knew him from?"

"I'm not sure," Angus said. "Earl Rivers, from upstate?"

"Frankly, it don't ring a bell—but you're welcome to come over later if you want."

Suddenly there was a squeal of recognition. "Earl Rivers!" Tequila screamed. "You mean Chicken!?" She laughed.

"Chicken?" Angus repeated.

"Yes, Chicken—a little knock-out with curly blond hair?"

"That's Earl," Angus confirmed.

"Where is he? Son-of-a-bitch ain't been by to see me in days. That ain't like him." Tequila sounded genuinely concerned.

"That's why I called," Angus said.

"Chicken's not in trouble again? I ain't bailing his ass out of nothing this time. I'm broke."

"He's not in jail," Angus said firmly. "And he's probably not going to get into anymore trouble. How do I get to your place?"

Tequila hesitated. "I'm in the Village. Didn't he give you the address?"

"No," Angus said.

Tequila gave him directions. "Come in an hour she suggested. "And look, if you think about it, pick me up a pack of smokes."

"What kind?"

"Surprise me," she said. "Anything but menthols." And hung up.

"Here we go, fellah," the driver said. The cab jerked to a halt, bringing Angus abruptly back to reality. He had been fantasizing that Earl wasn't dead after all and that they were back home roughhousing through the abandoned barn.

"Thanks," Angus said. He looked out the cab window. They had pulled up in front of a red brick apartment house with a shiny green canopy that stretched out to the curb. Angus expected to see a doorman, but there was none. He read the fare off the meter and handed the driver three singles. "Keep the change," he said and got out. The cab pulled away.

Tequila lived on the second floor. Angus stepped out of the elevator into a long narrow hallway carpeted bright red with white and gold-stenciled wallpaper. 2E marked the door at the end of the hall. Angus punched the buzzer; it chimed.

The door swung open, and a blond-haired Latin woman stood on the threshold. There was a short beat as the two strangers looked each other over.

"So you're Chicken's big brother!" she cried with a hint of a Spanish accent, and pulled Angus inside. She threw a furtive glance up and down the hall and closed the door. "Come on in and sit down," she said and escorted him through the small dining alcove into the dimly lit living room. A radio played rock music low. They sat on either end of a plastic-covered white sectional sofa. Angus smiled. Tequila smiled. But at first no one spoke.

"Can I offer you something?" Tequila said to break the ice. She sensed Angus had something serious on his mind.

"Not right now," Angus said. "Thank you."

"Are you really Chicken's brother?" she quizzed him, momentarily suspicious. "You're not a cop, are you?"

"No," Angus laughed. "I'm his brother all right, ma'am."

Tequila warmed up. She liked this guy's manner that's for sure. "You don't look much like your brother," she observed, "but you look just as good!" and she pretended to blush.

"So Chicken sent you by to see me," she continued in a familiar tone. "Where is he?"

"Earl," he began, and then corrected himself, "Chicken is dead."

"I'm not surprised!" Tequila retorted hotly. She threw her shoulders back and crossed her legs. She seemed irritated, distracted.

Her manner confused Angus. "I drove down today to claim the body." He didn't know what else to say.

"Spare me the 'Naked City' crap!" she snapped.

Then thinking Angus might misinterpret her attitude, she said, "I'm sorry—I mean—you know, condolences and all that." She turned away and began to shake; she was crying uncontrollably. "That son-of-a-bitch!" she managed between sobs. "Even when he's dead he gives me grief."

Now Angus understood where she was coming from and he touched her shoulder to console her. Wiping at her face with one hand, she reached around with the other to pat his fingertips.

"What can I tell you," she said, looking deeply into Angus's eyes. "He was having some tough times but he didn't deserve to die." Instantly she regained her composure, and asked, "What did he die from?" Then in a tiny voice: "Somebody cut his throat?"

Angus gasped and pulled away. What a ghoulish thought! "An overdose," he choked out. "They found him dead from an overdose."

Tequila gesticulated and shook her head until finally the words came. "Forgive, forgive…" she groped for the right phrase, "my frankness. It's just my way." Explanations out of the way, she continued. "I used to tell that little bastard: 'Give it up! It's gonna kill you!' You think he would listen, pay the slightest attention. None of them listen. I grew up in this garbage can. I'm Puerto Rican-Italian. From the Bronx. I'm in show business now. But to this day I'll never understand why people let themselves get hooked. They ain't got no self-respect. That's got to be it!" Tequila had said her piece.

Angus detected a change in the woman's manner but he didn't quite know what it was yet.

Tequila stood up. "I need a drink. Can I get you something?"

"Sure," Angus nodded.

She disappeared into the kitchen. Angus could hear the opening and closing of the refrigerator, the banging of ice trays, the clinking of bottles and glasses. He looked around the room. The red and pink lights gave it a warm glow. Two bright yellow bucket chairs faced the sectional sofa he was sitting on; in between there was a low, marble coffee table topped with a heart-shaped candy dish and giant ashtrays. Over two matching end tables were suspended ornate bubble lights affixed to the ceiling by a cord-laced link chain.

Tequila returned from the kitchen with a highball glass in each hand. "I hope Scotch is all right," she said handing him one. "'Cause that's all there is." She took her seat on the couch and raised her glass. "Cheers!" she said, and was about to drink when she changed her mind. "No, let's drink to your brother." She gestured with her glass. "This one's for Chicken—may he rest in peace." Tequila took a long swallow.

Angus returned the toast and took a sip. "Did you know my brother a long time?" he asked.

"What's a 'long time' in this town?" she said, putting down her glass. "Couple of months? A year? I used to let him sleep here when he needed a place to crash." She indicated the sofa they were sitting on. "Now you probably want to know how I met him? For once I don't have to make up a story. He used to hang out at a club I performed in over on the Bowery. Wasn't open too long I'm sorry to say. New owners were trying out an entertainment policy. I did a couple of songs, told some jokes. I have a little routine I worked out." She gave Angus a penetrating look. "You've probably never heard of me, but I've got quite a following here in New York and up on the Cape. Right now I'm acting in a play."

She was seconds away from taking out a portfolio of pictures and clippings. "Anyway," she continued, "Chicken used to work there too. He was a busboy or something. He'd always come back to my dressing room between shows. A real sweetie pie. You know, lighting my cigarettes, zipping me up, bringing me drinks—the little courtesies you appreciate in this business." She crossed her legs, spread her fingers on her knees, and shook her head sadly.

Angus noticed what large hands she had. The fingers were quite thick, and though she wore several flashy rings and a rosy nail polish, they were not very delicate at all.

Tequila read Angus's thoughts from the expression in his eyes. She impulsively grabbed for her drink but misjudged the distance and knocked it over. The brownish liquid ran out and beaded across the marble surface of the coffee table.

"Shit!" she swore and ran off to get paper towels.

Angus noticed as she got up the second time how tall she was. He began to suspect that Tequila Sunrise was no woman. The thought intrigued and disturbed at the same time.

Tequila came back and went about sopping up the spilled drink.

"Did Earl—I mean Chicken—stay here a lot?" Angus asked.

"It was an on-again, off-again thing with us," she shrugged. "I sometimes have to go out of town once or twice a month."

"He stayed here when you were away?"

Tequila stopped wiping the table and reared up on her haunches. She put one hand to her waist and threw out her hips. She eyed Angus with exaggerated suspicion. "Honey," she began, "I may be a soft touch but I'm no jackass. 'Let him stay here when I was away?' she mimicked. "And where do you suppose I'd be sleeping now?" She rejoined him on the sofa. "He may have been your brother, so don't get me wrong—and I loved the little bastard—but it wouldn't take five seconds for him to let one of his junkie friends clean me out. And I mean everything including the plated faucets in the john!" Tequila shook her head. "Drug addicts can't help it. They gotta have their stuff." She laughed gently. "That brother of yours is sure too much. I'm gonna miss him." She meant it.

She reached for a cigarette pack on the end table. It was empty. She crushed it in her hand and tossed it into one of the big ceramic ashtrays. This reminded Angus that he had stopped to buy some on his way over.

"I got those smokes you wanted," he said.

"Ain't you a doll!" she squeaked and took the pack. She opened it and withdrew a long filtered cigarette. Angus picked up the table lighter and gave her a light.

Tequila took a deep puff. "You talk to Panda yet?" she asked.

"Panda?" Angus echoed. The name was on the list; he was certain.

"Yeah, *Panda*," she repeated emphasizing the P sound. "He 'discovered' Chicken. Panda came to see *me* but he discovered Chicken." She had to laugh. "What I did for your damn brother!" The martyr took another deep drag.

"What do you mean?"

"Panda's an artist, a filmmaker. Chicken got invited to the Studio a couple of times to shoot some film. Panda takes pictures all the time."

"I didn't know Earl was acting. In movies, no less!"

"Who says it was acting? It's more like posing. You know, that avant-garde stuff. Sometimes Panda takes hours of film of people sitting, or screwing, or whatever. He's like a major voyeur. That's 'Art! Who am I to judge?

"Anyway, Panda stopped by the club to catch *my* show. He'd been talking about using me in one of his movies. After the show he came back to my dressing room. I thought he came to see me! Ten minutes later he and your brother are waltzing out the door together. Ain't that a bitch?" She picked up her drink.

"Can I get you another, honey?" she asked, holding out her empty class.

"No, no," he insisted. "I'm fine." His mind reeled with a profusion of images and questions. "Where's this Panda located?"

Tequila was on her way to the kitchen. "He's got a couple of floors in an old factory building on Spring Street in Soho. I'm sure he's listed: Panda Artworks," she said to the sound accompaniment of the refrigerator opening and closing. "Sure I can't freshen your drink?"

"No," Angus said, "thanks." He took the opportunity to scan Chicken's list again. 'Panda' was the next-to-last name. He returned the paper to his pocket.

Tequila swished back into the room. "Oh!" she flashed, "Don't let me forget." She sat down on the sofa; the plastic-covered cushion squeaked.

"Forget what?" Angus asked.

"I got something belong to Chicken. He asked me to hold it. Guess I better give it to you now."

"What is it?" Angus asked casually. He didn't want to seem too anxious.

"I'll show you." Tequila sashayed over to the closet and pulled a beat-up green knapsack down from the shelf.

"I have no idea what's in it," she said, shaking the pack. "Here, I'll leave it on the chair. Take it on your way out." She returned to the sofa. This time she sat a little closer. "Now," she cooed. "Tell me about yourself, big brother. Chicken never mentioned family."

Angus smiled awkwardly. "Afraid there's not too much to tell." He stood up. "Tequila, you've really been fantastic. I can't thank you enough."

"What's your hurry?" she purred.

"It's getting late. I've got to get going."

"Are you sure there's nothing else I can do for you?" There was no mistaking what she meant.

"If I think of anything, I'll call you. Thanks for the drink and for telling me about Earl."

"My pleasure." She averted her eyes, then jumped up in a burst of pretended good spirits. "Do come back when you haven't got so much on your mind."

Angus nodded and moved toward the door. Tequila followed. They paused in the dining alcove. Bright fluorescent light spilled out from the kitchen. Angus could detect the elaborate makeup Tequila was wearing; the golden-colored hair was a wig, and he could see stray dark hair stubble above her lips.

She handed him the knapsack. Their glances met. She gave him a wink and a knowing smile. "Come see my show," she said and took a printed flier from the stack on the hall table and tucked it into his breast pocket.

"I'll try," he lied and left.

8

THE GLP MEETING DRAGGED ON UNTIL STAN realized the proceedings had slipped into irredeemable chaos. He made a motion to adjourn; Tyler seconded, and it was passed unanimously. Small knots of kibitzers lingered. Nicky had sat in the back waiting for a chance to approach Tyler. He hesitated before walking over because Tyler and a black activist were having an animated discussion. Nicky caught Tyler's eye, but he couldn't draw him out of the conversation. Finally, he interrupted. "Tyler, you can put me down to work on the pier proposal," he said in one quick breath.

"Sure thing," Tyler said and nodded to Seedy to hold on a minute. "Hey, how are you doing?" Tyler asked, recognizing Nicky from the other night.

Nicky sighed; Tyler had remembered him after all. He had been so afraid he wouldn't. "I'm doing all right," Nicky said, and they started talking, filling in Seedy and the group that was gathering on what had come down the other night on the pier. They all agreed that the proposal should be written as soon as possible. Nicky said he lived nearby and had a typewriter; they were invited to do it at his place. Tyler and Seedy came along readily. On the way they picked up a couple of six-packs. Nicky lived in a cozy rent-controlled apartment on a tree-lined street. The three activists wasted no time getting to work.

Nicky's cat, a Siamese throw-off called Meow—the Bitch!—was in heat. He could kill her. All she did was periodically let out a piercing wail and rub her crotch indiscriminately against him, visitors, furniture—whatever attracted her attention. He should get her fixed, but he was convinced he didn't have the right to make *that* decision for his pet. Instead he put up with the noise and the mess.

After all, she stayed around no matter what. That's more than he could say for most of the guys he met. But maybe tonight his luck was going to change; he just had a feeling.

Soon they had composed a draft of the proposal and got to work on a press release. The beer gave out just about the time Nicky was typing everything up. They agreed to go over the material again tomorrow before taking it around to the papers. Seedy looked at his watch. "I got to split." He got up and Tyler gave him a friendly hug. Nicky showed him to the door.

"See you guys tomorrow," he said and was gone.

Nicky joined Tyler on the couch. He got out some grass and rolled a joint. The two men passed it back and forth. The pot soon mellowed them out, and Nicky got talkative. "You got a job?" he asked.

"I do when I want to," Tyler replied. "I'm a carpenter—self-employed."

Nicky could feel goose bumps go up and down the back of his arms. "Your own boss? That's wonderful!" His words slurred slightly.

"Yep, I like it that way," Tyler agreed. "I'm not going to get rich, but it pays well when I work."

"I wish I had more independence. I'm an actor—but I work office temp to get by. Right now I'm collecting unemployment."

Meow rubbed up against Tyler's boot. Nicky pushed her away. This one's mine!

Nicky turned the radio on low and moved closer to Tyler. He leaned back and closed his eyes. Tyler slid his hand over and touched Nicky on the knee. The two men came together in an awkward embrace.

Seedy took a walk over to Christopher Street. He had a feeling it might be a good night for roaming. A calm returns to the Village on Monday nights, since weekends traditionally belong to the tourists—both straight and gay—who flock in from the outer boroughs and beyond. On weeknights more of the neighborhood regulars were visible as they move singly and in pairs up and down the strip or linger chatting in clusters on the narrow sidewalks and in doorways. Some of them have passed up and down these streets for decades. A few manage to keep in step with changing styles; others cling to the look, though perhaps no longer flattering, that gave them their initial successes in the game of love.

Through the years the face of the Village has changed as well. Where once men picked each other up in furtive anonymity, now a huge nightly party seems to flourish, especially in the warm weather months. Old-timers remember when boys met boys in the leafy shadows of Washington Square Park, but the area's popularity gave way to landscaping and modern lighting. The action moved down to Eighth Street and over to Greenwich Avenue, fueled by a couple of outrageous clothing boutiques and the notorious coffee shop on the corner of Tenth.

After Stonewall, "hanging out" on Christopher Street—from Sheridan Square to the River—was *de rigueur* in international gay circles. To the dismay of residents and straight pedestrians, the curbs and stoops were constantly mobbed with gays socializing and flirting. Street musicians, playing everything from Corelli to Coltrane add to the general conviviality. Nearby, a white-faced mime or perhaps a top-hatted magician entertains atop a milk crate, and a drag on roller skates waltzes in and out of traffic: a slow honking caravan of gawking straights and prowling gays. On the corner of Hudson a lone drug dealer hawks his wares in hushed tones: "Grass—acid—speed."

The bars fill up around eleven, and by one a.m. patrons spill out to the curb. Those who have made out are leaving together, and those still looking head deeper into the Village. A casual observer might wonder how so many slim fit young men have the resources to play all night, every night. Of course, some do work from nine to five; grab a nap, then play till dawn. And there are those who live by their wits, possessing a trade or talent that allows them to work only when they want. Others are on public assistance, collect unemployment, receive allowances from generous relatives, or are kept by lovers or several loyal johns. And there are even a few with no visible means of support whatsoever—social workers routinely label them *artists. They* survive, too.

Some go on to be legends, mostly because they always seem to be out on the street, in the bars, leaning in doorways. It's not rare to overhear one gay remark to another as a legend passes them, "My god, I see that number every time I come to the Village!" "Kiss off, you fucking tourists!" the Legend hisses and gives them the finger. Affronted, he makes his way down the street dejected, running a veritable obstacle course of casual strollers in tight denims or army fatigues, Frye boots or straw wedgies. The Legend walks hurriedly, and listens to snatches of exchanges as he passes:

"Have you seen that mad show on The Bowery? What's her name, you know, it sounds like a cocktail—she's in the cast'…"Oh. I'm afraid I can't right now. I'm waiting for somebody. He should be along any moment."…"What do you mean, that's tacky? And I suppose that red thing you always wear with the faux fox trim—that's fashion?"…"I'm sorry, what's your name again?…How'd you make out?" "Don't ask!"…"The moon's full tonight; I can feel it."…"Joints, nickel bags, dimes: Columbian gold."…"Another bar? So what! More of the same."

Finally, in some dark doorway just off the strip, the Legend pauses to compose himself. He shouldn't let those cracks shake him up so much. After all, notoriety comes with the territory. He laughs and gives a passing number the eye.

TUESDAY

THE BIRDS CHIRPING IN THE TREES OUTside the window almost brought him to consciousness. He heard the bird song under the effect of a sedative that kept random patterns racing through his head at break-neck pace. He opened his eyes, then closed them; sleep's pull was stronger.

A firm knock on the door.

"Thank you, Joseph," he called automatically, still within the sleeping pill's seductive grip.

The manservant soundlessly entered the Bishop's bedchamber. He shuffled over to the bed with a steaming cup of black coffee in one hand and a copy of the morning paper in the other. The Bishop pulled himself out of bed with a start and lurched into the bathroom. Joseph nodded respectfully. He set the coffee on the night table and arranged the bed pillows into a cozy mound.

His Grace moved to the window and pulled one curtain open. His mood seemed expansive as he bathed in the bright daylight, intoning his morning prayers. Then the Bishop crawled back into bed and arranged himself against the pillows. Joseph finished opening the draperies. As the room filled with light, the birds grew noisier. His Grace reached for the coffee cup and saucer and brought it delicately to his lips. He took a tiny, audible sip. Elegantly yawning, he picked up the newspaper but did not open it. Instead his glance drifted dreamily toward the latticed window: how stunning the intricate patterns of stained glass when illuminated by the morning sun!

Joseph moved noiselessly from cupboard to closet about his tasks. He laid out the Bishop's morning garments and red velvet slippers. He stepped into the bath and started the tub; the water's roar roused His Grace sufficiently to turn to the morning paper. As always, he scanned the headlines on the front pages before turning to the death notices. After a quick reading of all the names of the day's obituaries he was drawn to a story on the opposite page: AUTOPSY CON-FIRMS OVERDOSE FOR TEENAGE RUNAWAY. Beneath the headline there was a large photograph of a handsome fellow looking somewhat distracted and annoyed. The photo was captioned: "Grief-strickened brother leaves City Medical Examiner's on First Avenue." The man was getting into a car, and in the foreground his hand was firmly gripping the door. The long thick fingers excited the Bishop's prurience, and he began reading the accompanying story. When he came across the name "Earl Rivers," a shadow of recognition came over him. He didn't quite realize what he knew until he read on to, "tattooed on his forearm the nickname…

"Chicken!" he exclaimed.

"I'm sorry, your Grace?" Joseph inquired.

"Nothing, Joseph. Nothing." His Grace returned to the newspaper, his jowls growing flush.

There were several paragraphs, peppered with quotes, about the brother of the dead boy driving in from upstate to identify and claim the remains. There was also mention of Chicken having a police record. The story went on to discuss the initial speculation in the gay community that the boy had been a crime victim due to a spate of muggings and other random violence that had been occurring on the waterfront in recent months. Police officials were quoted as saying, "Patrols will be stepped up to deter crime in the area."

The Bishop reread the first few paragraphs, especially the part about Chicken's police record. He should have expected as much. How blinding was his infatuation! It was a good thing that the police knew their place and didn't ask too many questions. Otherwise it could have been a very unpleasant interview.

Agitated, His Grace paced to the bay and threw the window open. The harsh sunlight, unencumbered by the leaded glass, assaulted him, violating the serenity of room.

Joseph emerged from the lavatory and beckoned to His Grace. It was not unusual for the Bishop to get lost in his meditations and forget the time. "Thank you, Joseph," he sighed, and so as to not arouse the servant's suspicions, he did what was expected.

The Bishop eased his flaccid body into the steamy water; momentarily it lulled all his cares away. He wasn't concerned about Chicken anymore. After all, he had done nothing to be ashamed of. He had reached out to touch another human being and been burned. He was considerably calmed by the soothing vapors. Now he could view the whole incident more objectively.

His Grace was strolling about the cathedral grounds noting the first buds of spring. He glimpsed the mop of blond ringlets and then saw the boy in a green fatigue jacket perched on the high stonewall. Struck by the boy's angelic visage in the pastoral setting, he couldn't resist an impulse to speak.

"Tell me, young fellow, is the view any better from up there?" he called, raising both arms slightly in order to give his cape full play in a passing gust of wind.

The boy was startled by the dramatic figure and almost lost his balance.

"Careful there, don't fall!" His Grace admonished gently.

The lad smiled and admitted sheepishly, "I guess I shouldn't be up here."

"That depends," the Bishop toyed, "on what has drawn you to such great heights."

"The birds," the boy exclaimed. "I'm waiting for one to start building a nest."

The Bishop roared. "City birds are a lot smarter than that, young man," he managed between guffaws. "They always build their nests far from probing eyes like yours!"

Chicken jumped down with an assist from His Grace. The two fell easily into conversation, and soon the Bishop was pointing out the different varieties of plantings that garlanded the grounds. Before long they were back in the pantry enjoying cookies and soft drinks. The cleric was seduced by the sweetness of temperament that complemented the boy's equally appealing countenance. The visitor was ravenous, and His Grace found him self extending a dinner invitation. The youngster accepted readily.

The Bishop got very sad and misty as he recalled how badly everything had turned out. He should never have let the boy wear the ring in the first place. But it was such an innocent request. He never imagined the boy would seriously believe it was a gift and leave with it. Yes, it all got very awkward. Especially when the police returned it. Of course, he had already reported losing it "tramping about the garden." Then, when it turned up in a West Side pawnshop and the man who was trying to pawn it said he bought it from some kid in the Village.... Yes, the police were very understanding. No, there was no need to press the case. He was glad to have the signet back and would be more careful next time. The matter was closed.

Why, he had actually thought about making arrangements for Chicken to room on the grounds, perhaps help Miss Munson part-time in the gift shop. What plans he had had and only after a few days' acquaintance! Now the Bishop wished he had taken Polaroids. He was ashamed of giving in to the excesses of his imaginings, yet he found repentance all the more glorious for it.

It was better to think of something else, the Bishop decided. No—it was better to think of nothing at all. He closed his eyes and concentrated on his breathing. Immersed up to the neck, he was very cozy indeed....

Next thing he knew Joseph was gently shaking his shoulder. He must have drifted off. What if he had slipped under the water and drowned?

"Joseph," the Bishop sighed. "What would I do without you?"

The retainer beamed.

2

ANNIE GORDON HAD BARELY FINISHED HER second cup and already the intercom was buzzing. She pressed the talk switch. "Yes, ma'am?"

"Good morning, Annie," came the well-bred tones of Alice Rhodes. "Just coffee for Mr. Rhodes and my usual bran and juice. Has the paper come?"

"Yes, ma'am."

"Thank you."

Annie released the button and pushed her chair away from the table. She carefully folded the newspaper that she had been reading and put it on the breakfast tray. She retrieved a tumbler of juice from the refrigerator and filled the serving pot with fresh coffee.

Alice heard Annie lying breakfast on the terrace. She was still in bed and wanted to stay there. She had awakened with an uneasy feeling deep in her gut but couldn't put a finger on the cause. Porter hummed to himself as he dressed. She wished he were back in bed with her. Lately it seemed they had so little time together. He was always off campaigning. She clung to the memories of the early years: the endless walks along the Drive, summers on the Cape. Then there was plenty of time for everything…. Porter was no longer the lover she married. The change paralleled his mounting political ambitions. If it were another woman, she could understand and be confident of winning him back. But his mistress was Politics, and Alice was helpless in the face of such a formidable rival.

The cotton percale sheets felt cool and soft against her naked body. She closed her eyes tight and squirmed and stretched, grinding her buttocks against the firm mattress. Her hand gently stroked her inner thighs. Now she remembered what had given her the uneasy feeling. She had wanted to make love this morning. Porter had acknowledged her caresses briefly, but then mumbled he'd be late for a breakfast meeting at Gracie Mansion and bolted into the shower.

Annie tapped lightly at the glass door to signal that the table was set.

"Porter," Alice called, pulling herself out of bed and into a pale satin robe and slippers. There was nothing she hated more than warm orange juice. "I'll get your coffee."

Buttoning his collar, he stuck his head in from the dressing room. "Do I have time?"

Make time! she thought, but turned away so he wouldn't read it on her face. "Whatever you say, darling," she said coolly and crossed to the terrace door. At her touch it slid the rest of the way open. Putting on his jacket, he came out a few steps behind her. He kissed her on the mouth hard.

"Maybe a quick cup," he said and reached for the paper.

She filled his cup, adding two lumps of sugar and a splash of cream. Porter automatically stirred the mixture while reading the front page. He put down the spoon and opened the paper. Alice poured cream on her cereal. She took a sip of the juice. It was icy cold, just the way she liked it. Her eyes strayed across the table to a full-page airlines ad on the back page. Huge bold-faced print asked: HAD ANY...LATELY?

She laughed aloud at the irony of the message.

"What's so funny?" Porter asked, curious enough to put his paper down.

"You are!" she said jokingly and reached across the table to tweak his nose. "Do I still get you all to myself tonight?" she asked playfully.

"What's that supposed to mean?" he asked, knowing full well the answer.

"Nothing. I didn't say it." Complaining would only make matters worse.

"Honey, some of these people are very important. I need the endorsements."

"I know, Porter, I know. The last thing she wanted was for him to start defending himself. They had so little time together and she hated to spend it at odds.

He took a sip of the coffee. "I think Mother wants us for cocktails. We'll be out of there by six-thirty the latest."

"Anything special?" she asked flatly.

"It's a kick-off for some benefit or another. You know my mother."

"What time?"

"Five-thirty. Meet me there." He wanted to suggest that she go over a little earlier to spend some time alone with his mother but thought better of it. "I'll be thinking about you," he said, rising from the table and blowing her a kiss.

She got up instantly and walked with him to the terrace door. They embraced. He pulled her very close.

"Maybe we can get away for a couple of days this weekend," he whispered. "Go out to the beach and lie in the sun."

The thought of the Island and the closeness of his body aroused her. He licked behind her ear. The moist tip of his tongue sent a shiver through her. She felt like an amorphous form waiting to be molded by his touch.

"Later," he murmured, and his arms slowly dropped away.

She knew better than to cling, to force herself on him. For a second she tightened her hold, then released him, letting her arms fall away like deadweights. She grabbed at the terrace door to steady herself.

"I mean it," he smiled, and gave her another kiss

He was gone almost before she realized it. Still warm from his touch, she drifted back to the table. For the first time since she woke up she saw what a gorgeous sunny day it was. The park below was a verdant mat. In the clear blue horizon, beyond the tops of buildings, she could see the New Jersey hills. Alice felt moist and pulsating. She sat down and pulled her chair close to the table. Partially concealed by the folds in her robe, she started working two fingers between her legs. Her other hand gripped the lip of the table. Throwing one cautious look about her even though the canopy shielded her from prying eyes, she slumped over, moaning and whimpering….

3

ANGUS RECEIVED A 9 A.M. WAKE-UP CALL from the front desk. He didn't get up right away but lay there in a dreamy state of half-sleep. His meeting with Tequila crept into his thoughts. He could smile about it now: the preposterousness of the situation, and how he was completely taken in until practically the last minute. He had done some casual reading in national magazines on transvestitism and sex-change operations, but as far as he knew that was his first face-to-face encounter. In Nam a German magazine with graphic illustrations had been passed around the hutch: men in women's clothing exposing their genitals. The freakiness of the explicit pictures was vivid in his memory.

He wondered about Earl's relationship to Tequila. Had they been lovers? Probably—but then again she had intimated that Chicken slept on the sofa. He tried to picture them in bed together, but all he could see was the tow-haired ten-year-old whose sneakers needed tying. He remembered picking him up on his shoulders and trotting around the yard jousting with low-hanging tree branches, his peals of laughter ringing through the neighborhood.

Now how little he knew this same brother. He blamed it on the years that separated them. He should have tried harder to keep in touch. But for Angus, manhood came early. When Angus was discovering girls, Earl was learning how to walk. Working part-time, he earned enough to know a certain amount of independence. He was married and starting his own family before Earl was out of elementary school. Then the draft, two years active duty…. When he came back he hardly knew Earl at all.

There was a period, a few years, when he and Earl were the best of pals. It was when his mother returned to work and Earl was put in day care. It was Angus's responsibility to pick the boy up after school and stay with him until their mother got home. At first Angus resented the loss of his free time, but not for long. Earl proved a sympathetic and undemanding charge. They had a couple of games they played, silly simple stuff like Angus hiding and Earl seeking him out, or just tossing a basketball, but it gave Angus a strong sense of satisfaction to remember. And how could he forget the stray cat Earl brought home? How heartbroken he was when the old man wouldn't let him keep it because he said black cats spooked him.

"I'm the winner, I'm the winner, I'm the winner! Angus remembered Earl's shouts of joy over winning a foot race that Angus had let him win. That time now seemed too brief and so far away.

There was almost a dozen years difference in age between the two boys. Edna Rivers called Earl her "late child" because he was born just before her 48th birthday. Moe Rivers was nearly 60 and knew he wasn't the father, though he was too proud to admit it to anyone—except Edna. He made her pay dearly for her indiscretion. Angus sensed the change in his parents after Earl was born. His father rarely had a good word for "the kid," as Angus came to think of him. Angus believed it was because the old man was going senile until he overheard an exchange between his parents, just a few words, some snide references to Earl's blond hair. He gradually figured out what his father meant.

Moe Rivers was a dark swarthy man, descendant of immigrant Slavs who lost their real name during processing on Ellis Island. Angus inherited his father's mane of fine dark hair and solid physique. Edna's people were so-called "lace-curtain Irish," they gave their daughter a good convent education only to have her take up with a common laborer. Moe earned a good living but he had no pretenses to middle-class respectability.

Why did Edna marry him? She was a 36-year-old librarian in a small upstate town when Moe came along and proposed. It was her only offer, and she grabbed it. Moe was a good-looking man in his way and a charmer. While they were courting he showed her every deference; it was noticeably absent after they wed. The same desperation for the touch of a man 12 years later led to a brief affair with a stranger. Her second son was an ever-present reminder of her husband's humiliation.

Edna raised Earl dutifully, but her heart wasn't in it. In her loneliness and shame, she began keeping discreet company with "a little drink." First it was wine or sherry, but she moved on to harder stuff and was soon filtering the world through a deepening haze of alcohol. Sometimes she would sober up long enough to get her self together to go to church. The solemn ritual and well-meaning parishioners would only serve to increase her guilt, and the only way to assuage her conscience was to obliterate it.

His wife an embarrassment to him, and with his own inflexible attitudes, Moe built an impenetrable wall that kept his family at arm's distance. Theirs became a house of discordant strangers living in uneasy proximity.

Somehow through it all Earl grew to adolescence, and whatever scars there were never marred his sweet nature. If anything he seemed to grow more beautiful, like a golden blossom sprouting in a junkyard. Yet there was something of the devil in him, and from very early on he seemed always to be getting into trouble. At home, at school, with neighbors—but no one ever stayed mad at him for long. He had such a winning way of accepting his faults and standing ready to receive his punishment.

Suddenly Angus remembered the knapsack Tequila had given him. He had planned to examine it right away last night, but had been too tired to do much else but fall into bed when he got back. He pushed the sheet aside and got out of bed. The bag was in the chair where he had dropped it. It was the standard green imitation of a Government-issue backpack; the kind he had used when he was a Boy Scout. His thick fingers deftly undid the buckles and sash, and parted the opening. He felt around inside, then dumped the contents on the foot of the bed.

A ball of clothes, bits of paper and other miscellaneous items tumbled out. Among them a comb, hairbrush, and a frayed yellow toothbrush—all the personal things Angus had wondered about. There was also a brown leather pouch and a red spiral notebook. Angus opened the pouch. It contained a clay hash pipe, rolling papers, a metal clip, an eyedropper, and a length of cord.

He reached for the notebook and opened it. The first few pages were filled with indecipherable notes in an unrecognizable scrawl. It was the same kind of paper on which Earl had recorded the list of names and phone numbers. Angus kept flipping through the small book. The writing stopped and there were blank pages. He was about to close the notebook, but suddenly there was more writing—and in Earl's precise even script.

Angus turned a couple of pages. Earl had used the book to keep a diary. Many of the entries were just a few lines, and sometimes there was more than one to the page. Above each paragraph he had marked the day of the week. He read the first few entries, and then flipped through to the last one. All together he estimated there weren't more than twenty or thirty separate entries.

Angus didn't feel like reading any more. He closed the notebook and put it down. He went into the bathroom, turned the shower spigots on full blast, and stepped into the tub. The needles of cold water felt good against his back and shoulders. He turned into the spray, pushing his face into the rushing water. Whatever the intensity of the water he couldn't divert his thoughts from Earl. How amazing it all was: this life he had lived in the city. What more could there be? The possibilities now seemed vaster than he could imagine.

Toweling off, he returned to the bedroom, went over to the bureau, and glanced at the list once more. The name Panda struck his fancy. Tequila said he had made movies of Earl. Why not give him a call? Angus picked up the phone, got on an outside line and dialed. An answering service picked up and the solicitous feminine voice explained, "They never get in before noon. I'll take your number and have somebody get back to you." Angus decided not to leave a message; he was toying with the idea of just dropping by.

The name after Panda's was Ted. Again he got an outside line, and dialed.

"Mr. Hughes' wire," came a crisp female voice.

"Is he there?" Angus asked.

"Mr. Hughes is out of town. Can I take a message?"

What sort of office is this, he wanted to know, but asked instead, "When's he due back?"

"Sometime Wednesday. Whom shall I say called, sir?'

"Angus Rivers," he found himself saying and reading off the motel phone number. Her cool efficiency intimidated him.

"I'll see that he gets the message," she said and hung up.

Angus wondered why he bothered to leave a message. Maybe this guy Hughes would get back to him and maybe he wouldn't. Either way Angus had nothing to lose. In this frame of mind he looked over the list and decided to make another call.

4

A CAR HONKED AND A TRUCK RUMBLED BY. A gentle breeze brought the sounds through the open windows. The glass chimes hanging in the archway tinkled. Fritz lay stiffly across the low bed like a pale ivory Buddha. He was fully awake and staring at the telephone. The call had come a while ago. Since hanging up the receiver he had not stirred. He was wondering if he had done the right thing. He reconstructed the conversation.

The caller said that he was Chicken's brother and he wanted to come over. Fritz was hesitant. The brother said he had some news, some bad news, and wanted to deliver it personally. Fritz insisted on hearing it over the phone. "Chicken is dead," the man blurted out. The words still echoed inside Fritz's head. In his initial grief and confusion, he gave the caller the address. Now it wasn't quite clear to him what this brother was coming over for.

Fritz looked out the window at the slate-gray building that blocked out most of the sky. His thoughts turned to Chicken and that first night. Liking Chicken as much as he did broke all the rules. Though he could smile about the way they met, he was convinced he should never have let it happen.

Coming home late one night, he discovered the boy curled up asleep in the doorway. His first impulse was to give the tattered little beggar a boot and retreat quickly inside. But the boy's golden halo of hair sparked Fritz's curiosity and softened his usual hostility. He paused to admire the young sleeper. Emotions long banished from his consciousness began struggling inside him for expression. The boy's eyes opened. He smiled sleepily and moved to make way, like a stray dog used to letting strangers pass. Fritz fumbled with his keys. He stole another glimpse of the young beauty, and his eyes shone with desire.

"Got someplace I can crash tonight, Mister?" the boy asked.

How many times had Fritz been approached by scruffy little delinquents looking for a place to stay; he usually turned them down instantly. Certainly the offers tantalized, and once or twice he had later regretted not saying yes, but generally he was intimidated by the awkwardness of the situation. He'd be embarrassed to walk down the street with some obvious adolescent in tow. His intentions would be transparent, and he was deathly afraid of what passersby would think. But now a young supplicant lay on his very threshold.

"Come in if you want," Fritz said simply.

The boy he came to know as Chicken silently followed him up the stairs….

Fritz wanted to get out of bed. He should start dressing, have something to eat, but he was beginning to resent the coming intrusion. Was this brother of Chicken's looking for someplace to stay too? Or was his visit a prelude to inquiries from the police? This last thought made him shudder. He was afraid of losing his green card and being deported.

The buzzer sounded. He'd soon know his fate.

Fritz pulled himself heavily out of bed and padded over the floor to ring the caller in. He retrieved his robe and slippers from the closet and put them on. He waited by the door for the knock.

"Mr. Hilton?" the man asked as Fritz opened the door. "I'm Angus Rivers," he said, and extended his hand.

Fritz looked at the man a long moment before shaking. He gestured for him to come in and closed the door. "Have a seat," Fritz sighed and pointed to a chair at the small dining table.

Angus sat down. He felt disoriented in the cluttered little apartment. The old man moved heavily across the room to retrieve another chair. Angus used the moment to take a quick look around. Every available surface was crowded with assorted knickknacks: souvenir mugs, painted ashtrays, plastic dolls and stuffed animals, miniature statues, pennants, and plastic flowers. All the lights were shaded with paper Chinese lanterns; chimes and pinwheels were situated near the windows to take advantage of stray gusts of wind.

Fritz returned with a matching chair and sat down. He was a great mountain of a man swaddled in a soiled terry-cloth robe. He eyed the visitor but said nothing.

"So you were a friend of my brother's," Angus began tentatively.

"Chicken was a good friend; I'll miss him," Fritz said sadly. "How did it happen?"

Angus told Fritz as much as he knew about the overdose, the pier, and the possibility that his body may have been brought there from someplace else. "How did you get to know my brother?" he asked Fritz.

"I let him—how you say?—crash here when he needed a place to stay. He stayed here on and off for a couple of months."

"When was that?" Angus asked.

"Oh, it's been over a year, last winter. Last time we talked, he was sharing a place in the East Village with some other boys."

"Do you know who?"

"No, not really. He once brought a fellow around. It wasn't too long ago, maybe a month or so. But I don't know whether they were living together or not."

"What was his name?"

"I'm afraid I've forgotten. Actually I put the whole ugly episode out of my mind."

"What do you mean?" Angus asked.

"I'm afraid matters got a bit out of hand. I caught the boy Chicken had brought going through things in the bedroom. That's when I suspected that he and Chicken were using drugs. Not that Chicken would ever knowingly take anything. No, he'd never do that. But this friend of his was definitely bad company."

"And you're sure you can't remember his name?"

"It was an odd name; I'd certainly remember if I heard it again. It was not a usual name but a nickname, you know."

"You remember what he looked like?"

The old man vigorously shook his head. "A real snake. Something about his eyes: piercing, crazy. And his skin was very pale with a greenish tone."

"What color was his hair?"

"Black. Stringy coils of shiny black hair." He gestured with his hands to suggest the length. "I took an instant dislike to him and Chicken knew it."

"When did you last see my brother?"

"Why, now that you ask, it was probably the time he came around with this awful...Snicker! That's his name. I told you it was an odd one."

"Snicker," Angus repeated. He was certain it was nowhere on the list. Maybe Chicken had mentioned him somewhere in the diary.

"That was around the early part of May," Fritz continued. "Of course he could have come by since and I missed him. I been working double shifts for over a month now."

"What kind of work do you do?" Angus asked to keep him talking.

"I'm a licensed massage therapist. I work for a health club." There was no mistaking the old man's sudden irritation at answering personal questions.

Angus shifted uncomfortably. He was trying to think of something else to ask.

"Are you conducting your own investigation?" Fritz asked Angus.

"In a way you can say that," Angus conceded, though he hadn't quite put it to himself that way yet. "I'm just tracking down people my brother knew. You know how the police are. What's another dead body in a big city like this? Well, he was my brother, and me and my parents are kind of upset." Angus was growing defensive.

"Chicken was a good boy," Fritz calmly assured him. "But it's hard to stay away from trouble in this city. Especially when you're young and finding your way."

The old man seemed genuinely concerned, but there was no more reason for Angus to hang around. And he found the narrow flat more and more oppressive. Angus thanked Fritz for seeing him and added: "If you think of anything else that might help me locate this buddy of my brother's, I'd appreciate a call. I'm staying at the Westside Motor Inn till the end of the week." He fished in his shirt pocket. "Here," he said and handed him a printed book of matches, "the phone number's on there."

The old man wished him luck and showed him to the door.

As Angus was coming out onto the sidewalk he heard some loud shouting and the crash of garbage cans. The cause of the disturbance was a large buxom woman with steel-gray hair wildly wielding a broom on the opposite curb. She was chasing a big orange tomcat that apparently had overturned the trash cans foraging for scraps. "Son-of-a-bitch!" she screamed. The battered animal skittered across the street past Angus and dove beneath a parked car.

"Looks like lunch is a little late today, fellah," Angus whispered sympathetically and started walking up the street.

5

THE WILY TOMCAT REMAINED HIDDEN BEhind the auto's furthest wheel. After a short breather to get his bearings, he slinked up the street beneath the row of parked cars. Halfway up the block he made a break for a familiar alley. Squeezing effortlessly through the gate rails, he moved along at a swift jaunt staying close to the wall. Arriving in the rear courtyard, he mounted a narrow ledge leading to an adjoining yard. He paused to survey his surroundings.

The backyard landscape was green and tranquil, a sharp comparison to the hurly-burly of cars and pedestrians in the street. The chatter of birds punctuated the stillness. A soft breeze murmured through the trees. A sparrow lighted on a nearby bush and chirped playfully, jerking its head in a rush of curious little flutters. The bird skipped from branch to branch, moving unawares nearer the preying tom, which had crouched down in the grass waiting for his chance to pounce. A fly landed on the cat's nose. He responded with an involuntary jerk of his head and a swat of his paw. The movements alerted the sparrow, which instantly soared up to a window ledge.

Thwarted once more, the tom made a hasty retreat along the adjoining back fences of several yards until he reached his own. He paused and craned his neck to watch the sky a moment, then slipped through the broken cellar window into the apartment building. In the basement's cool dark labyrinth he headed for the old super's subterranean lair. He stepped soundlessly through the torn meshing of the screened door.

A radio propped up on top of the refrigerator blared easy-listening music interrupted by occasional bursts of static. The cat padded over to his bowl and nosed the paltry remains of dry food. Dissatisfied, he leapt onto the sink and poked around the stacks of dirty dishes. An odor aroused his senses, and he sniffed the air for a direction. It was a greasy frying pan sitting on one of the front burners; he jumped smoothly from the edge the sink to the top of the stove.

He lapped ravenously at the residue of bacon fat in the bottom of the cast iron skillet. Each lapping stroke of his tongue pushed the pan a little closer to the edge of the burner till finally it toppled over and crashed to the floor. The tom perked up his ears and froze, ready to spring.

"Son-of-a-bitch!" came a terrible yowl from the next room followed by the crash of china and cutlery. "Damn you, Samson! Damn youuuu!" the voice cried out.

Marlowe had dozed off in his favorite armchair after completing a late morning meal. Rudely awakened by the noise in the kitchen and knowing full well the culprit, he stood up, forgetting the dishes and silver balanced precariously in his lap. Kicking the broken shards from underfoot, he lunged toward the kitchen in a fit of rage. He was intent on closing the kitchen door before Samson could escape his punishment.

"Where are you—you bastard?" Marlowe snarled, bursting into the kitchen. He glimpsed a streak of orange fur disappear through the rotted screening. He banged the inner door shut. "I'll fix your ass—just you wait."

He tottered unsteadily about the room exhausted. He already had on the best part of a good drunk. Cursing his pet, he stumbled into the other room. Amidst the debris on the bedside table sat an open pint of red wine. He raised the half-empty bottle to his lips, took a good swig, wiped his mouth with the back of his hand, and cleaned the hand on the seat of his stained coveralls. He put the bottle down and crumpled into the vinyl-covered armchair. Trying to focus his thoughts through the haze of alcohol that clouded them, he remained immobile. Soon he dozed off. His head fell forward, his mouth dropped open, and a string of spittle hung precariously from his jaw.

The phone rang. He stirred, but the brain was unable to make out the message. The phone rang again. On the third ring he comprehended and lurched over to the wall instrument with Pavlovian alacrity.

"Yeahhh," he breathed into the receiver. No answer.

"Yeah!" he demanded, raising his voice.

"That you, Marlowe?" the caller whispered hoarsely.

Marlowe recognized the voice. In the background he could hear a loud-playing television and a baby crying.

"What do you want?" he growled. "I told you not to call here."

"I had to," the voice pleaded. "I gotta see you." In the pause Marlowe could clearly hear the noises on the other end: a woman's angry threats punctuated by children laughing and squealing.

"You there?" the caller shouted. Marlowe grunted.

"Listen," the voice begged. "My sister's kids are driving me nuts. I gotta get out of here. I'm taking the train in tonight."

"You can't stay here," Marlowe warned.

"Just a couple of days. I'll keep out of your way. You won't know I'm there."

"Give it another week, huh?" Marlowe urged. "You stay in Jersey the week, then we'll see."

"I gotta get out tonight." There was a desperate quiver in his voice. "You hear me, Marlowe? Tonight!"

The connection was broken. Marlowe dropped the receiver into its cradle. He wasn't anxious to see Snicker or to have him around anymore, especially after last Friday. He had to get rid of him. Stake him if necessary, but anything to get him to leave town.

6

IT WAS HIGH NOON, TEMPERATURE BROILing, as the black station wagon pulled into the garage of the Medical Examiner's building. The three occupants slid leisurely out of the front seat. Nathaniel A. Linden had made the trip personally, accompanied by his regular driver, Johnson, and a part-time helper nicknamed Loco. A surly orderly at the processing desk informed them with a certain satisfaction that it was "Lunchtime, babee—and a coupl'a more ahead'a you."

The funeral director told his men to go get a sandwich. He was above letting petty annoyances disturb him. He located the water fountain, took a long drink, and then waited patiently in the corridor. He casually noted the regular pattern of the gray-tiled walls and the well-worn flooring. The faint odor of disinfectant hanging in the air caused him to nervously sniff the white carnation in his lapel. He pictured himself standing there in his black-and-white seersucker with black accessories. What a sharp contrast his presence was to the drab institutional surroundings. He took great pride in his personal appearance and had all his suits custom-cut. He made a good living; it was his privilege to dress well.

He plucked a discarded newspaper from a bench and thumbed through it. Suddenly looking up at him was the older Rivers boy and a story about finding the younger one on the West Village piers. The story said the younger boy's street name was Chicken and that he was mixed up in dope and prostitution. Nathaniel was impressed. He had no idea his clients were so celebrated. He tore the article out and carefully folded it into his wallet. His thoughts turned to the frail mother who had come to see him the night before. Till now he had known her as the local librarian; they had what could be best described as a nodding acquaintance. He also knew she had two handsome sons.

Mr. Linden noticed how heavily scented she was and realized she was masking the smell of alcohol. Who was he to judge; so when she stumbled or lost the thread of what she was saying, he lent steadfast support. He had been there himself and knew how small kindnesses were appreciated.

"You can be certain, Mrs. Rivers," he suavely assured her, "we'll make all the arrangements. I'll go down to New York and personally take charge." The solicitous manner came easily but it hadn't always been that way. Once he was full of large dreams for another kind of a future. Begrudgingly he had taken over the family business from his ailing father. Certainly his attitude toward the work had changed, but the truth was he'd been contemplating a pleasure trip to New York and now he had a legitimate business deduction.

His men returned from lunch. The processing desk resumed business. He presented his authorization papers, and the clerk handed over the necessary release forms. Johnson and Loco retrieved the transport casket and wheeled it to the receiving area, where they were met by Nathaniel and a morgue attendant who led them back to cooler drawer #78 and unlocked it. While the attendant double-checked the cadaver's identity against tags and photos attached to the file, Loco and Johnson transferred Chicken from the cooler tray to the unornamented pine box. The plastic wrapper caught on a corner and pulled away, revealing the boy's slightly muscular arms and upper torso. Nathaniel found that the sight aroused him.

Loco and Johnson wheeled the box out to the station wagon and loaded it on. After taking care of the final details of processing, Nathaniel joined his two employees in the garage. "Johnson, I think the Palisades route is your best bet this time of day," he instructed the graying driver.

"Yes, sir."

Nathaniel pulled his briefcase out of the boot. "Look for me around noon tomorrow. Tell Henderson to get started on this one right away. We're showing him Thursday."

"Yes, sir, Mr. Linden."

"Drive carefully," Nathaniel cautioned and waited while the two men got into the car. He walked alongside as they moved out of the garage. Nodding goodbye at the curb, he watched the vehicle turn into the flow of traffic. He walked to the corner and hailed a cab. Settling into the high back seat he told the cabbie to drop him at a particular intersection, a discreet distance from his favorite bathhouse.

7

PANDA ARTWORKS WAS LOCATED IN AN OLD warehouse off lower Broadway. Angus rode a rickety freight elevator to the tenth floor. He stepped out into a narrow corridor with a door at either end. One door was painted bright green with gold lettering that read CYBRITSKY NUTS & BOLTS, M. CYBRITSKY, PRESIDENT. The other door was black with PANDA ART-WORKS dramatically scrawled in silver sparkles.

Angus tried the PANDA ARTWORKS door. It was locked. He knocked.

After a moment the WO in ARTWORKS opened up, and a mouth and nose demanded, "Who's there?"

"I'm here to see Mr. Panda," Angus said.

"Yeah, well, who are you?"

"Tell him," Angus began, and then thought for a moment. "Tell him Chicken sent me."

"Hey!" the inquisitor chirped in a complete change of tone. "Hang in there a sec." The peephole snapped shut, and the door swung open. A willowy fellow in coveralls and frizzy red hair ushered Angus in.

"Man, you should've mentioned Chicken right away and I wouldn't have hassled you. You wouldn't believe the bums trying to get in here all the time. Grab a seat, I'll get a message to Number One. What's your name?"

"Angus, Angus Rivers."

"Hey, you're not the guy in the paper today, are you?"

The guy in the paper? The desk clerk at the motor inn had shouted, "Your picture's in the paper!" when he was going out. He had meant to pick up a newspaper at a corner stand. "I haven't seen it myself yet," Angus admitted. "You got an extra copy around I could look at?"

"It was around here earlier, but you know how fast something like that disappears." The lanky lad crossed to a clear Lucite desk and leaned over to speak into the intercom. "Tell Number One a friend of—I mean, Chicken's brother wants to see him. His name's Rivers, Angus Rivers." He turned to Angus and said, "Myrna will be out in a minute. Relax."

Angus settled into one of the plush modular seating units. The redhead returned to some typing. The ultra-modern decor was quite a surprise, Angus found, after the peeling paint and general seediness of the entry, elevator and hall. The floor and walls were covered with deep blue carpeting, and all the furnishings were stark white. Office doors were concealed behind vertical panels.

A short stout woman wearing large, thick "fish-eye" glasses emerged from behind a panel. She was as wide as she was high, and almost seemed to be waddling through the thick carpeting as she came toward Angus. "Hi, I'm Myrna, Panda's assistant," she said with throaty resonance. "Can I help you?"

Angus stood up. He literally towered over her, and he wasn't that tall. "I'm Angus Rivers," he said. "Chicken was my brother."

"Yes, I know; we read about it in the papers," she sadly acknowledged, and gestured for Angus to sit back down. She sat opposite. "I know how sorry Panda is about all this. Chicken was quite a favorite around here."

"Did Chicken work here?"

"Well," she began, choosing her words carefully, "Panda worked with him on a couple of projects."

"Projects?" Angus repeated.

"Yes, film projects, photography." Then, realizing that Angus might not know what she meant explained, "Panda's a visual artist, a filmmaker. Certainly you've heard about, or even seen, 'Parking Lot'? That was last year's big release; it was widely acclaimed. Now he's getting more into video, too." There was a touch of condescension in her tone.

"We don't get too many of those 'art movies' up my way, ma'am," he apologized. "You say Chicken was in a movie?"

"Panda shot some footage, but I don't believe any of it's been used yet."

"I didn't know my brother wanted to be an actor, and I sure didn't know that he made any movies. I'd sure appreciate seeing them if I could."

"Why, of course, of course," Myrna agreed coolly. "I don't know what arrangements can be made today. Excuse me while I go check the schedule." Myrna eased herself out of the seat and waddled off. Shortly, she returned.

"Panda wants to meet you," she announced as if it were a call from the Almighty. "I'll take you back."

Angus followed Myrna through a crowded maze of offices and studios. He didn't know what to make of what he saw. Overhead were cribs of abstract canvases and huge blow-ups of photographs, some of which on closer inspection turned out to be paintings as well. There were scurrying assistants and apprentices everywhere, some silk-screening and drying prints while others hung intently over drawing tables or videolas. In one studio life-size tableaux—a family in resort attire at breakfast, a wino curled up in the gutter—were being carefully uncrated. A massive metal sculpture was dollied past. At last they came to a pair of chrome doors with round, mirrored windows. Myrna pushed the right door open, holding it for Angus.

The room was cool and dimly lit. It took a few seconds for Angus's eyes to adjust. He was confused. Though he knew it was the middle of the day, there seemed to be a party going on. Several groups of men and women were draped around the room engrossed in conversation. Most were drinking cocktails and smoking. Some curious glances met his. Angus surmised from their expensive clothes and exaggerated postures that most of the women were fashion models or actresses. About the men he was less certain. They were of various ages and in attire that ranged from work clothes to dark business suits. The far wall was mirrored from ceiling to floor, and a massive glass and chrome conference table in the center of the room seemed infinite.

Casually leaning against the table was a white-haired man dressed in a white suit. He was talking animatedly to a circle of intimates who automatically moved aside as Myrna approached with Angus. The man dressed all in white immediately turned and spoke to Angus. "You must be Chicken's brother," he said warmly in a high-pitched wavering voice. The room was reflected dramatically in the mirror behind him. And though his hair was chalk-white, his face was youthful. Only his eyes seemed privy to the knowledge that had turned his hair prematurely white.

Angus offered his hand but Panda ignored it and gave him a smile instead. "What kind of a place do you have here?" Angus asked in honest amazement.

"Well, I suppose you could call us a 'multi-media center.' We're involved in all aspects of electronic and applied visual arts."

"Something like an art factory?" Angus suggested.

"Sort of," Panda allowed. Then to business: "Myrna tells me you'd like to see some footage."

"I'd sure appreciate it."

"Myrna, see if one of the crew can scare some up," Panda lazily instructed.

"Done!" she said and would have clicked her heels had her two melon-like calves not been in the way.

"In the meantime," Panda turned back to Angus, "Can we offer you something—coffee or a cocktail?"

"Not right now, thank you," Angus declined. Panda smiled; Angus smiled back.

"So how does it feel to be the 'celebrity of the day'?" Panda tossed off.

"What?"

"Your picture in the morning paper. Surely you've seen it?"

"No," Angus admitted.

Panda retrieved a newspaper from a pile on the table. It was already folded open to the right page. "Why, you got more coverage today than most people who try to get press all their lives." Angus stared incredulously at his photographic image. He appeared much larger physically than he imagined himself. He needed a shave, his hair was uncombed and his suit was rumpled. Still, the expression on his face was far from unflattering, he noticed, and he shyly appreciated the picture. He returned the paper to Panda.

"Why, if you're not careful, Angus—I may call you Angus?—you could become a celebrity!" Panda was virtually gushing. Angus laughed uneasily.

Suddenly the chrome doors flew open. A woman sheathed in studded black leather from her throat to her spiked high heels swept in. She paused to preen and get her bearings. A low murmur rippled across the room. The intruder spotted Panda. Her eyes widened and her nostrils flared. She tossed back her head of closely cropped dark hair and put her hands on her hips. Like a slow-charging bull she strutted toward Panda. Several of his entourage stepped into her path and whispered hurried warnings. She paid no heed and shoved them out of the way.

"So you think I'm a crazy has been?"' she sputtered. "I will show you who has been!" She wiped out a glistening revolver from the folds of her black cape. "I will give you what you deserve!"' she screamed, and, before anybody could stop her, she pulled the trigger. "Bang! Bang! Bang!" she spat in time to three quick clicks of the gun's empty chambers.

Panda, who had seemed as frightened as everyone else, started laughing. The laughter spread around the room in a rush of general relief. Angus was confounded. Instinctively he had reached out to stop this crazy woman, but had caught himself when she made it clear that the gun was harmless.

The leather-clad lady stowed the pistol away. She began laughing and gesturing dismissively at Angus. "I fooled your ass, Mr. Macho," she taunted. "You should've seen the look on your face." She practically collapsed in convulsions of laughter.

Angus was the butt of some enormous joke that he did not get. He felt cornered, yet he resisted the urge to lash out. "What's going on here?" he demanded of Panda.

Panda eyed Angus with veiled contempt. "Your screen test, silly boy," he playfully reprimanded. "Tanya's your co-star."

"My what?" Angus gasped.

"Panda films everything, darling," the pistol-toting female chimed in on cue. "Art is life, and life is art!" she declared. But, in case he didn't get it, she added, "Violence can be art too."

Angus was certain the woman was deranged. In fact, these people were all mad. He was determined not to lose his cool.

"We better run the tape before there really is a murder," Panda chided ruefully. He could read the confusion in Angus's eyes. At the touch of a remote the mirrored panels slide open to reveal a wall of television monitors. He flipped another switch and each screen pictured a different aspect of the operation. One screen showed the reception area, others the various offices and studios. One whole row was devoted to various angles in the room where they were standing. Angus saw two close-up views of his own face as well as long and medium shots.

Panda rewound the tapes and pressed the play button. Angus stared at the screens in shock. He had never quite experienced anything like it before. The camera had captured every move he had made from the reception area through the studios and into Panda's office. The entrance of the would-be murderess and his responses were all graphically recorded. "Turn it off, turn it off!" he found himself shouting. "TURN IT OFF!" he screamed directly at Panda.

Panda touched a remote. The screens went blank. He motioned the crowd out of the room; they obeyed noiselessly.

"Didn't mean to scare you," he confided, not bothering to mask his astonishment. "Most people are flattered." He moved insolently around the table and sat in the high-backed swivel chair.

Angus was furious. "Look, mister, I don't know anything about who you are or what you do. I'm just checking out anyone who knew my brother."

"Sit down." Panda motioned to one of several chrome and leather chairs spaced around the table. Angus did so reluctantly.

"Yes, we knew your brother," Panda allowed. "At one time we considered Chicken quite promising. But not everyone is *star material.*" Panda flipped open a cigarette box and removed a thick joint. He lit it, inhaled deeply, and passed it. Angus took the joint and automatically puffed. They passed the reefer silently for several moments.

"Now, you'd like to see some of the film we shot," Panda began expansively. "I'll be glad to show you what we've got though I really haven't been able to use it yet. I was planning to splice it together with different footage and create a fantasy montage. Let me check to see if the projection room is ready." Panda lifted the silver phone and hit two of the buttons. "Ready?" he queried, and listened. "Oh, not again!" he said with annoyance. "Well, take care of it." He hung up and looked petulantly at Angus. "I'm afraid there's some problem with the equipment again. It'll take a little while to fix it. Why don't you relax? We'll be going to dinner soon. You can come along."

"No thanks," Angus snapped.

"Oh, don't be ridiculous. I know some marvelous places. Anyway, we've got to make full use of your new-found celebrity." He picked up the phone again.

"Myrna, make reservations at Max's…Oh, that's right, isn't it?…Well, I'm sure Angus will want to join us." He hung up. "Have I got a treat for you," he gurgled. "How would you like to go to a cocktail party first?" He flung up his hands in an excited frenzy. "The timing is perfect! Priscilla Rhodes is having a little sip at her East Side townhouse to kick off a benefit for one of those ubiquitous little dance companies. You simply have to come along. Everybody will be there. I won't take no for an answer."

The reefer was pretty potent, and Angus had mellowed out. He hadn't turned on much since Nam. He'd forgotten how wonderfully pot blurred the rough edges. So by now he was game for practically anything.

"I'll order some drinks. What would you like?" Panda chatted on non-stop. "Smoke as much as you want. We'll hang out here for another couple of hours. We'll let the others come back—a few at a time, of course, so you can get to know them. They don't bite—really!"

In his own way Panda could be totally ingratiating, especially when he wanted something.

8

NICKY WAS TIRED OF ONE-NIGHT STANDS. He was tired of coming home alone after long hours cruising the streets and bars. He was afraid of becoming forgotten and undesirable. When he was younger, new friends came easy. There was always someone around, not necessarily the Ideal Someone—but someone to share meals with, to cuddle with in bed at night, someone he might even learn to love. Still, he could be terribly cruel when he wanted, lie to those he didn't want to see again, and at times be downright rude and vicious. Then it didn't matter, and now certainly it was too late for regrets.

He was old enough to remember the way things were before "gay liberation": furtive cruising in parks and side streets; the unmarked bars with postage stamp-sized dance floors concealed behind threadbare curtains and how when the lights flashed everybody stopped dancing; anonymous encounters in bathhouses and public toilets. He remembered going home with tricks that didn't kiss or didn't suck or didn't do anything, and yet he didn't mind because it was better than nothing.

Then the young kids and radical gays came on the scene with their "I don't give a damn" swagger, shoulder-length hair, and colorful outfits. He remembered the first time he really made love to another human being, a no-holds-barred, all-enveloping encounter that marked, more than any other experience preceding it, Nicky's "coming out".

Lately his sexual appetites were insatiable. He felt a need to be always active and was thankful for the time spent with Tyler that at least diverted him but never satisfied him. Nicky knew he wasn't going to get many more chances for a real relationship. Once the thought of growing old alone and by himself scared him. But not anymore. He was comfortably slipping into a companionless life pattern that would sustain him should his fate take such a turn.

Of course, it was nice to fantasize about life with Tyler. He was the first trick Nicky had brought back to the apartment in ages—not that Nicky had been abstaining, not in the least. Life in the Village afforded numerous opportunities to be intimate with the most desirable stranger and yet ignore all the rituals of civil intercourse. Tyler was the first person to come along in a long while who genuinely seemed to want to know Nicky better.

The night before, after Seedy had left, they had made love for hours. But after a mutual climax Nicky detected a subtle change in Tyler's ardor that made him feel alone and insecure. Certainly they were physically compatible. From the first caress he could tell that Tyler was an experienced lover; the way Tyler's body fit so perfectly against his, the deliberate measure of Tyler's strokes: all attested to the man's facility and mutual pleasure. Still, when they were done, in the calm that followed, Nicky felt in Tyler a pulling away, an inexplicable estrangement. Before easing into sleep, they shared a single cigarette, silently, in the ash's orange glow.

In the first moments of awakening today they tried to make love again, but the heat of early afternoon was less inspiring than the dark, cool night had been. Finally, Tyler bolted out of bed and stretched his long arms and lean torso. "I'm anxious to get that stuff run off and over to the papers."

Nicky eyed his new lover admiringly. "You want me to help?"

"You meet me over at Party headquarters later," Tyler suggested. He started pulling his clothes on. "I'm gonna need some help addressing and stuffing envelopes."

"Oh, goody!" chirped Nicky, just as if he'd been offered an all-expense paid week on Fire Island.

Tyler gave Nicky a good-bye feel on the ass and after a stop in the john was gone. Nicky sat up in bed. The day stretched before him like every other one now that he was on unemployment and was playing out what he fondly referred to as his "youth": he'd sleep late, then fuss around the apartment until it was time to go out. How long could he keep this up? In the fall he would definitely have to get serious about a new career, one economically securer than the dream that had brought him East.

Voted "best actor" by his high school graduating class, he majored in theatre for two years at a hometown college before dropping out. Bankrolled with a couple of hundred dollars from his older sister, he came to New York to "make it." The first couple of years in the city were his best; everything seemed so promising. He enrolled in classes at one of the highly regarded studios of stage technique, read the trade papers faithfully, and auditioned for everything. He got ensemble work easily enough and eventually, a small part in a long-running Broadway show. It seemed he was on his way when things suddenly started drying up. A lot of actors he knew were going to the West Coast to do television, but no offers came his way.

Soon he was going to fewer auditions. No longer a new face, his work was familiar to most of the casting agents around town. Without ever really "making it," he had become a has-been. To support his self he took temporary jobs, mostly office work—regarding restaurant work as beneath him, though the money was better. For years he wallowed in self-pity, unable to move ahead in his chosen career and helpless to make any constructive changes in any other direction. The decision to try elsewhere was the eventual outcome of his frustration.

Nicky pulled himself languidly out of bed. He checked the time. It was nearly four: plenty of time for a long hot bath and the essential hair and skin treatments before his date with Tyler. He turned on the tub faucets and paused to examine his reflection in the mirror. Not bad! he complimented himself and carefully arranged the shiny brown hair that fell across his forehead. He didn't want to admit it, but his hair was getting thinner and receding ever so slightly. He knew when the time came he would have to do something, transplants probably, since they were the closest to real growth. There, he had another good reason to begin a new and more lucrative career.

Nicky turned on the radio and tuned in his favorite classical station. He picked up a magazine and lowered himself into the steamy vapors. Meow jumped up on the edge of the tub and walked completely around the perimeter. Carefully poised, she lowered her head almost to the water's surface and let out a disgruntled "Meooow!"

"Shut up," Nicky snapped and pushed her to the floor. He thought she had finished the cycle, but the raised hairs at the base of her tail indicated otherwise.

"I'm going to get your tubes tied one of these days," he warned his pet and settled back to enjoy his bath.

9

THE CLOSING OF THE GLP FACILITIES during the day to casual hanging out caused the derelict population in the West Village to swell accordingly. In the late afternoon men and boys—winos, crazies, hustlers, street transvestites, panhandlers—squatted in Washington Square Park or Sheridan Square or cadged quarters from passersby on Eighth Street. Sloven, unkempt vagabonds, up from flophouse beds or sidewalk grates, they congregated in packs like stray dogs snapping at each other or momentarily subdued by the ritual of passing a pint or a joint.

Amidst a group on Fourth Street sat Lourdes, dejected and withdrawn in the bright afternoon sun. The drag queen's appearance was a barometer for his feelings. When he felt bad he looked terrible. He fingered his tattered finery and wished he had something else to wear. Nothing raised his spirits faster than a new outfit or a pair of shoes. When he worked at the public library, he could afford to indulge fashion's whim. No irregulars or seconds in his wardrobe. He shopped the best department stores, and what he couldn't shoplift he paid for. Indeed, it was having so many fine things that got him in trouble at the library. He started neglecting to buy gender clothes to work in and began improvising with selections from his closet of feminine attire he thought discreet and suitable for daytime wear.

He started casually, with softly tailored blouses and slack sets, and just a touch of shadow to bring up the eyes. Since he worked in the stacks and had little public contact, no one said anything at first. The security guards joked among themselves and got to nicknaming him "Brunhilde" because of his formidable falsetto and the way his large biceps and thick neck bulged out of the dainty tops he wore.

The first time he wore a dress to work he wore a pair of pants underneath— a fashion he claims to have originated long before Seventh Avenue. Thinking the dress and pants combination a subtle beginning, he gradually worked up to mesh stockings and high-heels. Apparently not everyone agreed. Mr. Schultz, the floor supervisor, called Lourdes into his cubicle "for a little chat."

"Are you having difficulties at home, Mr. LeFleur?" Schultz inquired patiently.

Lourdes dumbly returned the fixed stare and shook his head no.

"How would you describe your clothes today?" pressed Schultz, since he knew only one way: the direct one.

Lourdes motioned aimlessly with his arms and head as he tried to come up with something to say.

"What we do on our off hours is nobody's business but our own," Schultz continued sternly. "However in future please wear proper attire to your place of work. And let's keep it that way. Thank you." Mr. Schultz had settled the matter.

Lourdes was glad to get the hell out of the office, and for a while he resisted the temptation to deviate from the accepted attire he'd previously worn to work. However, not being able to dress up, he started getting a bit shabby, and his mood darkened proportionately. He didn't even have fun dressing up on weekends anymore. A spirit had gone out of his life—the sublime feeling of accomplishment a tastefully contrived ensemble gave him. His creativity had been stifled.

The showdown came the Monday Lourdes casually sauntered up the granite steps of the library and through the main lobby wearing four-inch spike heels and a designer original he'd picked up for nickels in a thrift shop and meticulously let out. He was sure nobody recognized him at first glance. After punching in his time card, he picked up his cart and wheeled it into the stacks dramatically humming the *Gloria al Egitto* chorus from Verdi's "Aïda."

Co-workers gasped incredulously. And none other than the director himself had witnessed Lourdes' entrance. Shortly after 9:30 a.m. Schultz caught up with him as he was returning from a coffee break. Lourdes had paused to check his makeup in a small compact mirror.

"Uh hummm!" Schultz cleared his throat.

Lourdes whirled around, startled. "Oh, it's only you, Mr. Schultz," he gasped coyly.

"What's going on here?" Schultz demanded.

Lourdes looked about inquiringly, then back at Mr. Schultz and shrugged; he had no idea.

"What…what…" Schultz groped for the words as he gesticulated fiercely. "What are you wearing today?" he finally brought out with all of the indignation he could muster.

"Ummmmmmmm," Lourdes purred thoughtfully. "Just a little number I picked up off the rack at Bonwit's. Do you like it?" He demurely picked up a corner of the hem and proceeded to model the garment.

Mr. Schultz turned a deep crimson. "Very good!" he managed and backed off slowly. Payday there was a pink slip in Lourdes' envelope.

So what! he laughed. He got to wear some fabulous duds that week, and they let him collect unemployment besides. At last he was free, free to live in drag all the time, and he went to great lengths to enjoy it. He set his wigs every night, and in the morning put himself through a brutal regimen of exercise and beauty treatments. He spent hours coordinating accessories and when he'd finally got together a smart look he'd go shopping, to the post office, or for a well-mapped-out stroll. Occasionally he entered amateur drag contests, once making third runner-up for his Diana Ross impression.

When unemployment ran out, he started looking for legitimate work—secretary, waitress, cocktail hostess—but was often humiliated by the discourteous brush-offs he received. Some interviewers laughed right his face; others refused to talk to him. He gave up looking for work and got more completely into dressing. Soon he was running night and day with some shaky queens in the Village. As his resources dwindled, he lost his apartment and most of his belongings. ("Ever try maintaining your wardrobe from a shopping bag?" as he like to put it)—but what did he care, moving from uppers to downers to pot and to whomever was standing on the next corner and interested.

Lourdes yawned rudely into the bright sunshine, and wrapped his arms around the back of the bench. In the odorous debris of the small park he and his cronies sat or lay waiting for something to happen, anything to distinguish one day from another.

"You got some change?" Dido asked Lourdes. "Let's chip in for a pint."

Lourdes stared at him blankly unable to focus.

"What'd'ya want?" he snarled.

"Chip in for a pint," Dido repeated. "You got any change?"

A pint? Lourdes could do with a little taste; his throat was dry. "Yes. That would be nice." He dug down into the bottom of his big carryall and fished among the numerous makeup and hair articles for change. His fingers touched a coin and withdrew it. It was a subway token slug. He tossed it back and felt around some more. There had to be at least fifty cents in there, he couldn't have spent all the change already. Sure enough, in a side pocket he found a quarter, three nickels and a dime. "Here," he contributed. "You got enough?"

"We've got fifty cents. That's a good start," Dido replied.

"That ain't enough for a pint? Hasn't anybody else got change?" He looked at each of his companions. In turn each shrugged No. "Then wait a minute," Lourdes concluded. "Gimme back my fifty cents until you get the rest." *This* Diva was no fool!

"I'll get it, I'll get it," Dido insisted.

"Show me when you do. In the meantime I'm holding on to my pesos."

"Damn," Dido moaned. "You mean between the six of us we can't come up with enough for a pint?"

"It sure looks that way," came back Lourdes, equal to the challenge. "And thank you for your two-cent contribution!"

For a moment Lourdes felt like his old sassy self.

10

PRISCILLA RHODES LIVED IN ONE OF THOSE discreet well-tended townhouses in the East 70's just off Central Park. This valuable piece of real estate—and a shrewd housekeeper named Bessie—represented her major assets. Nevertheless, the one-time Broadway chorus girl turned East Side dowager gave the illusion of means by wisely managing the small income left by her late husband. Of course, remaining in town so long into the summer season was unusual. Luckily this evening's little affair provided the perfect excuse. This year she passed on a rental in the East End and was planning on staying with friends when she went out for July and August. After playing gracious hostess for so many years she figured it was time to be a gracious guest.

She ordered cocktails set out for her son and daughter-in-law in the upstairs sitting room while the party below was getting under way. A portrait of her late husband dominated the wall above the fireplace. He eyed proceedings with his usual bemused detachment. After drinks were served all around and pleasantries passed, Priscilla began the interview.

Radiant in a cocktail length pink *peau de soie* original, she lit a cigarette. Who'd believe she'd been up since dawn overseeing party details?

"How's the campaign going?" she asked in a calculated manner.

"Everything considered," Porter allowed, recognizing all too well his mother's tone, "it could be going better." He laughed defensively.

Forever in character, she announced, "If victory's uncertain, withdraw! You can always run again."

"It's not that simple, Mother. I'd lose the respect-and support of a lot of people if I pulled out now."

"Well, keep the issues simple. Stay away from unpopular positions." The Ps in the last two words rolled over her tongue with deliberate emphasis.

"Right now I'm taking votes where I can get them."

"Well, I don't think all this publicity linking you to the homosexual rights controversy will do any good in the long run." Why beat around the bush!

"Mother," Porter admonished gently, "don't you think you're being just a tiny bit hypocritical?"

"What do you mean?"

"You're frequently seen socially—and mentioned in the columns—with that outrageous artist Panda."

"Him," she tossed off with a laugh. "He's perfectly harmless. Why, I don't think the dear man has any sort sexual identity at all. At least he's never intimated such in all the years I've known him. Anyway, there's no comparison. Hobnobbing for worthwhile causes is about the only thing that gets me out nowadays. But you putting yourself out for that group can only work against you. That life style will never be acceptable."

Much of what she was saying now she had rehearsed earlier. In the back of her mind she was wondering how the party was going.

"Gay rights are just another minority issue, Mother. Like Blacks and air pollution. I get better coverage as a result of my stands on those issues."

"Still, you're treading in dangerous waters and the whole matter could ultimately have adverse effects. Think of your father." She had played her trump.

"That's unfair, Mother. Certainly Dad would have stood behind what's right."

Agitated, Priscilla turned on her daughter-in-law and demanded, "What are your feelings about all this, Alice?"

Alice wasn't listening. "I'm sorry," she apologized.

The older woman remained undaunted. "I want to know what you think of Porter supporting this homosexual bill?"

"Mother, I hardly interfere with Porter's political decisions."

"I think you should have more to say, my dear. It affects your future as well."

Priscilla Rhodes had never been ecstatic over Porter's choice of a bride. She thought the girl ordinary and not clever enough for the brilliant son she raised. Alice had always sensed her mother-in-law's misgivings. And so did Porter. He spoke up.

"Leave Alice out of this, Mother."

"No, Porter," Alice began slowly. "Your mother has made a good point. Let me answer her." She eyed the elderly woman evenly. "The last thing Porter needs is both his wife and mother telling him what he should and should not do."

Porter took a good look at his wife. She had never used this tone with his mother before. He was secretly proud of her.

"This is a family concern," Priscilla protested. "I'm merely offering reasonable advice."

"You give orders, Mother Rhodes—never advice."

Priscilla didn't quite know what to make of her daughter-in-law's newfound belligerence. "Well, my dear," she demurred tactfully, "if Porter has your full support, then I'll be the last to question his tactics." She smiled beatifically.

After countless confrontations Alice finally won a point with her mother-in-law. There was an awkward pause. Priscilla rose. She took a couple of quick steps to flare out her dress. "Shall we descend?"

When Priscilla emerged from the room and posed briefly at the top of the landing on the arm of her handsome son, all eyes turned to watch them. Alice wisely lingered behind, and as her husband and his mother swept down the circular stair, she waited a couple of beats before following.

The parlor and garden floors were festooned with fresh flower arrangements. Guests, drinks in hand, were scattered throughout. A string quartet, tucked cozily in the bay window, played selections from Boccherini concerti. Bessie beamed approvingly as "Madam" passed, then turned her probing eye on the hired bartender and two maids, the latter serving great silver trays of hot and cold hors d'oeuvres. Priscilla and Porter, full of warm smiles and personal greetings, gradually moved through the double drawing room and down the trellised covered steps into the garden. Never was there a more stunning mother-son couple! Obviously he got his striking good looks from her, but there was no mistaking the aristocratic bearing inherited from his father's side.

Priscilla noted exactly who was where and whom they were talking to. She was a little anxious about the tendency of the dance company members to shy away from the other guests and socialize only among themselves. She'd long observed that personal contact tended to make donors give more generous contributions. Having come to share the choreographer-guru's dream of a major season, she was determined to raise the funding. The company had a small but excellent reputation, all they needed was proper showcasing.

The arrival of Panda and his entourage was calculated for maximum effect. He always traveled with a pack of fashion and art types who, if they weren't good-looking enough to be an ornament, usually had something interesting to say. Priscilla could see that today was no exception. As the gang of seven—Panda and Tanya arm in arm, followed by two bizarrely made-up mannequins, a greasy prole type, and a pair of nattily dressed pretty boys—came over to present themselves to Priscilla and her son, there was a perceptible flutter in the room. Every eye seemed to be saying if anybody's name makes the columns tomorrow, it will certainly be Panda's.

Angus was unaccustomed to such severe but discreet scrutiny. Since he had arrived with Panda, there was rampant speculation about him. Angus had no idea what was going on; he was, however, very uncomfortable and he kept his eyes averted. Panda, on the other hand, loved being the center of attention. He introduced Porter and Priscilla to his entourage. Alice caught up with her husband and was included in the general introduction. Immediately she sensed there was something about Angus that was different from the other men in Panda's circle. She eyed him closely and he returned her gaze; his glance devoured her.

"Angus is our newest celebrity," Panda piped bitchily, sensing the magnetism between the two heterosexuals. "He could be a Valentino for the new age."

"In that case you can give a benefit screening of his first film for Porter's campaign treasure chest," Alice suggested icily.

Porter missed that one. He had moved on pumping hands in his mother's wake. Alice fell into step, giving the group a farewell nod, her eye lingering a fraction longer on Angus.

Announcements were made about the upcoming season, and the choreographer was introduced along with the principal dancers. The party was over when Panda picked up his entourage and headed for the door.

As the Princess was leaving she asked Alice *sotto voce,* "Who was that odd guy with Panda?"

"Which one?" Alice played dumb.

"The Polyester Apollo—who else?"

"Tell you when I find out," Alice teased.

11

SNICKER WAITED FOR THE SUN TO SET BEfore he ventured out of his sister's Jersey City flat. The cover of night stoked his confidence, made him feel secure. He took a roundabout route along back streets and alleys to the train terminal. He was "carrying," and the local cops knew him well enough to stop and frisk him. He clung close to a pillar at the far end of the platform until the New York-bound train rumbled into the station. Taking a front seat in the near-empty first car, he settled into a glazed-eye stupor. His last fix had been administered in the pre-dawn. By late afternoon his body ached. There was no privacy to shoot up with his nephew and nieces under foot. He dropped a couple of reds and the sleeping pills temporarily dulled his craving.

He had to get it together, he kept telling himself. He couldn't go on with this feeling of desperation eating away at his guts. He had to stop it, but he didn't know how. Struggling from day to day was getting harder and harder. He wished he could get back on welfare. At least then he'd have something steady coming in and time to think. Now he was living from one rip-off to the next.

"Bullshit!" That's what he told the bitch when she said that they would no longer honor his claim because of some new ruling. "What new ruling? I'm still crazy!" he kept trying to tell her. Didn't they lock him up in Bellevue for ninety days and then wasn't he going to the shrink every week like he was supposed to? There was just no way he could get a job. And what about the steel plate in his head? That had to count for something. The bitch tells him again, "Your case is closed!" and he tells her he ain't leaving until its reopened again 'cause he's eligible. Before he knew what was happening, the security guards were bouncing his

butt out the front door and onto the curb. He swore and screamed like a mad-
man, raving along 14th Street until he calmed down and started plotting his
revenge.

Snicker snorted to clear his nose, rubbing the nostril hard with the back of
his index finger. Maybe he should get back into a rehab program. There was always some kind of bread to be had in one of the programs. He'd sell the
methadone from the treatments and make a little more money on the side. Lots
of cats were doing the same thing and getting by. He'd be able to find himself a
room in one of those hotels in the Village. All he needed was time and some
money to get it together.

Snicker looked warily around the car. No one was paying any attention to
him. What did he have to worry about? he asked himself. So what if it was in the
papers. He'd made the papers before and nobody knew it was he. He was only
sorry now about how they'd handled the body. Having had time to review one
by one the events of that night, he realized how much smarter it would have been
to make it look like Chicken wandered in on his own. Nobody OD's and in the
process falls into an empty barrel feet first.

His ineptness cracked him up. It was all Marlowe's fault for rushing him.
Still, there was nothing the police knew or would find that would trace back to
him—at least as far as he could figure. Sure he and Chicken hung out together,
but they hung out with other people too. The only one who knew something for
sure was Marlowe. And he's going to keep his mouth shut because he was there.

Snicker calculated he had known Chicken no more than a couple of months.
They hooked up with each other a few days after Snicker got out of jail. Well,
not really a jail but more like a halfway house for drug-addicted offenders. Still
there was a head count and a lock-up every night. That's the part Snicker found
roughest. He had always been a night person and not being able to get about at
night freaked him the worst during the six months he was confined. The night
he met up with Chicken they were both working Third Avenue. It was late, practically dawn. They got to talking about one thing or another when a dude in a
big Cadillac rolled up and said he was looking for a threesome. They were game.
After the john dropped them off, they went for breakfast and hit it off real well.
Snicker promised to turn the kid on to some dynamite dope.

Soon Snicker was copping regularly for both of them, and they were spending a lot of time together, mostly in coffee shops and hotel rooms. When there was no money they would sleep at Marlowe's or Chicken would stay with the drag queen Tequila and Snicker went out to his sister's. Snicker was pretty much of a loner, and having a Main Man like Chicken around was a new and not altogether unattractive experience. It was good to share a joke or a meal but to stay casual and undemanding too. The ritual of shooting up each other was their only act of mutual affection. Snicker was starting to miss the little bastard.

The first stop on the New York side of the Tubes was Christopher Street, and Snicker was the only passenger exiting. A strong gust of wind greeted him as he emerged from the station. He turned the corner as jukebox music blared out the opening door of a bar and the Supremes taunted, "You better run run run…"

Maybe he ought to stop and down a beer to kill some time? He backtracked a bit and sauntered into the bar. There were maybe a dozen or so guys scattered throughout the place. He bellied up to the counter and mumbled, "A beer." He looked at his reflection in the mirror over the booze bottles lining the shelf behind the cash register. His eyes were like two black pits set deep inside his head; his cheeks and jowls were puffy. The sight repulsed him and he turned away. He wondered what had happened to his damn shades, and he started feeling around in his pockets again though he'd already checked several times.

The bartender put the beer in front of him and Snicker paid. He picked up the change and his beer and strolled over to the jukebox, drawn by the bright light and vibrating waves of loud music. He read down the lists of song titles without registering one; he wanted to give the impression his eyes were busy. Soon the bright light was bothering them, and he moved into a shadowy corner near the men's room. A guy came out pulling up his zipper and gave him a heavy cruise. Snicker instantly sized him up: he didn't look like he could afford to buy and probably didn't have enough in his wallet to go through the hassle of taking. Snicker bluntly ignored him and continued sipping his beer.

For some reason or another he started thinking about his father. When he was a kid, the only time he'd see the old bastard was when he was out of jail and had a load on. His father would come visiting then pretend to pass out on the couch, and when everybody was asleep, he'd slide into bed with Snicker. Too afraid to call out to his older sister sleeping in the next room, he'd let his father have his way with him. They didn't know where their mother was any more. One day she put on her coat and never came back. Anyway, if he didn't give in to the old man, he'd get back at him some way. At fourteen, Snicker was old enough go live on his own, and he did. Even sleeping on rooftops, he never had second thoughts about his decision to leave.

He was better off without the stupid son-of-a-bitch. One time like an ass he told the old man where he was living, and Pops showed up asking for money and trying to get cozy. When he told the old wino he didn't have a dime, his father called him "a liar" and swore up and down at him.

Snicker told him to shut up and get the hell out! The son-of-a-bitch started swinging at him like he was a punching bag or something. Snicker pretty damn near pushed him out the window. He managed to get him to the door and out into the hall. He grabbed his own coat and started down the stairs because the only way the old man was going to leave was to follow him out.

"My own damn son trying to kill me!" the father crowed to the curious neighbors who fearfully darted behind their door when he reeled past.

The last time Snicker saw the old man he was bumming quarters on a street corner in Yorkville. Snicker was out tipping around the East Side with Chicken. They crossed the street and kept on going. His father never saw them.

Snicker wondered why he was thinking about that mess. All it did was bring him down more. He got another beer and stumbled over to the pool table. He hadn't held a cue stick in ages, and it felt good walking around the table doing mock set-ups. He chugged down the beer and bought another. After finishing that one, he casually walked into the toilet and threw up.

12

THE MOOD IN THE GAY LIBERATION PARTY storefront was calm, like the deceptive period of tranquility just before a tempest. As usual Stan was anxious, but this evening he had good reason. It seemed that the good Rev. Tunney-Brown and Joey were hitting it off a bit too well. When he'd got back to the apartment, Stan had walked in on the two of them standing before the open refrigerator in naked embrace. It was all he could do to keep from crying.

Nicky wandered into the storefront late and kept up his nonstop chatter until he had exhausted everything bright and amusing he could think of to say; then he settled down to riffle through a fashion magazine. He didn't mind waiting for Tyler; he enjoyed playing dutiful spouse.

Too bad Tyler didn't share the sentiment. When he arrived his thoughts were all business. Not only was he disappointed with the small number of people who'd turned out to help stuff envelopes and distribute fliers, he was seriously questioning his political ambitions. Ever since he had made a conscious decision to get more active in the Movement, he had strived to make a splashy contribution. Sensing that the ranks of the Gay Liberation Party were splintering, he was making a last ditch bid for recognition. He regretted having remained on the sidelines during those first months of recruiting and organizing after the Stonewall riots. Like so many on the street that night, he didn't believe anything of lasting importance would come of Stonewall. It would just be an outburst of anger and resistance that would quickly fade under legal and social pressures.

Now he was beginning to feel nostalgic about how far the movement had come since the Stonewall fell. He looked around the dilapidated storefront and remembered the heated meetings and strategy planning that had gone on there in the past year. He sensed a change coming and suddenly realized that things in the storefront would never be quite the same again. The Movement was entering a new phase, and he was part of making it happen. He looked at his gathered comrades with new affection.

"Seedy, can you help me hand deliver these to the media offices tomorrow. We'll split it up; they're mostly in midtown."

"Sure thing, Tyler."

"There's this one guy over at the *Record* I want to see in particular. He wrote the story about the kid they found down on the pier. Maybe he's interested in doing some follow-up."

"Sounds good to me," Seedy encouraged.

"Now, can the rest of you put the flier up in bars and restaurants or any other place you can think of. And then we'll pass the rest of them out tomorrow in Sheridan Square."

"Count me in for around noon," Nicky sighed, looking up from his magazine. Everyone else agreed that noon was a good time.

Tyler suddenly felt a great surge of confidence that literally had him vibrating. Once more he was feeling secure about the future of the Movement and his place in it. He was so swollen with his own importance that he hadn't noticed that Stan was unusually quiet.

The older man was trying to convince himself that nothing had changed between him and his lover, but the strain of waiting was becoming too much. Joey was supposed to pick him up for dinner, and he was more than an hour late.

"Hey, Stan," Seedy shouted from the office. "I got this guy from the Black People's Coalition on the phone. He wants to know what kind of a sound system we've got for the rally Thursday."

"At the moment none but don't tell him that. Just say we'll call him back. Get the number."

Out of the corner of his eye Stan saw his lover and the good Reverend drift in. He feared an ugly confrontation.

"Sorry, we're too late to help you guys," the Reverend apologized. "Joey took me on a little mini-tour of the West Village. Are there always so many people on the streets?"

"The good weather helps," Stan managed. "Did Joey take you over to the pier?"

"Yeah. We got there about sunset. It was spectacular!"

Stan felt more despondent than ever. Sunset was one of the special times he and Joey shared.

"Well, I bet the sun wasn't the only thing that was going *down* while you were over there," joked Nicky. Seedy laughed but stopped when he saw that he was the only one.

"Is there anything left for us to do?" the Reverend asked to fill the awkward silence.

"I think it's all under control for the moment, but you can help us pass them out in Sheridan Square tomorrow around noon."

"Oh, OK" the Reverend said, remaining oddly noncommittal.

"You eat yet, Stan?" It was Joey who had come over to stand beside his lover. He gave Stan's shoulder a playful squeeze.

"I was waiting for you," Stan admitted. "You still wanna eat at that Mexican place?"

"We—we already ate," Joey explained. "We stopped off and had some pizza. Hope you don't mind. Maybe Tyler could go to Pancho's with you. You eat yet, Tyler?"

"Nay—but I can't afford Pancho's. A couple of hot dogs from Nathan's is more my budget tonight."

"Mine, too," Nicky hastened to add. He wasn't crazy about Mexican food anyway.

"Come on, Stan, we'll have one of those dining islands all to ourselves," Tyler prompted, as he finally caught on to what was going on between Joey and the Reverend.

"I'll catch up," Stan called as the others started leaving. "What're you guys going to do?" he asked Joey as if it was the most natural question in the world.

"I don't know. Maybe hang out here for a while. Anyway we'll meet you back at the apartment later."

"You sure you two had enough to eat? Why don't you come along and keep me company," Stan pressed. "You know how silly those guys get in public places."

"I'm not hungry. Are you, Bob?" Joey asked the Reverend. He shook his head no.

"All right," Stan said, his voice cracking, "You be sure to lock up. I'll see you at the apartment."

Joey walked his lover to the door and gave him a lingering kiss on the mouth and a big hug. "We won't be long," he whispered.

Joey's signals were confusing Stan. It was obvious Joey wanted to be alone with the Reverend, but he was acting as if nothing had changed between them. Couldn't Joey see how unhappy Stan was about seeing them together? Stan realized that at nineteen Joey was chronologically still an adolescent. How could he expect Joey to be as committed to the relationship as he was? Although he believed it was the first real love for both of them, Joey's life was just beginning; but still, in a way, so was Stan's.

Stan had negotiated some emotionally rugged terrain through the years. He had come to this relationship after long, unhappy experience. Joey had not. Joey knew nothing of hurt and loneliness, the long periods of desperation and self-doubt. Joey knew nothing about people wanting to be your friend because, "You're such a nice guy," and yet never reaching you in a one-to-one relationship that was emotionally fulfilling. Most guys he encountered, especially of his own generation, rarely made the effort to get really close. So many of them were leading double lives or feeling insecure and guilt-ridden about the nature of their sexuality. Joey's love was spontaneous and natural. Coming along when it did for Stan, to a man who was glad to drop a facade that he had reluctantly built to protect himself, this love and the fear of losing it made him terribly vulnerable.

Standing there, Stan finally decided that Joey still wanted a stake in the relationship and maybe he was just being too possessive. He was glad he hadn't let Joey realize how upset he was by doing something silly or embarrassing. After all, which one of them was the *kid* anyway?

13

SHOWING ANGUS A GOOD TIME—AND showing him off—gave Panda inestimable delight. They descended upon the currently favored restaurant where Panda ordered a sumptuous meal with a new wine for each course. The liquor consumed during the Rhodes party and the wine at dinner loosened Angus's reserve completely: there was nothing like getting ripped on good booze to make him his most charming self. He grew very protective of Panda and Tanya, which they both found extremely amusing, but understandably, for different reasons.

After dinner, it was on to a popular discotheque, where Angus conspicuously ogled the scantily clad women who gyrated to the pulsating music with complete abandon. Panda and Tanya writhed absently through several numbers, while Angus opted to stay on the sidelines and drool. Several more drinks were tossed down, and in the wee hours they were bumping serenely through dark Manhattan streets in the back seat of a taxi.

The driver pulled up in front of Panda's studio. Angus jumped out to hold the door open for Tanya.

"Darling," she drawled sadly, "I'm afraid this is my ride home. You boys are going to have to excuse me."

"If you must, you must," Panda chirped as he de-cabbed and gallantly slammed the door behind him. "I'll talk to you after lunch tomorrow, dahling!"

"Night-night, Handsome!" Tanya called, waving out the window as the car pulled away.

Angus was so plastered that he was barely able to follow what was happening. He did know that Tanya had left and was sorry he wasn't going with her.

"Well, I guess…I better be going too?" It was almost a question.

"And miss the movies!" Panda teased. "They must've gotten the projection equipment fixed by now. You did want to see the film of your brother? Here," Panda handed him a key attached to a ring with several others. "Open the door." It was a side entrance to the building.

Angus obeyed wordlessly. They entered a small alcove and then into an elevator. The doors opened directly into Panda's private office.

"May I fix you another drink?" Panda asked graciously.

"Why not!" Angus readily agreed.

Panda made Angus a vodka tonic and poured plain mineral water on the rocks for himself. He led Angus into the adjoining screening room, where they made themselves comfortable in two of the dozen or so overstuffed armchairs; it was like a big living room. Panda touched a series of buttons on a panel set in the armrest of his chair that caused the screen to lower, the lights to dim, and the projector to turn on.

"The piece of film you're about to see is what I call a 'study,'" he explained carefully. "In order to get an idea of a subject's potential we put him in a costume and setting and just let the camera roll—the equivalent of an improvisation." Panda couldn't help feeling slightly superior to this hick from upstate.

On the screen appeared a Western setting. A painted desert dotted with cactus served as the backdrop for a hitching post and corral fencing. An assistant carrying a saddle came into view, and the film abruptly cut to the same scene with the saddle in place on the hitching post.

Earl sauntered into view. He was dressed in skin-tight jeans, rawhide chaps, cowboy boots, and a wide-brimmed hat. A leather vest framed his trim smooth torso, and a red bandana was tied around his throat. He seemed self-conscious and kept talking nervously to someone off-camera. He laughed, and then seemed to be disagreeing about something by shaking his head and motioning with his hands. Obviously coaxed by the off-camera presence, he started assuming a cowboy persona. He eased over to the corral fence and struck several rakish poses. Defiantly he threw his ass out at the camera. He moved over to the hitching post and climbed into the saddle. Using imaginary reins and arching his body he simulated riding a horse at a gallop. Hastening his pace, he lashed the horse and leaned low in the saddle.

The screen went white. Angus took advantage of the few seconds to sort out his thoughts. He had never before experienced the power of a filmed image this way. It was his brother Earl all right but it was the manner and stance that Angus did not recognize.

Chicken appeared on the screen again. The camera held a very tight close-up of his face. Momentarily, the natural flaws and blemishes in his complexion made him repulsive. The camera eased back and his features softened; the lens slowly caressed his neck and shoulders and paused for a leisurely examination of his smooth hairless chest.

The camera pulled back. Chicken was sitting on the fence, each hand resting seductively on his inner thighs. His crotch was accentuated by the contrast between the dark leather chaps and the faded denims. The camera moved down his leg and in closer to examine his boots.

Angus recognized the details in the stitching. When the film was made the boots were brand-new, shiny, the soles and heels barely soiled—a startling contrast to the beat-up pair back at the motel.

Chicken jumped down from the fence. The camera shakily moved to get him back into frame.

Panda smothered a chuckle.

Chicken started dancing. Apparently some music had started playing. He began by throwing his feet back and forth in a crude Charleston, but soon he was dipping and bumping and grinding his hips wildly. He tossed his hat into the air and flailed his arms above his head. The picture jumped and went out of focus for a moment. When it cleared, Chicken's mood had changed. He was somber, seductive. He turned to one side and teasingly peeled the leather vest back to reveal his well-formed bicep and shoulder. The look in his eye was coy, seductive. He turned his rear to the camera and slide the leather vest up and down his rippling back muscles. He turned back around and after shimmying the garment against his pectorals to redden his nipples he tossed it off. He was naked to the waist except for the bandana about his throat. He looked menacingly into the camera and belligerently put his hands on his hips. He slowly gyrated his middle, moving closer and closer until his groin dominated the screen.

The screen went white. Angus was jolted back to the reality of the screening room. Panda was rolling with laughter, almost to the point of tears.

"What a clown, what a clown!" he sobbed. "Wasted, wasted!"

The lights came up slightly. Panda gave Angus a heavy-lidded stare then casually reached over and pressed his full palm on Angus's leg just above the knee. "Are you comfortable?" he asked. "Is there anything I can do for you?"

There was an awkward moment; Angus diplomatically brushed the hand away.

"What's the matter?" Panda snapped. "Don't your buddies pat you on the leg?" Panda was used to getting what he wanted. After all, he'd been very generous with both his time and money. "Just sit back and enjoy yourself," he suggested quietly.

Angus smiled nervously and got up. He crossed to the door into Panda's office and checked his watch against the clock.

Angus's action only made Panda more sullen. "What's the matter," he demanded bitchily. "Don't you swing like everybody else?"

Angus sensed a confrontation building and he wanted to extricate himself as quickly and painlessly as possible. "I'd better be going," he said and glanced toward the double mummy case that housed the private elevator they rode up in.

"Don't you want to see some more?" Panda was up from his chair and on his way over.

"Maybe some other time. I gotta get going. Thanks for dinner and showing me around tonight."

"Any brother of Chicken's is a friend of mine," Panda shrugged with controlled nonchalance.

"Only you don't seem to want to be too friendly." Panda reached over and made a blatant attempt to grope Angus. He was quickly rebuffed.

"Come off it, Panda. It's not my scene." Angus had sobered up considerably.

"I thought it ran in families—like freckles." That was nasty, he knew, but Panda had managed to feel the enormous bulge of Angus's groin and was willing to risk everything to have him.

Angus had no fight with the man; all he wanted was *out*. "Get the elevator for me, Panda," he said politely eyeing Panda and at the same time trying to figure out the trick that would bring the elevator. "I'm gonna call it a night."

"Is that what you're going to call it?" Panda bristled and came toward him again. His white silk shirt was disheveled, and there were food stains on his pleated white trousers.

Angus noticed a small figure in relief to one side of the elevator casing. It was the head of a bird, and he touched it. The twin mummy case parted to reveal the waiting elevator. Angus stepped inside.

"Go! Get the hell out! What do I care? You're just another hunk of meat," Panda sneered. "And meat is cheap." He watched the mummy case come back together. "You're just another piece," he yelled. "Like your brother!"

The elevator doors opened at street level, and Angus hastily exited. He barely made it to the curb, where he vomited, as if cleansing him self of this night.

14

MARLOWE PUT THE TRASH CANS ON THE curb earlier than usual. He wanted the routine chores out of the way before Snicker showed up. The orange tom rubbed affectionately against his master's soiled boots. They had reached a truce earlier, and Marlowe had treated his pet to a supper of canned mackerel. The old super leaned over to scratch the animal's ear. Samson purred and arched his back. Like Snicker, the wily tom had discovered the old man's weaknesses and played upon them; strays sensed behind all the gruffness he was a soft touch.

Snicker had been one of Cookie's boys. When Marlowe worked himself into a roaring drunk and was unable to suppress his longings, he found the courage to pay for his pleasure. Cookie ran a neighborhood bar, The Cookie Box, and on the premises maintained a stable of young boys. Cookie's specialty was chicken—the younger the better and it was rumored he owned a share in a baby mill in the Midwest.

Marlowe would go in and wait conspicuously by the bar. Cookie or one of the bartenders would come over and talk to him, and soon a deal was struck. Too timid to select, Marlowe took whoever was suggested. The bartered flesh would follow him back to his subterranean lair. Snicker was introduced to him this way, and Marlowe paid to see him a few times more. When Cookie tired of Snicker—junkies have but so much shelf life—and kicked him out, Marlowe let the boy sleep back by the furnace in exchange for a little companionship.

Soon Marlowe wearied of Snicker too and told him he'd have to look for someplace else to live. Then Snicker started bringing back other boys, mostly runaways and dropouts he'd connected with on the street. A few months ago he brought Chicken. Marlowe found the new boy bewitching and could hardly contain his lust. Unlike the others Snicker had pandered, this one was neither dirty nor half-crazed. He proved even more agreeable than the super's wildest imaginings. Encouraged to make him self at home, Chicken used to take long baths in the afternoon and then parade around for hours in a towel as he dried his hair and preened in the full-length mirror. Cigarette dangling from the side of his mouth, he regaled Marlowe and Snicker with tales of the year he hitch-hiked back and forth across the country or with stories of the johns who picked him up.

"I once met this guy in a white Rolls-Royce. And you know what he told me after I jumped in? He said 'I was standing in that same spot 15 years ago, and to-day I got a million dollars!' He's a big fashion designer—you'd know his name if I told you!"

Chicken moved in close to the glass and gently fluffed his eyebrows out with the tips of his fingers. Then he combed his hair, and stepped back at arm's length, and turned his head first to the left then to the right to make certain the part was evenly centered.

"I think I'll dye it black like a vampire!" he teased. "I'll die my hair black and wear it in a pompadour. You remember pompadours? My brother had one."

Sometimes the towel would fall away and Chicken would take his sweet time to replace it. Or he'd do his dance exercises in a pair of skimpy briefs. Marlowe encouraged Chicken's exhibitionist tendencies. He didn't give two thoughts to the hard drugs Chicken was using. What did he care? A narcotic stupor made Chicken more amenable to his kinkier desires.

There was a knock at the door. Marlowe remained immobile, listening intently to see if the caller was alone. Satisfied, he got up to answer.

Snicker stumbled in without so much as a nod. He was sweating profusely, and there was a haunted look in his eye. He crossed to the table and looked around suspiciously. "Hey, man," he whined, "I gotta get fixed." He was sniffling and kept scratching his face and nose. "Gimme a few bucks, I'll pay you back. You know I'm good for it," he lied, never looking directly at Marlowe.

The old man opened a kitchen cabinet and rummaged through some debris collected on a lower shelf. "You dropped this!" he spat contemptuously and tossed a glassine packet of white powder at Snicker's feet.

Shaking uncontrollably, Snicker made a fumbled attempt to catch it. Failing, he fell on his knees to the floor and after some grappling scooped it up. He studied the packet closely, and a pleased grin tightened the corners of his mouth. "This looks like good shit. Where did you get it?" he asked greedily.

Snicker didn't wait for an answer. He was back on his feet, retrieving his works and cooking spoon from a folded paper sack he kept inside the elastic of his socks. Marlowe watched wordlessly as the addict went through the ritual of preparing the drug for injection with a makeshift syringe. Snicker straddled a kitchen chair, tied his belt securely around his left bicep, and held the two ends between his teeth. He made a fist and pumped his arm up and down until a small blue-green blood vessel swelled prominently amidst the scars. He punctured the vein just below the bend in his elbow, and there was a flash of red in the needle reservoir. He slowly worked the blood and the drug back into the vein by gently tapping the rubber nipple of the eyedropper attached to the needle. As the last of the solution drained into his arm, he let the ends of the belt fall from his mouth. He put the "spike" down and loosened the knot.

He soon experienced a rich warm feeling circulating through his body followed by several mild rushes. He calmed considerably, his mood growing more expansive.

Finally, Marlowe spoke up: "How long are you planning to sit there?" he demanded.

Snicker looked over at Marlowe as if realizing for the first time he was not alone. His lips spread into a big smile; there was a glassy glint in his eyes.

"How long?" Marlowe repeated, after waiting what seemed like an eternity for an answer.

"What's your rush…?" he asked in a singsong that trailed off inaudibly. His head rolled back, and he slowly raised his hand to scratch his throat.

"You can't stay here, that's all!" Marlowe exclaimed.

Snicker tried to focus on what the old man was saying, but the words seemed incoherent. The best he could manage was a silly grin.

"The fire inspector's been poking around," Marlowe lied. "That mattress and stuff you got back behind the furnace he says we got to throw it out. You can't stay here."

"Take it easy, man. We can talk about it." Snicker was feeling real nice. "You don't want to bring me down do you?"

"Why don't you take a trip? Go to San Francisco. You need a change. I need a change."

Snicker laughed. Now he got it. The old man was scared, and trying to get rid of him. "I don't know anybody in San Francisco, old man. You got somebody you want me to look up?"

"You'll make friends all right." Marlowe's tone was solicitous.

"Bug off!" Snicker's mood turned vicious. "I told you: you got nothing to worry about." He closed his eyes and rubbed his hair and face to soothe the agitation. "What happened happened." He was whispering. "Nothing to do with you; nothing to do with me."

Snicker slumped back in the chair and loosened his trousers. "Now why don't you come over here and sit next to me," he winked and rubbed his groin. He knew how to quiet the old man.

15

ANGUS DIDN'T KNOW HOW LONG HE'D BEEN walking. He was somewhere in the Village when a cab with a naked man sitting in the back seat sped by. At least that's what he thought he saw. It broke him up. He looked around to see if anyone else shared his amusement. The street was deserted. He laughed out loud anyway and turned to follow the cab's progress. Once it was out of sight he was about to continue walking when he realized he didn't know where he was or where he was going. At the corner he floundered as the traffic light turned red and a waiting car bolted into motion. He moved to the adjacent curb and crossed. Before his foot touched the opposite pavement, the thoughts that had plagued his mind since leaving Panda's loft returned.

For the first time in his life he was beginning to comprehend the passions that can set one man sexually upon another. Drunk as he was, he could see the lubricious glint of lust that emanated from Panda's eyes and radiated his whole predatory being. So well Angus recognized the manifestations, for he had known similar extremes in his pursuit of women, especially women with whom he planned to have no more than a casual, but totally erotic encounter. He had once been equally crude, thinking nothing of grabbing a broad by her ass or giving her tits a squeeze just to let her know he was ready when she was.

Harder for him to deal with was the footage of 'Chicken' he had viewed. He was having difficulty distinguishing the little brother he remembered from the celluloid image of who he had become. That they were one and the same person, there was no question, yet he wanted to believe none of it was possible, or at least that a series of uncontrollable circumstances was responsible for the bizarre twist

Earl's life had taken. Earl, the baby brother of his late adolescence, was still a kid in Angus's mind's eye, yet the film he had seen cruelly disputed this recollection. Now Earl was dead, and the life he had ended up living amazed and shocked his older sibling.

When Earl was seven he had to go into hospital for minor surgery. The little guy was scared stiff and had made Angus promise to take care of some last bequests, which he prefaced with "If I don't make it through..." Angus hugged the reluctant patient to give him courage and hurried back the next day to be there when he came out from under the anesthesia.

One summer he put Earl on the train for a two-week trip to one of the charity camps. Earl was eleven and none too happy about going. Angus tried to explain what it would be like when he got there: the swimming, the campfires, and the counselors. Earl needed a lot of convincing. He was crying when the train pulled out of the station. In the first day he called twice, pleading to come home, but then the calls stopped. When he came back from camp there was a marked change in his manner. Angus assumed the kid had gotten himself laid by some seductive older girl. Actually, Earl had discovered drugs.

The first time Earl ran away, he was thirteen. He was suspended from school for refusing to get his hair cut, and he and the old man practically came to blows over it. It seemed like a simple matter to Angus, who learned about the situation in letters from his mother. By then he'd been drafted and was stationed in West Germany. Indeed, the entire hair controversy always struck Angus as absurd. Reading about the confrontations over long hair in newspapers and magazines, he deemed it an issue created by an insatiable media. It was only after returning to the States that he was able to appreciate the importance of the longhair question in American life. Overseas he was better off believing what he wanted to believe.

After all he was busy making the world safe for democracy. What a laugh! He had really believed all that bull crap too. How else could he justify his so willing presence in Vietnam, the glee with which he made heroic gestures with the butt of his rifle, the casual destruction of people and property? It was an elaborate game and he was a grand player: the instincts of a true sportsman.

Sure, there was talk about the dissent at home, but you never wanted to believe it was any more than a vocal minority. This was like the other great world wars, and he was only a soldier doing his duty. Hell, aren't we the rightist damn country there ever was? The war was going to be Angus's chance to even the score. If he could do well in combat, he could extend the sense of achievement into every avenue of his life. Secretly, he'd always wanted to be a good athlete, but he'd proved pretty mediocre in whatever sport he went out for. With a sports scholarship he could've gone to college, and then he wouldn't have had to go to war to prove himself.

Then it was time to come home. Damn! He didn't expect the whole town and a brass band to turn out like in an Audie Murphy movie, but nothing prepared him for the reception he did get. He processed out in the middle of the night and really didn't sense anything was wrong until the flight back to the U.S. The false cheerfulness of the stewardesses was the tip-off. Stateside there was a wait for housing and little transitional assistance. It was like it didn't matter he'd left a chunk of his psyche in a rice paddy in Southeast Asia. He was proud of his uniform and proud to wear it until some freaked-out longhaired, yelling obscenities, ran up to him in a crowded street and spat on him.

The V.A. was less than grateful. They catered to the vets of other wars. You were trained going into the service; they should train you to leave. He didn't ask to go; the Government told him to go. Then they discouraged him from talking about his experiences. Vietnam veterans trickled back; there were no heroes' parades. If you're a Vietnam vet, you're suspect. On TV you're a demented misfit, unstable, dangerous: some kill-crazy freak that should have been left over there in the jungle.

When he got home, he was too wrapped up in his own turmoil to notice that his brother had become a veritable pharmacy of hallucinogens and amphetamines. But what did Angus know; he was too busy sorting out the pieces of his own life. Sometimes he'd get up in the middle of the night, turn on all the lights, and just sit. He drifted from job to job. Day-to-day relations with Sally were rapidly deteriorating. He hardly gave Earl a second thought, even when he dropped out of school and announced he was moving to New York.

The old man didn't give a damn, and nothing Ma said would change Earl's mind. He got in touch a couple of times when he needed money for emergencies. He called at Christmas for no apparent reason other than to wish everybody a merry holiday. Sometimes there would be a postcard, a color picture of a New

York tourist attraction, the Empire State Building or the Statue of Liberty, an incoherent message scrawled across the back, signed "Earl."

Angus was walking along the waterfront. The one time bustling harbor was a ghost of its former self. The long line of municipal piers, massive structures with facades of molded tin and roughhewn timber, stood boarded up or left to waste. Scavengers had pilfered nautical souvenirs and anything else of value, including utility pipes and wiring. Close on their heels, derelicts sought refuge from the elements in musty, debris-strewn offices and storerooms. Eventually hordes of adolescent gangs descended upon the rotting wharves, defacing them with their makeshift clubs and graffiti scrawls.

He paused to study the twisted ruins of one pier. It occurred to him that this was the area where Earl's body had been discovered. He heard voices and turned to see two men exiting through a break in the facade. Angus tentatively approached the opening and impulsively went inside.

He was awe-struck by the stillness and cathedral-like proportions of the interior. The space was as long as a city block. Moving slowly, he gazed in wonder at the vastness, his emotions inexplicably aroused by the lofty expanse. Beneath his feet the pitted planking was littered with broken glass, bits of rusting metal, and refuse. Sections had buckled up, and in places whole boards seemed literally to have been torn out, exposing the sludge-gray waters below.

Up ahead an imposing verandah dominated the pier's far end. After inspecting the sagging dock and storage cribs below, Angus climbed to the upper level, where a large bay window overlooked the water. He positioned himself in the center frame and looked out over the horizon as rosy morning light illuminated the Palisades. He closed his eyes, and a gentle breeze tousled his mane of auburn hair. He took a deep breath of the salty air and slowly exhaled.

Angus had no idea how long his eyes were closed. When he opened them he discovered two men hovering nearby. One man gave him a wink and a friendly nod; the other threw him a hard glance and looked away. Angus eyed them for a moment and sensing no danger, returned his gaze to the harbor.

He looked at his watch. It was nearly 5 a.m.

"What time you got?" he heard one of the men say. Angus wasn't sure whom he was talking to.

The man touched his shoulder and repeated the request. Angus flinched. "Almost five," he said.

"Wanna smoke a joint?" the man asked.

"Pardon?" Angus said; he wasn't listening.

"Pot. Reefer, man. I got a stick in my pocket that'll blow the three of us to hell."

"No thanks," Angus smiled.

In the shadows a match flared as a cigarette was lit. Besides these two, Angus was now aware of other men lingering in the vicinity. He realized they were stalking him: he was sexual prey.

Slowly Angus let himself down from the sill. Guarding his movement so as not to seem abrupt or hostile, he walked away from the window toward the stairs. In the distance was a slash of bright daylight marking the way he'd come in. His hand gripped the balustrade. He descended slowly but lost his footing on a broken step and fell forward, finally managing to catch himself on the banister. The noise he made seemed thunderous. At the bottom of the steps broken glass crunched underfoot. He was reminded that planks were out of the flooring and a misstep could land him in the river.

The stillness was broken by laughter and animated conversation. Angus saw two men dressed in black leather and chains approaching. One shushed the other and they separated. Angus quickened his step, bracing for an encounter. One man seemed to be coming directly at him, and Angus veered to avoid contact only to lose track of the other. A ripple in the buckled planks tripped him, and he stumbled helplessly into the arms of the second man.

"You all right?" the stranger queried, his helping hands lingering too long.

"Fine, fine," Angus said, pulling free and getting on his way.

"What's your hurry?" the man snarled.

Angus said nothing. He got his bearings and kept moving.

WEDNESDAY

THE LINDEN FUNERAL HOME & MORTUARY occupied the first two floors of an imposing Victorian mansion. Formerly the stately residence of one of the town's prominent lumber families, the property had been purchased by Nathaniel's father in the late 1930's from the sole descendant, a reclusive spinster. The house sat on a grassy half-acre plot at the corner of two tree-lined streets in what was once a fashionable neighborhood but now fringed the sprawling commercial district. The upper two floors the elder Linden had converted for family living, a circumstance Nathaniel's mother never quite reconciled. This discontent was underlined for the impressionable young son by her premature demise. For months after the funeral Nathaniel would let himself in to the slumber room that had housed her bier and meditate throughout the night. To this day when he enters No. 2 his mother enters his thoughts, almost as if her spirit had chosen that room for its final resting place.

Nathaniel took the midnight bus up from New York. He walked the short distance from the bus depot in the company of the rising sun. He used the back door, which gave access to a little office he used, and after checking the previous day's mail, he retrieved the passkey and let himself into the business side of the house. The mingled scents of fresh flowers and furniture polish hung in the air. He casually strolled through the slumber rooms and took a turn pass the chapel to see that all was well. He climbed downstairs to the laboratory and flicked on the light.

The moment he had been anticipating had finally come. The boy's partially draped body was laid out on the worktable. Nathaniel slowly walked into the room, relishing the sublime intimacy the boy and he now shared. His assistants had completed most of the technical preparations for burial; all that was still needed were a cosmetic touch-up and suitable attire. The mortician turned the bright work lights on, and walking around the table studied the boy's face from every angle. He pulled back the cover to reveal the sutured torso, pubic area, and lean muscular legs. He was repulsed by the scarred tracks of needle marks on the inside of both arms, and yet couldn't help noticing how nicely formed the limbs were. He found himself running a single caressing finger along the bare skin of the cadaver's upper arm and shoulders: it felt like velvet.

Suddenly a memory that had long lain dormant came back to him. He was stumbling along a dirt road by the rail yards after stealing off to have a couple of drinks. It was not an attractive period in his life. He was nearing the end of a binge that had begun ten years earlier when he flunked out of college and ran off to New York for an extended sojourn into sodden promiscuity. He'd periodically come home to dry out but with varying success; there was always the subtle pressure from his father to "come into the business."

He remembered it was summer and at the end of the road was a little clearing where he liked to take a little snooze. As he approached, he could see that his place had been usurped by—could he believe his eyes?—a nude sunbather; and the most attractive kind: male. The sight titillated Nathaniel, and he quickly concealed himself in some bushes. Spread-eagle atop his discarded clothes, the sun-worshipper was the younger Rivers boy. Seemingly on cue, the boy flipped over, flaunting an enormous erection that drove Nathaniel to masturbatory excitement. Oblivious, the teenager manipulated himself to an ejaculation considerably less prodigious than that of his unseen partner.

Nathaniel wondered how he could have forgotten the incident, so much fodder for erotic imaginings it might have provided. Then he remembered what had followed. He passed out, only to be rudely awakened by his father, who came looking for him when Nathaniel failed to keep a lunch appointment. Not a pretty picture: he imagined himself disheveled, asleep in the bushes with his pecker hanging out and semen residue all over his hands and trousers. Under the circumstances, the elder Linden proved extremely diplomatic. He helped his son to his feet and even offered to dust him off and button his pants. So great was

Nathaniel's humiliation that he knew why he had wiped all memories of that day out of his mind, even the erotic part.

Thoughts of his father depressed Nathaniel, and he wanted to push them back into his subconscious. He turned his full attention to a small tray of cosmetics he was preparing—blush, a liquid base, eye shadow, and a blemish cover. He was proud of his flair for makeup artistry and also of the little discoveries he'd made to facilitate application. He combed the golden ringlets away from Chicken's brow and swabbed the face with a cleanser. While it dried, he studied the face from various aspects, using the palms of his hands to deflect and soften the light. Meticulously he applied foundation and eyeliner. The skin's pasty pallor assumed a more natural glow. He subtly rosed each cheek with blush and pinkened the lips with a small amount of blush dabbed on the tip of his index finger. He arranged the hair casually so that the shimmering ringlets fringed and framed the face. He stepped back to admire his handiwork.

The face was fine but the blotches in the crook of either arm were hideous! Nathaniel found himself painting over the needle marks with gobs of blemish cover. Of course no one would notice them once the body was dressed, but that did not matter to his aesthetic sense. He would know that all was not perfect, and that was enough. Nathaniel felt a great tide of emotion erupt inside him, but it did not show on the calm facade he wore like a suffocating second skin.

"What a waste!" he grumbled and turned away.

There were sounds of a door opening and closing above. His staff was starting to arrive. He looked at his watch; it was ten o'clock already. Suddenly he felt very tired, and he quickly tidied up his work area. Carefully he replaced the shroud. Before turning off the light he took a long last look at the boy's face. How silly, he thought, "But it's true," he said aloud. "He does look like he's only sleeping."

2

SUSTENANCE—EXCEPT FOR AN OCCASIONAL glass of milk to line the stomach—rarely passed Panda's lips before three o'clock. So what on earth was he doing at The Fatted Calf with a chef's salad gaping up at him; it wasn't even noon! The sight of neatly arranged cuts of Swiss cheese, boiled ham, and turkey strips on a bed of crisp lettuce made him wince. He looked around the sprawling dining room to see if anyone else was really eating. The restaurant had filled considerably since his arrival and indeed several patrons were already enjoying their meals.

"Oh, that looks yummy," gurgled Skip Karlson, returning from the ladies' room. Ordering the salad was her idea; ditto, dining so early.

"You eat it then," Panda suggested drily.

She laughed and took her place opposite him. Eyeing her own order suspiciously, she lit a cigarette.

"Service is certainly improving around here," she announced in the general direction of Michael, the maitre d'. "I haven't finished my drink yet." It was her second.

"Let's send the food back then." Panda seemed a bit too eager. "It's getting cold."

Skip threw him a withering glance. "Yours will keep." She exhaled a long shaft of smoke that upon hitting the table billowed into soft clouds. From her own dish she broke off a bit of fish with her fingers and popped it into her mouth. Her pretty features contorted in mock disgust.

"Tasty." She munched with little enthusiasm and took one more puff of the cigarette, before crushing it out. Three lipstick-stained butts already crowded the little ashtray.

"So what' s the item you were going to give me before I rushed off to my 'little emergency?'" She took another bite from her dish, using the fork this time.

Panda smiled devilishly. He was instantly revived. Talking about himself always did that. He bit off a piece of the cheese wedge he was fiddling with, popped it in his mouth and slowly chewed; the look of revulsion on his face was more for effect.

"I hope it's good; I haven't got a lead for tomorrow's column." Skip had a reputation to maintain. She knew that better than anybody else.

"Don't I always take care of you?" he fawned.

"No comment."

"What do you mean 'No comment!'" he pouted.

"I mean just that. In this business one hand washes the other, darling." It was a veiled reference to the benefits he had most certainly reaped from earlier mentions in her syndicated column. "So what's the item already?"

He was still sulking. "I just signed a million-dollar linen deal—that's all!" he whined.

For old times' sake Skip didn't laugh in his face. "Quite an item," she deadpanned and tossed down the rest of her drink.

"I'll say," Panda jumped on the defensive. "It'll freak everybody out."

"And what if it backfires. A lot of people still take your work very seriously."

"That's exactly why I want to blow their minds." He laughed smugly. "Who cares? Either way I stand to make a mint. I've got hundreds of old abstracts to pull designs from. You can say I'm 'bringing art into the most intimate moment of people's lives,' 'recycling my earlier work,' you know, make it sound significant."

"All right, I'll print it, but you owe me."

Panda knew better than to say any more. The bitch had agreed to use the item, so what else did he want.

Skip ate some more fish and looked up just as two women were being seated at a nearby table. The morsel caught in her throat. She put her fork down and coughed to dislodge the food before she started choking. She'd recognized Alice

Rhodes and was experiencing a long-suppressed flood of memories. But she was-n't a schoolgirl any more and could handle it.

"You okay?" her luncheon companion inquired.

"Well, there goes an old college chum," she managed with forced casualness, after clearing her throat.

"Oh where?" Panda turned to look, all eager-eyed.

He'd been too busy counting future sales to notice Skip's reaction.

"Calm down," Skip snapped in a low, even voice. "Don't attract attention."

Panda turned back around. "You mean Alice Rhodes?" he asked.

Skip looked over his shoulder to see if Alice had noticed them. As if sensing Skip's eyes, Alice threw a casual look their way. Skip stiffened. Alice returned to conversation with her lunch date seemingly unfazed. Satisfied that Alice hadn't especially noticed her, Skip collapsed against the banquette in a cold sweat. The man-tailored suit and tie she was wearing seemed unbearably confining.

"Want me to invite her over for a drink? Maybe she can cheer up this dull gathering," Panda jeered.

"Don't you dare!" Skip came back harshly; then regaining full control explained, "I use the word 'chum' loosely. She was a year ahead of me at board-ing school. A chemistry lab was as close as we got."

"You went to one of those horse-y *girls* schools?" he read like an indictment.

"Yeah, and I got the calluses to prove it," she joked, then picking up on the implication of his tone added, "Alice Quincy was too busy being Sorority Sue to notice an intense number like me."

"So that's why you missed Priscilla's party!" he pounced. "An old crush dies hard."

"I sent my spies. I can't be everywhere at once."

"What a divine lady, Priscilla Rhodes." Panda knew better than to push his luck. "She really knows how to do it—give a party, I mean. Too bad only the B-list ever shows. I'm sure I was the only name there yesterday. Me and the Princess, of course."

"And her son Porter?"

Panda brightened. "Oh yes, *he* was there! He's got my vote."

"Too bad you don't live in the South Bronx."

"I may not have to. He spoke at a Gay Liberation Party meeting in the Village the other night. Perhaps he's got more than Congress on his mind. How about our next Mayor?"

"Wait, did you say Rhodes campaigned at that dismal GLP storefront in the Village?"

Panda nodded.

"Scout's honor?" Skip pressed. Completely abandoning the rest of her lunch, she lit a cigarette.

"Would I steer you wrong?" Panda ruffled playfully.

"*That's* an item!" Skip intoned. "Now we're square."

She watched Alice give her order to the waiter. Panda couldn't believe his eyes. Skip was gloating like a sated cat.

3

HE WAS KNEELING IN A MUDDY TRENCH AND mortar shells were bursting nearby, blasting sand and debris overhead. It was raining on and off, and he hadn't had a bath in days. The enemy was moving closer, and the returning rifle fire was getting louder. Suddenly a magnesium flare lit up the night sky, and he saw that two of his buddies were slumped over. It happened so fast he thought he was hit too, but when he realized he wasn't, he crawled over to Lopack and tried to help him.

"Lopack," he said shaking the soldier's limp body. "Lopack. Lopack," he pleaded…

The blast of a siren burst his ears and for another few more seconds he relived the agony of the night his two pals had died somewhere near the Cambodian border….

The phone rang again, his eyes opened, and the morning lit motel room jarred his memory. He wasn't back in the jungle. The telephone was ringing. He reached over to answer it.

"Hello," he croaked.

"Ted Hughes here," boomed the caller. "Did I wake you?"

"No, no," Angus insisted, struggling to gain coherence. "Who's calling?"

"Ted Hughes of Doyle, Merrill and Terrence. You left a message with my secretary. I was out of town." Ted's manner was crisp and precise.

"Oh, yeah, right, right." Angus was still pretty groggy. "Can you hold on a minute?" he begged.

"Sure," Ted said.'

Like a wild animal set free, Angus fled into the bathroom and relieved himself. His head was throbbing with a hangover. He got back on the line.

"Hello, Ted Hughes," he began, uncertain. Then it all came back to him. "Ted Hughes—you're a friend of my brother Earl."

"Earl," Ted repeated with a big question mark.

"I mean Chicken," Angus corrected himself.

"Chicken!" came a bemused tone of recognition. There was an awkward pause, then nervous laughter. "You're Chicken's brother, are you?"

"Sure am," Angus assured him. "I'm his brother."

"Well," Ted began then paused. "He gave you my number?"

"Sort of."

"What's the little devil been up to?"

"That's why I'm calling," Angus said.

"Oh I see," Ted said playfully. Then, "Can you hold on a minute?"

Angus overheard Ted give some brief instruction to someone called Sue, probably his secretary.

Ted got back on the line, "How long are you in town for, Angus?"

"I don't know," Angus admitted. "Maybe another day or so."

"Look," he said, "something urgent has come up. Why don't you and that brother of yours meet me for lunch? I bet you guys haven't had a decent meal all week. There's a great seafood place called Murphy's Clam House on Water Street. Think you can be there in an hour?"

"Sure," Angus said as he scribbled down the name and address.

"See you there," Ted said and hung up.

The ride downtown cost Angus almost five bucks plus tip. Murphy's was an unpretentious fish place near the city fish market. There was a bar in front with tables in the back. As Angus entered, the smiling hostess greeted him.

"How many?" she asked.

"I'm meeting someone for lunch," Angus explained.

"What name?"

Angus thought for a second. "Hughes," he recalled. "Ted Hughes."

"Of course, Mr. Hughes. He's waiting for you." She turned briskly to one of the hovering waiters. "Table 14, Pio. Mr. Hughes." She turned back to Angus. "Pio will show you the way."

Angus fell into step behind the wiry Latin who led him through a maze of tiny tables to a corner booth. Angus spotted a guy in a blue suit and red tie studying the menu. Sensing Angus's approach, he looked up.

Ted Hughes had a big friendly smile and was immediately up out of his seat with his hand extended. "So glad you could come, Angus." The two men clasped hands. "Please sit down." Angus did so, and Ted returned to his own seat.

"May I bring you a cocktail?" Pio asked. Ted had already been served.

"Bloody Mary, thank you." He had taken a couple of aspirin, but his head still felt pretty bad.

The waiter nodded and turning to leave practically knocked over the extra chair. "Sorry," he said and rushed off.

The two men eyed each other a moment, both with great difficulty containing broad grins.

Finally, Ted spoke up. "So you're Chicken's *older* brother?"

"That I be," Angus nodded. "And I guess you're wondering 'where's Chicken?'"

"I have to admit the thought has crossed my mind," Ted said good-humoredly. The thought that this was going to be some kind of a shakedown had also passed. Ted was in his early 40's, a little overweight, but immaculately groomed. Deeply tanned with red-brown hair graying at the temples, there was an unmistakable "air" about him.

"Well, that's why I called you in the first place," Angus began. Measuring his words carefully he told Ted Hughes what had happened to his brother, even mentioning the write-up in the newspaper.

Ted was stunned. "It seems like only a couple of weeks ago he went out to the beach to help me open the house." He shook his head, incredulous.

"Now I guess you're wondering why I was so quick to take you up on your luncheon invitation?"

"Don't worry about it. I'm always glad for the company."

After a big lunch of fresh seafood and a bottle of wine, the two men, if not cozy, certainly trusted each other. Angus got around to his questions.

"I'm trying to find somebody else Earl—Chicken—knew. I think he might be able to tell me who dumped my brother on the pier."

"I'd sure like to help, but there's not too much I can tell you. We got together a few times, but he never introduced me to any of his buddies."

"How did you meet my brother?" Angus asked point-blank.

"Boy, you picked a good one. Look, Angus, there' something I want to tell you first. I don't know what you're up to, but I've got a family to consider, and they are going to have to come first."

"I'm not threatening you, Ted. I'm just trying to track down a guy who knew my brother. His name is Snicker. Ever hear of him?"

Ted thought a moment and shook his head. "Afraid not. There are a lot of kids on the street. I never ran into one called Snicker."

"Do you know any places my brother hung out? I know about Third Avenue."

Ted laughed. "You ask some very direct questions there, fellah. Yes, there's a place called Cookie's. Matter of fact, that's where I met your brother."

"Where's Cookie's?"

"It's a bar down in the Village. Guy named Cookie is the owner. He keeps a crew of kids around who work out of there. Chicken told me he was in there on and off. That's why I gave him the office number. You must've gotten hold of his address book?"

"Something like that. Where'd you say this Cookie's is?"

A side street in the Village, just off West." Angus looked blank so Ted said, "I'll draw you a map," and proceeded to do so on a cocktail napkin. "You start at Sheridan Square and just follow this route. You can't miss it."

"What's a good time to go by there?" Angus asked.

Ted looked at his watch. "They're open now. It's a lunch stop for some of the Street crowd." Ted started to rise. "Now, if you'll excuse me, I have a one-thirty."

Angus also got up. "Look, I want to thank you for lunch, for everything."

"My pleasure," Ted said. "Again, I'm very sorry to hear about your brother."

Ted paid the tab, and the two men parted at the curb. Ted got into the first passing cab and headed south. Angus hailed the next one and told the driver to take him to Sheridan Square.

4

NICKY SPENT ANOTHER NIGHT ENTWINED IN the arms of his gay activist. He might as well have slept alone. Tyler was "too tired" and went right to sleep when they got home. His host tossed and fumed, feeling that an orgasm was the least he was entitled to for all the time he was devoting to the Cause. Nicky was for gay *rights* all right—and his came first.

At various intervals throughout the night and morning Nicky did his best to arouse Tyler—all for naught. The best he managed was to get Tyler up and into the bathroom. When he came out, he started getting dressed.

Puzzled, Nicky got out of bed and went over to him. "Where you going so early?" he purred, making it quite obvious what he was after.

Tyler took Nicky's hand and gently cradled it between his own. "Early?" he teased. "It's after twelve. Noon! Anyway I've got to get up to the *Record* to see that reporter Shriner."

"You know, I don't get you!" Nicky steamed. He was angered by the rebuff. "Here you are screaming for gay rights, all that political bullshit, but when you get right down to it, you're just out for yourself!"

What do you mean?" Tyler demanded, startled by the outburst.

"Oh, nothing. Forget it!" Nicky spun away and sprinted into bed. He lit a cigarette.

"Oh, I get it," Tyler sighed and followed him over. He put his arms around Nicky's shoulder. "I'm not in the mood this morning, baby," he said sweetly and gave Nicky a tender peck on the forehead.

"You bastard!" Nicky grumbled under his breath He refused to be assuaged, and struggled clear of Tyler's embrace. Then suddenly he softened. "Okay," he said. "Go keep your appointment. I'll see you later."

"You mean it?" Tyler pleaded and blew him a kiss. He opened the door and went out but had to turn around and come back for the package of flyers. "Don't forget you're suppose to be giving these out in Sheridan Square today!" he commanded and was gone.

Nicky remained perfectly still. He listened closely to Tyler's heavy boots clopping down the stairs and the sound of the street door opening and slamming shut. He crossed to the window and opened the curtain. Tyler came into view on the street below as he walked to the corner and turned out of sight.

Nicky closed the curtain and started getting dressed. If Tyler weren't interested, he'd stroll over to the pier and find somebody who was. He pulled on a pair of skintight black Levis, grimy work shoes, and a ripped T-shirt. He raked a comb through his hair and slapped some cold water on his face. He was out the door but came back to use some mouthwash.

Meow, who had been quietly rutting under a chair, saw her chance and quickly escaped into the hall. She ran up the stairs toward the roof. Nicky didn't notice the cat's departure and went out, locking the door behind him. The waterfront was a couple of blocks away and then through a maze of unloading trailer trucks. In the dark interior of a warehouse he glimpsed a group of lunching workmen swigging beers and devouring hero sandwiches wrapped in white butcher paper. Soon he was walking along the wharf. He saw a figure in light blue disappear into a break in the facade of the cruisy pier. Nicky quickened his pace. The police had closed off the former entry, but a new and better one had been made by someone breaking open an existing door. Nicky went in.

The interior was serene and bright with afternoon light. In one sweeping glance he searched for a trace of the other trespasser. He saw a shadow ascend out of sight on the stairs leading to the second level. Nicky followed. He paused on that first landing to check out a small office that commanded a view of the street and old highway. He looked inside the abandoned toilet. Nothing.

He climbed the second flight of stairs to a freight loft with storerooms and offices letting off of it. He checked each one methodically and then headed toward a far door, moving cautiously over the rotting planks. It was the last of the storerooms, and it too was empty.

He lingered a moment to examine the space. There were loading doors at either end. The one overlooking the water was missing. He crossed to the open hatch and looked out into the harbor. There must've been a fifty-foot drop to the murky waters below. A tremor of fear passed through him, but then he dissolved into a smile. There was nothing to be afraid of. He studied the far shore and the deteriorating pier next door.

An instinct made him turn. A man had come up behind him; he appeared menacing. It was the man in blue. For an instant Nicky was certain that he was about to be pushed, and he panicked. He abruptly moved away from the opening. The man stopped cold and pretended to be looking around.

Nicky calmed down. He'd overreacted. This was the man he'd been following. The man was wearing a blue uniform with the name of a car-leasing concern blazoned in white across the back and over the breast pocket. Nicky guessed he was on his lunch break. Their eyes met. The man threw Nicky a hard look then looked away. He was unshaven, and his hands were dirty. He started pulling at the fly of his oil-stained trousers.

That was all the invitation Nicky needed. He moved toward the number, but the number moved away. He continued to grope himself and watch Nicky. Nicky pounced, and again the man wouldn't let him get near.

They stood watching each other for a while. The man continued pulling at what had become a prominent lump outlined against his inner thigh. Nicky couldn't resist any longer. He fell to his knees and slowly crawled over.

5

ALICE RHODES COULDN'T HELP BUT NOTICE the mannishly attired woman who kept staring at her from across the restaurant. When the woman was leaving, Alice got a better look at her and recognized the columnist Skip Karlson and her escort Panda. They exchanged a flutter of fingers and tepid smiles as they passed. Alice hadn't time to give them a second thought. The demands of her own luncheon date were enough of a strain. It was becoming more and more difficult to mask her contempt for the woman.

The ordeal facing Alice was a courtesy lunch arranged by Porter's campaign manager. Tillie Gold was the wife of the Congressman whose seat Porter was campaigning for. It wasn't the first time Alice had to endure an arranged lunch. The way she managed to get through them was to go to the chicest and most expensive watering holes. Thankfully, there seemed to be a new "in" place opening practically every month, and the novelty of changing decor and menu kept up her enthusiasm. Usually her guest was sufficiently impressed, and Alice felt that she came off as something of a jetsetter.

They had just completed the main course and the busboy was clearing off the dishes. The waiter passed out dessert menus. He stood with pencil poised to take the order.

Tillie scanned the card. "Oh, Alice, honey," she gushed in her strident Bronx accent. "I don't think I should have any dessert. They all look very, very fattening," she sighed. "Wait till l I tell my daughter I had lunch at The Fatted Calf."

She was so tacky Alice couldn't believe it. Alice's response was a tight smile as she returned to her perusal of the dessert list. The concoctions had outrageously lush sounding names, and each seemed richer than the one before.

"What are you going to have, dear?" Tillie inquired in a voice she thought sounded charming.

"I don't know," Alice admitted. "I'm caught between the chocolate ice cream éclair and the tutti-frutti cobbler."

"Both excellent choices, madam," the waiter prompted.

"Just hearing them adds pounds." Tillie batted her false eyelashes and showed her stained uneven teeth.

The last comments Alice wanted to hear about this woman's attempts at dieting had been made long before lunch.

Tillie began absently humming to herself. She was so engrossed in making a selection she hadn't noticed the look of mortification on Alice's face or the waiter pretending not to see or hear anything.

Tillie Gold had come a long way for a girl from the South Bronx. And she'd be the first to tell you. A good 20 years her husband's junior, she had started out as a clerk-typist in his real estate office. The smartest move she ever made was taking a secretarial course in high school. She loved Shakespeare, but for a girl with no chance of college things had turned out even better. Now, though, she was a little worried.

Lunch had been her idea and passed through proper channels. Now that Morris was being forced to retire with a heart ailment, she was looking to make and keep friends in the right places. Tillie had grown accustomed to the position of power her status afforded her as the wife of a congressman; she would dearly miss the prestige.

"I'll go with the éclair," she said at last. "No, wait!" she changed her mind. "The cobbler. Fresh fruit, less calories."

"Very good, madam," proclaimed the waiter with his heavy continental accent. She couldn't decide whether he was French, Spanish, or Italian.

"The éclair, please," Alice said and smiled demurely as she returned the card.

"Very good, madam," the waiter echoed, collected the menus, and disappeared.

"Oh, I'm so glad you ordered that. I'm dying to see what it looks like. We can taste," Tillie confided.

Alice mustered another one of her polite smiles. Now what else could they possibly talk about? Alice rummaged through her mind for some innocuous topic.

"Alice, you're gonna love Washington," Tillie decided. "Of course, it took me a couple of terms to get into the swing of things. You know bow standoffish those Southerners are. But after I was around for a while, they started to warm up. I made friends." She was unconsciously twirling her teaspoon. "Honey, I just know they gonna love you right away. Remind me to call you with a list of some of the shops you ought to try. There's one hair salon in Georgetown where everybody goes."

From the look of Tillie's coiffure Alice decided it was a place to definitely avoid. "Sure thing," Alice said. By the barest determination she refrained from laughing out loud.

Tillie was too dense to pick up on Alice's true sentiments; she just hoped for the best.

The waiter returned with dessert. His timing couldn't have been better. He set the orders down, serving Tillie first.

"Oh, Alice," Tillie exclaimed. "Yours looks so good!" She eyed her own choice with disappointment.

"Oh, here," Alice said, seeing that the woman was truly crestfallen. "You take the éclair; I'll have the cobbler."

Actually Alice's generosity had more to do with the fact that the éclair looked like a gooey brown mess while the cobbler was in fact a shortcake with a variety of fresh berries: much more appetizing.

"Are you sure you don't mind?" Tillie asked in a tiny apologetic voice. There was no mistaking the glint of gluttony shining in her eyes. She was already holding her plate in preparation for the exchange.

Alice pushed the chocolate mass across the table into Tillie's place while Tillie set her dish down in front of Alice.

Tillie looked at her new dessert with undisguised relish. "Would you like a little taste, dearie?" she proffered her poised fork.

"No, no, you go ahead," Alice declined graciously.

Tillie plunged right in; as it had been with her earlier course, when eating she wasted no time small talking. Alice was relieved that the burden of conversation had once more been lifted.

6

CITY ROOM ATTITUDES TOWARD SHRINER took a turn for the better when he turned in the story on the teenage overdose. After it was printed, there was a perceptible difference in the way Irma the receptionist chimed "Good morning, Frank" and how some of the older guys went out of their way to say "Hello". There were even a couple of ribs about his becoming the paper's expert on 'homosexual affairs.' Ha. Ha."

The innuendo didn't faze Shriner either way. Until recently he'd been tossing helplessly about trying to deal with his new job and other matters of living from day to day. It was only of late that he had become aware of the big void in his life.

He had never been particularly popular with women, though he could certainly get a date when he wanted one. He dated a couple of girls pretty steadily in college but never got farther than some heavy petting. Anyway, his course work kept him busy most of the time. His first sexual experience was with a female hitchhiker he picked up on the highway near his family's home. She matter-of-factly offered to blow him for ten dollars. He took her back to the house—his parents were conveniently away—and banged her on the pool table in the family room. It wasn't what he thought it was going to be like, but it got him off, and wasn't that what it was supposed to do?

He had a strictly carnal relationship with a nymphomaniac he met in a singles bar when he first came to New York to work. But after a few weeks found the physical-only side wanting. Lately he'd been channeling his energies into the job and a daily jog around the reservoir near the furnished studio he rented in a good block on the Upper West Side. When he was lonely for someone to talk to, he'd drop by the local tavern and join a cross-section of the paper's employees for laughs and a few drinks. When he got loaded, he'd go home and sleep it off. That was the way his life was going at the moment, and he didn't let it bother him too much because at least he had a "career"; it consumed and distracted him.

And now finally he'd by-lined a story that got him some attention.

"I like your eye for details, Shriner," complimented the wizened crime columnist at the next desk. They'd been sitting this close for over a month and the nearest the old man had come to addressing Shriner before this was when he'd sneezed on him by the water cooler. "You dwelled on the facts, but you didn't discourage speculation. They like that kind of writing around here," the veteran reporter advised.

Shriner was flattered by the old man's unexpected outburst, but he couldn't think of anything to say, and he certainly wasn't going to say "thank you." He smiled and nodded, and was saved by the bell: his desk phone rang.

"Yes, Irma, send him back." This—he looked at the notation on his calendar—Tyler Leeds had called earlier for an appointment. Secretly, Shriner thought of it as his first "fan call." From where he was sitting he had a clear view of the reception area, so while his visitor ran interference through the sea of desks in the city room he watched him approach. Shriner was struck most immediately by the casual clothes he wore, and observed secondly that the guy might invest in a supporter or at least a pair of underwear. He could damage himself seriously walking around like that.

Shriner got up to shake hands. He cleared the pile of papers off the extra chair and Tyler sat down.

"So this is where it all happens?" Tyler jested. "I've never been up to a newspaper office before."

"Come back on a less hectic day and I'll show you around the press room." Shriner never had had what could be described as "a normal red-blooded aversion to queers." If he had not known his guest's sexual orientation beforehand, Shriner would have said that Tyler Leeds was just another guy off the street. Time for business: "So what've you got for me?"

Tyler handed him a copy of his press release and the petition form. Shriner speed-read the materials over.

"I'm afraid this isn't my beat, pal. When you called, you mentioned the piece on the overdose."

"Well, it was the way you captured the whole feeling for the pier area where the body was found. I thought if you do a follow-up, you could discuss this proposal to convert the piers."

"The only way I could do a follow-up is if I get assigned to do one. And chances are they'll give it to whoever covers that precinct. I happened to be at the morgue when the brother showed up That's the way they do things around here."

Tyler was disappointed.

"But look, let me find out who you should talk to and you can go see him." Shriner wanted to be helpful.

He made a couple of phone calls. "The guy you want to see is out to lunch now. His name's Logan, I'll pass these along to him if you like."

"Thanks," Tyler managed. "By the way, while I'm here, is there any way to find out if the paper's covering the rally at City Hall tomorrow?"

"I'll check the daybook for you. When did you send the tip?"

Tyler smiled awkwardly. "Stan usually calls it in but aren't City Council sessions automatically covered?"

"We'll see." Shriner walked across the city room and flipped through some pages on a clipboard near the reception area. He came back.

"I don't see anything listed, but there's a regular guy who's assigned to that beat. I'm sure he'll be covering."

"And the rally, too?" Tyler pushed.

"Look, give me the details and I'll give the editor a note."

Tyler quickly ran down the march and rally plans. He liked the way the reporter was going out of his way to be helpful.

"Say," Tyler thought. "Are you sure there's no way you could do a story? I know you told me you had to be assigned, but couldn't you freelance it, and the paper might use it anyway since you work here? I really think you're a terrific writer."

"Anything's possible," Shriner offered, trying not to let the flattery get to him. He sure had to admire the guy's persistence. He didn't quite know why yet, but there was something about his visitor that attracted him.

"If you think about it, this could be one really terrific story about the gay rights movement. Certainly the City Council vote is crucial, but what about all the people who've been working to get it passed?"

"Well, you've already sold me." On that much Shriner would agree.

"So what'd'ya think?"

Shriner smiled sheepishly. "Actually, tomorrow's my day off." He usually spent it sleeping off the night before. "I could do it." Then he quickly added, "Let me give it some thought."

After Tyler left, Shriner made sure that the assignment editor had a detailed note about the rally. He was on his way out to grab a bite when he ran into Tyler waiting in the lobby for Logan to come back from lunch. One thing led to another, and they ended up in a nearby coffee shop. Soon it was as if they were old pals.

7

MID-AFTERNOON IN SHERIDAN SQUARE. THE air was hot and thick with dust and exhaust fumes. On the park benches senior citizens chatted and sunned themselves amidst derelict winos sprawled out half conscious and a cluster of street queens having an animated exchange punctuated by piercing shrieks. Waves of pedestrians—tourists, area workers and residents—crisscrossed broad Seventh Avenue and disappeared down the various narrow streets that jut off the square like spokes in a surreal pinwheel. The rumble of the subway rose over the din of motor traffic and the faint staccato of a jackhammer at a nearby construction site.

Outside the bank at the corner of Christopher Street a petition table and chairs had been set up. Stan, waving a ballpoint pen and clipboard, vigilantly accosted passersby, saying provocatively, "Sign up to liberate the piers!" Several signers lingered, talking.

A yellow Checker pulled up to the curb. Inside, Angus pushed the fare through the slot in the partition and waited for his change. He took one last look at the diagram on the napkin and shoved it into his pocket. He couldn't afford to tip the driver, so he didn't. The moment he slammed the door, the disgruntled driver pulled away yelling, "Son-of-a-bitch!"

"You signed yet?" Stan demanded, practically shoving the clipboard into Angus's stomach.

The aggressive stranger caught Angus off-guard. He shrugged, his thoughts elsewhere.

"We're petitioning the city to convert the abandoned piers on the water-front," went Stan's spiel. "They're a menace to the community." He misread the blank expression on his prospect's face and continued, "Some kid was found dead down there last week. People are constantly being ripped off. It's outrageous. So we're asking the city to demolish those piers or convert them into something the community can use."

Angus managed to shake his head agreeably. He was struck by the coincidence of him mentioning Earl's death.

"We want a feasibility study made on using them for recreational facilities. If we get enough signatures, the city has to respond."

"Before you go any further," Angus finally managed, "I better tell you something. I'm not from around here. I'm not a city resident. I don't think my signing will do you much good."

Stan smiled ruefully. "You can't win them all," he said philosophically and then winked. "Here," he said. "Take some of this literature with you." He handed Angus a packet of pamphlets and fliers. Angus stuffed them into his pocket and lost no time getting on his way.

The roughly sketched map that Ted Hughes had given Angus led him directly to the door of The Cookie Box. A wooden sign hung over the entry. It was carved and painted to look like a partially opened box of cookies tilted with its contents spilling out. A silhouette of the logo was etched in the door's smoky glass. Angus tried to see inside, but all he saw was his own distorted reflection. He hesitated, his hand on the knob.

"Pull!" a cheerful voice from behind directed.

Angus turned to look at the speaker, and in the same motion swung the door open. He moved aside to let the nattily dressed gent pass. "Thank you," the man said and stepped quickly inside. Angus followed. The man's manner was not unlike that of his luncheon host's: genial, civilized. Angus was acquiring an eye for types.

The premises were dimly lit, and harsh strains of rock music assaulted his ears. It took a moment for his eyes to adjust to the dark interior. He could make out neon beer signs and Day-Glo posters decorating the walls. Several patrons were being served at a long bar. A jukebox lit up one corner. Farther back were tables, cozy booths, and in the center, a pool table.

Angus grabbed a stool at the bar and ordered a beer. The bartender nodded agreeably. He opened a bottle and made change.

"Say, maybe you can help me," Angus began cautiously.

"Do my best," said the bartender with a wink. "Snicker been in here today?" He asked nonchalantly.

"Snicker?" the barman asked. "Who's looking for him?"

"Just wondering if he's around, that's all," Angus hedged.

"Ain't seen him. Not lately, anyway." He looked Angus over. "What's your name? Next time I do I'll tell him you came by."

"That's O.K.," Angus said. "I'm just passing through."

"Maybe Cookie can help you," the bartender suggested. He snapped his fingers at one of the pool players. The taller sauntered over to the bar, cue stick in hand.

"Yeah, Rich?" he said, pushing tousled hair out of his eyes. Taking a good look now that his eyes had adjusted to the black light, Angus could see he was a teenager.

"Tell Cookie there's a guy out here looking for Snicker," Rich instructed.

The kid gave Angus a curious once-over. "Will do," he said and disappeared behind a partition at the back of the bar.

Angus took a couple of sips from the frosty beer. The bartender wandered off to take care of other customers. The record on the jukebox changed. It was a slow pulsating number sung by a sultry female vocalist. Angus looked around. There were several men in business suits, including the guy who had come through the door with him. He was standing at the end of the bar talking to a dark-haired youth. Most of the men in the bar were older, though one or two were certainly about his age.

"Can I be of any help, baby?" boomed a rich baritone. "Mr. Cookie Hightower at your service."

Angus swung around. A great black man in a powder blue casual suit and floppy tan fedora loomed over him. He had large dazzling white teeth studded with a glistening gold cap, smiling eyes, and smooth brown skin. But there was potential for menace in his body language.

"Hey, bro," Angus said smoothly. He' d served with dudes like this in Nam. "I'm looking for Snicker. He been around?"

"Mannn, Snicker don't come 'round here no more," Cookie said in a lilting Jamaican accent. It was as if Angus should know better. "But maybe I can help you out. What'cha looking for?"

"What you got?" Angus played along.

A big grin broke through Cookie's thick purplish lips. "Are you putting me on, mannn? Everybody know Cookie got the best of everything. How much you wanna spend?"

Angus shrugged. He was glad he was wearing a tie and jacket. He fit the part better.

"Last of the big-time spenders, huh?" Cookie laughed and gestured toward the pool table. "You like one of them?"

Angus gave the two boys a cursory glance and looked back at Cookie.

"Too old, huh?" was how Cookie read the expression on Angus's face. "Well, why don't you step over here with me," Cookie said with a grand sweep of his bejeweled hand. He was determined to show off his wares.

Angus took the last swig and put the empty down on the bar.

"You're not into S and M, are you?" Cookie asked matter-of-factly on the way back.

Angus automatically shook his head, though he wasn't certain of what Cookie meant.

"Good. I don't want any marks on my boys."

The back of the bar consisted of more tables, mostly empty. Cookie led Angus to a corner booth where four adolescent boys were lounging on a red leather banquette. They couldn't have been more than 14 or 15 years old, and one little blonde moppet could pass for still younger. He was the only one to turn a glazed eye as Angus approached but his attention soon drifted away. The others continued laughing and plotting among themselves. "The two blonds are brothers—if you can dig that," he said and gave Angus a knowing wink.

Until now Angus had controlled himself. He had tried not to make any judgment on the information Cookie imparted. He had gone along passively playing a john. But now these young boys, mere babies, being offered like so much merchandise disgusted and disturbed him.

"What'd'ya get for all of them?" he snapped sarcastically.

Cookie was taken aback. "I never thought about it," he admitted. "Gimme a minute." He ushered Angus away from the table. The boys hardly noticed their departure.

"Tell me something," Angus began, measuring each syllable. "There is a kid I'd like to see. Another one. Maybe you know how I can reach him." He paused for emphasis. "Chicken. His name's Chicken."

"Chicken," Cookie repeated, softly savoring the word. "They're all 'chicken'." Don't have nothing but *chicken.*" There was a perceptible edge to his voice.

Angus lost control. "I'm talking about a kid nicknamed Chicken!" he lashed out. "I'm talking about a kid called Chicken they found stuffed in a barrel over on the pier! Do you know anything about *that* Chicken?"

The jukebox had stopped, and Angus was the center of attention.

"Look, man," Cookie reasoned, not yet sure how to deal with Angus. "I did my best. If you don't like what you see, there're plenty other places to go." The room seemed considerably warmer to Angus. Cookie signaled the bartender with a nod toward the door.

Rich came over. "Hey, man, what's the matter?" he asked, real friendly. "Maybe you'd like to come and have another beer. Cool off."

"I'm already cool!" Angus said and pushed past.

"Hey, that's the dude from newspaper," Rich realized. "Hey, Cookie, its Chicken's brother."

"Yeah, I'm his brother all right. Is this how you sold my brother?"

"Hey, man, chill. If Cookie not pimping them somebody else will. These kids are on the street. Their families don't want them. I'm no social worker but when a boy lives with Cookie he live good." Cookie smiled, pleased with himself.

"I knew ya brudder for a minute. Your brudder, he was very independent. He liked doing his own business. He hung out here but he never really was one of my boys. Not that I didn't want him."

Angus didn't know what to say to that. Cookie had laid it out straight and whether Angus approved of what he did or not, it existed. "Yeah, well I still think it's a crappy way for you to make a living." He had to say it anyway.

Angus made an abrupt move and the bartender, thinking he might try to take a punch at Cookie, pounced on him. The threesome struggled, knocking over a table and some chairs. Soon Angus was overpowered and dragged, twisting and kicking, to the front of the bar.

Cookie was disappointed. "Nobody looking for trouble. Everybody just wants a good time. Cookie give 'em a good time. Why you gotta make trouble, man?" He held Angus's arms in his iron grip.

"Don't know nothing about Chicken than what I told you," Cookie rambled on. "They all do drugs, you can't control that. But maybe that's something you should talk to Snicker about. I don't know nothing except about the chicken in my coop."

The two burly men pushed Angus roughly out the door and onto the pavement. The bolt slammed behind him.

Angus picked himself up. His knee was skinned and his trousers ripped. He seethed with outrage. There was only one option. He was going to the police.

"Finnelli," announced the voice on the other end of the receiver. Angus had found a phone booth a block away and got the number from information.

"Detective Finnelli, this is Angus Rivers. I was in to see you Monday."

"Yes, I remember of course, Mr. Rivers. What can I do for you?

"I think I've, got something for you on my brother's case."

"You do?" Finnelli asked. "What've you been up to, Rivers—playing detective?"

Angus didn't like the sound of that at all, but he continued, "I'm getting in a cab and coming over to see you right away."

"Wait a minute, Rivers. I don't know what you been up to, but you best call the PIU unit at the Sixth Precinct. Ask for Lieutenant Casals. Remember I told you they handle the investigations. Once positive I.D. is made here it's out of my hands." He gave Angus the number, wished him luck, and hung up.

Angus didn't have another dime. It didn't help his already pissy mood being brushed off. He slammed the booth door open. He didn't know where he was, but a good guess was the wholesale meat district from the company names, the stench, and the meat hooks that hung menacingly overhead. He got over to a main street and hailed a passing cab.

"Sixth Precinct," he directed.

"Sixth Precinct," the cabbie echoed. "Sure, fellah. Hold on, it ain't far."

8

A CIGARETTE BUTT SAILED OUT OF A THIRD floor window of City Hall. Little did the passerby who noticed know that this marked the opening of a crucial Council Committee meeting. Chairwoman Pegeen Fitzpatrick, striking the gavel, had just called the General Welfare Committee to order. Before taking his seat, the good Councilman from Brooklyn, the Honorable Salvatore Antonucci, had taken a last puff of his cigarette and casually flicked the smoldering debris out the window, open due to an air-conditioning malfunction. The eight-member committee arranged themselves around the long mahogany conference table; the highly polished surface reflected the countenance of each officeholder. Several of the gentlemen had removed their jackets.

"Before we turn to the business at hand I would like to read from a letter written by the daughter of one of my constituents," declared Chairperson Pegeen as she unfolded some pink stationery. Pegeen was a large, stern woman with a crisp, no-nonsense manner.

"Many of you are well aware of my interest in the senior citizen programs which the City funds," she understated modestly. "The letter was written by the daughter of an elderly woman I placed." Pegeen lifted the spectacles onto the edge of her nose. "It reads, in part, 'Our mother is a new person and we owe it all to you. Joining the Merrimac Center has changed her life. My family and I would like to thank you for the tremendous job you are doing. Please find a check for $25 toward your campaign for re-election. The sum represents a contribution from every member of the family down to my youngest, Annette.'"

There were tears in Pegeen's eyes. "It's letters like this that make the job worth all the headache."

After the obligatory congratulations were sung all around, Councilman Antonucci's hand shot up. Pegeen recognized him with a nod.

"I move we start by taking a preliminary vote on Proposition 36. Then maybe I can get more contributions from the constituents in my district."

Proposition 36 was a pension proposal for city sanitation workers. It provided a new base for calculating retirement benefits, and if voted for one category of city employee it would eventually be adopted for all.

"I second," chimed Father Stiles, one of two clergymen sitting on the Council. He was cementing Antonucci's support on another issue.

Porter was furious. He could see what they were up to. He was against Proposition 36 from the beginning. It was sure to increase substantially the pension burden already carried by the City. If a vote was called and he didn't reverse his position, he was sure to lose Antonucci's vote on Intro 77.

"Before a vote is taken, Madam Chairwoman," spoke up Councilwoman Elvira Rhebas, putting her knitting to one side. Formerly an elementary school teacher, she had been recently elected to the Council from the Bedford-Stuyvesant district. "I would like to see a copy of the study on this proposition. If I'm not mistaken, weren't there long-range problems involved in realizing the increased revenue to make 36 feasible?"

Porter could have kissed her; he could have picked up all 350 pounds of her and danced her around the room. She had voiced his very objection to the proposition.

"No vote then until every member has a chance to study the report," acquiesced Chairwoman Fitzpatrick.

Councilman Antonucci was livid. He had some not too kind thoughts for his fellow councilperson from Brooklyn. He and Father Stiles shared a doleful look across the broad table.

"Before turning to the next order of business, I would like to bring up something of mutual concern to all members of the council and their respective staffs." It was Councilman Klein from Queens whom Pegeen had graciously recognized. He paused to shuffle some papers he was holding, then continued: "As you know, due to increased construction in the City Hall area, the number of reserved parking spaces is dwindling. And now with this new expense budget being considered by the Finance Committee, each of us will soon be forced to make other arrangements." This was a veiled reference to a clause that permitted the hiring of drivers under special considerations. "It seems to me the taxpayers' money could go to more pressing needs."

A murmur of concern rippled around the table. Even Councilman Rusk put down his newspaper. "Let's start carpooling!" he suggested drily.

No one laughed. Though parking was not a problem of utmost importance, it certainly plagued many visitors to City Hall.

"Phew," blew Mr. Hernandez, the scheming Councilman from the Bronx. "What's the problem?" he asked. "My staff can find us a group rate in a commercial garage. Don't worry, I'll get it worked out." He smiled conspiratorially.

Chairperson Fitzpatrick, usually cool as a cucumber, couldn't mask the look of horror on her face. Considering that he was currently under investigation for misuse of office, Mr. Hernandez was hardly the one to intercede in this matter.

"We certainly appreciate your efforts," Pegeen managed. "But perhaps there's some other way to handle this parking mess." Her eyes searched Porter's for an answer.

"Let's put it before the full Council," Porter came up with, breaking the deafening silence. He could give a damn about parking; he had a car and driver!

"I second!" Pegeen declared. A vote was quickly taken and passed with two abstentions. A proposal for a parking study would be presented to the Council.

"I move for a preliminary vote on Intro 77," Porter got out before somebody else sidetracked matters. It was time to get down to business.

"I second," said Mr. Rusk. A liberal from the Upper West Side, he was also an active supporter of the bill.

"Since there has already been a great deal of discussion on Intro 77, let's just try and take a vote," decided Pegeen. No one raised an objection.

"All right, all in favor of a committee recommendation to bring the bill to the full Council, say 'Aye.'"

"Aye," intoned Porter, Mrs. Rhebas, Ms. Fitzpatrick, and Messrs. Rush, Klein, Hernandez.

"Aye-yie-yie," conceded Antonucci.

"Nays?" asked Pegeen.

"Nay!" called Father Stiles loud and clear. He was uncomfortable with his distinct minority status. "I demand discussion," he bristled.

"It's been discussed to death," shrugged Mr. Klein. "Anyway it's too late."

"Nonetheless my conscience would never permit an endorsement," harangued the Father. "The Bible condemns the lifestyle."

"What's that got to do with fair employment and housing practices?" countered Porter.

"By inference, it would sanction that way of life." Father Stiles was firm.

Porter would like to have passed a snide remark about what he'd heard went on in those seminaries of the good Father's Church, not to mention the rumors circulated about a recently deceased prelate's predilection for chorus boys. Instead he solemnly asked, "What about basic civil rights? Would you deny a large number of your constituency their civil rights because of race or national origin?"

Father Stiles could barely contain himself. "Certainly not!" he snapped. "But that's not what we're talking about."

"What are we talking about?" Porter demanded, not liking the edge in his own voice.

"We talking about teachers, policemen, firemen—the very employees this city so heavily depends upon. The firemen's union has declared they'll oppose Intro 77 to the finish. I'm afraid, my fellow councilmen," he grandstanded, "that Intro 77 is a hornet's nest. It will never pass the full Council."

O.K.," determined Chairperson Pegeen. "We bring Intro 77 into the Council tomorrow with a seven-to-one recommendation." She gaveled the session to an end.

9

THE CAB RIDE TO THE SIXTH PRECINCT WAS a short one. Angus forked over the fare and walked into the spanking new facility. Finnelli had called ahead, and there was word at the desk to show Angus right up. In the squad room he was introduced to Lieutenant Casals, a short serious looking man who didn't smile.

"So what've you got, Mr. Rivers?" Casals got right to the point.

Undaunted by Casals' matter of fact tone, Angus told him everything: about the list he had found in Earl's boot; the various people on the list he had gone to see, the incident at Cookie's.

Casals was unimpressed. "So what've you got?"

"This guy Snicker's the key. You've got to find him."

"The key to what?"

"The key to whoever was supplying my brother with narcotics—that's what. And this character Cookie bears some looking into, too."

"Oh, now I get it, Rivers. You're telling us how to conduct investigations."

Angus suddenly recognized that the detective was not particularly enthused. If anything, he was hostile.

"Okay, lieutenant, maybe I'm overstepping my bounds a little."

"I'd say you overstepped them a whole lot. You been watching too much television."

"Gimme a break, will ya?" Angus growled. "Look, Finnelli over at the morgue gave me the impression that the department didn't have the manpower to conduct more than a paper investigation. I'd say I've done the legwork for a very interesting case. Even if you can't track down the dope connection, that place Cookie's is certainly worth a visit."

"Rivers," the lieutenant moaned, "there's dozens of Cookies in this town. And what makes you think we don't know about Cookie's operation or what we might be doing about it?"

If Casals had punched Angus in the stomach, he couldn't have hit him any harder. "Then why haven't you done something about it?" Angus demanded.

"Look, Rivers, I'll tell you this much: we've got everything under control. First of all, there was never any hard evidence of foul play in your brother's death, though the case remains open, of course. The best I can tell you is turn over the one piece of information you do have—the list."

"For what? So you can sit on it. Nothing doing. Look, Casals, I want to talk to your captain. I'll turn the names over to him."

"You're wasting time, Rivers."

"Yeah? Well, let him tell me that."

"Whatever you say," Casals shrugged. He was starting to feel sorry for the guy. After all, it was his brother who was dead. Casals got up from behind the desk. "Wait here," he said and disappeared into the hall.

Angus was mad, and he was damn sure he had a right to be. How could the cop treat his information so lightly? He'd practically got his head kicked in getting it. For a moment he could almost believe that the cops and crooks in this town were in cahoots. That was no joke; so far there was nothing to dispute the impression. Angus was more determined than ever to get action.

Casals stuck his head in the door of the office. "Follow me," he ordered. Angus joined Casals in the corridor, and the two men walked the length to the Captain's office. His secretary told them to go right in. The suite was spacious and ablaze with afternoon sunlight.

The Captain rose from his chair for the introductions. He was large and thickly built with a blond crew cut that made him look considerably younger than his 59 years. He wore regulation blues. "Have a seat," he said, gesturing to the two chairs facing his desk. Angus and Casals sat. "Now, what seems to be your problem, Mr. Rivers?" the Captain asked.

Angus didn't like the sound of that, but he ignored it.

"Look," he began, taking the offensive. "I've tracked down a male prostitution set-up practically on your doorstep. I've also got a lead on a guy who might know something about the local drug traffic. And your detective here tells me 'Thanks a lot' and 'It's none of your business.' I don t get it."

"Well, we certainly appreciate you coming forward with the information, Mr. Rivers."

Angus was incredulous. "And what are you going to do about it?" he demanded.

"Look at it this way," the Captain said, choosing his words carefully. "We've got a number of ongoing investigations under way, and we are well aware of much of the local activity. But there's quite a jump from an arrest to a conviction. We'll pick up a guy like Cookie when we have a better idea of what he can tell us."

"I don't get it!" There was a ring of desperation in Angus's voice. "What about those kids he's selling? You're not going to do anything to stop that! What happens to them?" He stiffened and got a faraway look in his eye. "Do you want me to tell you?"

The Captain cleared his throat. "Look, son, I understand you're upset because your brother was involved in this sordid mess. You feel you have to find someone responsible so you can stop blaming yourself for what happened; you should have been there when he needed you. I understand."

"Thanks," Angus spat.

"Now, son, don't get nasty. I'm telling you this for your own good. Until our investigation's complete, there's no way we can act on your information."

Angus wanted to jump out of his seat and scream, "Why not, you bastard?" but he contained himself.

The Captain's tone softened. "Look, son, I'm going to tell you something, mostly because I don't want you to think we're not doing our job. But you repeat anything I'm about to tell you and I'll say you're a liar. Got that?"

Angus's curiosity was aroused, yet he didn't want to seem too anxious. He shook his head in agreement.

"Right now the word from City Hall is 'hands off the gays'. If we stir up any more controversy down here, they're afraid it could affect a bill currently before the City Council. Our hands are tied. Any sort of publicity could tip passage of the bill. If things stay quiet, there's a better chance of defeating it."

The Captain looked uncomfortably at the two silent men sitting opposite him. He shifted around in his seat. "Now, I've given it to you straight."

"I appreciate it, Captain," Angus forced himself to say, but he was far from satisfied. It was useless to push further; the man had gone out of his way to appease him.

"And remember you never heard a thing," the Captain warned. "Ain't that right, Casals?"

"I don't even know what you're talking about," Casals answered sheepishly.

A call came in on the Captain's private line. Before picking up, he wished Angus luck and excused himself. Casals showed Angus down to the street exit. Shifts were changing, and the stairs and corridors were crawling with blue uniforms.

"Guess you'll be heading back upstate now, Rivers?" It was more a piece of advice than a question.

"Guess so," Angus said, noncommittal.

They shook hands and parted at the double-glass doors. Casals headed back upstairs and Angus out to the street.

They forgot to take the list! he exploded to himself, but kept on going.

10

ALICE ASKED THE DRIVER TO KEEP THE air-conditioning running while she waited. She'd just come from a rough session with her shrink, and at the moment didn't give a damn about ecology. They were parked across from City Hall waiting for Porter. She pulled nervously at the strand of pearls around her throat.

Today's fifty minutes with Dr. Hopewell had been like no other session. The cathartic realization deeply troubled her, but also made her wonder if indeed there was a light at the end of the tunnel. She'd been in therapy for years, thinking it should be like this, but it never was— until now. She tried to put her finger on what had triggered the breakthrough.

Certainly lunch had been an irritating factor in her day—but no, the meeting had been less dreary than her worst expectation. She reconstructed everything that happened from the moment she arrived at her doctor's office.

Mrs. Phelps, the receptionist, was her usual cheery self. Alice was early; they chatted about the weather until the doctor was through with his earlier appointment. Alice thought she recognized the patient coming out, but the man hardly noticed her as he charged by, preoccupied. After a few minutes the doctor buzzed for Alice to come in.

The doctor's office was on the parlor floor of a brownstone in the East 60's. His windows overlooked a lush, well-tended garden. The large potted plants on the sills, the warm wood tones of the furnishings, and the bright-hued Oriental carpets gave the room an absolute feeling of tranquility. If there was any one sensation of her therapeutic experience that was vital, it was the security of his office.

She curled up in the overstuffed chair set to one side of his roll top desk and took a deep breath. Dr. Hopewell smoked a pipe, and she liked the smell of tobacco that lingered in the air. He continued writing, though he did look up and smile when she came in. Soon he put down the pen and said, "Hello." He had a warm way of saying "hello" that made her feel he was really glad to see her.

"I did it again!" she confessed right away like a precocious child who couldn't wait to admit some naughty but gratifying deed.

He smiled. "How was it?"

She shrugged. "I can think of something better—but if I could get it, I wouldn't be talking to you, would I?" She thought that sounded clever.

"Oh, I don't know about that," he said. It could have been a pass.

"It's degrading and I hate myself!" she declared. Then her voice softened to a whisper. "But it sure makes me feel better—for a while." She fumbled in her bag for a handkerchief. He gave her his. She used it to wipe the moisture from her brow and gave it back.

"Is it wrong?" she asked in a tiny voice.

"I keep telling you I'm no father confessor."

"You're right. I want somebody to tell me, 'Say ten Hail Marys and light a candle for a sick friend." She broke into a smile. "See, just hearing it helps."

"But is that how you're always going to deal with it?" he asked firmly.

She flared defensively. "I know he loves me. And there isn't anyone else. After eight years it can't all of a sudden be 'pinwheels and colored lights'." She buried her face in her hands and fought back the tear "What am I crying about?" she moaned.

"Tell me," he advised gently and gave her back the handkerchief.

"For myself!" she shrieked, and the words seemed to echo. "For the dumb, naive girl I was. Miss Varsity Virgin. Nobody told me," she whimpered. "Nobody told me sex was important. And it is. *It* so badly is...

The sight of a crazed, ill-kempt shrew scratching at the rolled-up window startled Alice. The beggar was gesturing for a handout with her dirty, calloused palm extended. She would not go away. Alice took a few bills from her purse and lowered the glass partition. "Give her this, Albert," she told the chauffeur.

Albert partially opened his window and pushed the money within the shopping-bag lady's greedy grasp The old woman squeezed the money tightly and looked up to acknowledge Alice. A dazed grin parted the lip of her toothless mouth. She looked around suspiciously to see if anyone was watching while she secreted the bills in her ragged bosom. Gradually she gathered up her shopping bags and bundles and drifted into the waves of pedestrians crossing City Hall Park.

Alice wondered what sort of circumstances had brought the woman to such a sorry plight. Perhaps in another way her own life was equally pitiable. She smiled. Maybe she was being a bit melodramatic. She closed the class partition.

A number of people appeared beneath the City Hall portico and spilled down the steps. Alice recognized several councilmen and especially Pegeen Fitzpatrick with her bright henna-red hair. Porter came into view. He was conversing animatedly with Father Stiles. "Oh don't bring him back with you," she found herself murmuring involuntarily, then she crossed herself and begged forgiveness for harboring the thought.

The chauffeur also saw Porter and pulled out of the parking space to meet him. A television news crew came out of nowhere. The reporter charged up to Porter and Father Stiles with his microphone poised like a bayonet. Camera rolling, soundman ready, he got off a volley of questions.

Alice couldn't hear a word, but Porter seemed to be fielding the interrogation smoothly. Father Stiles soon appeared to grow irritated and reddened. Finally Porter declined to answer any more questions and gestured toward the waiting car. Without further ado he skipped down the steps and into the car as Albert opened and closed the door for him.

Porter fell heavily into the seat next to Alice and issued a great groan. He kissed her on the cheek and then turned away. Alice tensed up; she tried not to.

"I should've studied medicine," he kidded, not noticing Alice's strained appearance.

"Of course," he said, answering his own question. "I faint at the sight of blood!" He laughed and looked over at her for the first time. He discovered her huddled in the corner, afraid to meet his glance.

"What's happened?" he asked and reached over to pull her to him.

"Nothing, nothing," she lied and started crying; her body trembled.

"Come on, tell me, baby," he soothed and held her tighter. The outburst scared him. He was glad Albert had wasted no time whisking them away from City Hall.

Porter patted her hair and cradled her head against his shoulder. "You can tell me, baby," he cooed.

"I just miss you, that's all," she said, regaining her composure and rummaging around for something to wipe her face with. He gave her his pocket-handkerchief.

"Really," she continued, looking deeply into his eyes. "I just miss you so much," and there was no mistaking the connotation of her words. An uncertain moment followed before he reached over and took her hands in his.

The sleek black limousine sailed off the approach ramp into northbound traffic on the East River Drive. Porter's eyes were drawn out the window past Alice to the gray battleships moored in the Brooklyn Navy Yard piers. He knew what she wanted and wondered whether she was consciously manipulating him, or whether her outburst truly reflected a deteriorating emotional state. He couldn't face another sanitarium especially with the primaries coming up in a matter weeks. His calendar was full for the next two days, and frankly he hated the long haul back and forth to Montauk.

Then again maybe he owed it to her. She was holding up pretty well under the pressure of the last couple of months when he was out practically every evening, returning too exhausted for anything but sleep. And hadn't she agreed to lunch with Tillie Gold? Having met the wife of the good Congressman from the Bronx, he was amused by visualizing the encounter between the two women at The Fatted Calf. He wished Alice shared his sense of humor, or at least had one her own.

"Hey, I got an idea," he said, finally making up his mind, and sounding gen- uinely excited. "Let's go to the beach, the way you wanted to. We can leave tomorrow night after the Council meeting."

"But I thought you have an interview, and what about that block festival on Saturday?"

"The hell with 'em. We can set the story for another time." The words stuck in his throat, even if it was only a limited circulation weekly. "And there'll be tons of festivals between now and November." He was determined to remain optimistic.

"You sure?" she asked, perceptibly cheered.

"Sure!" he said, and seeing her brighten, he really meant it.

11

THE ONE LUXURY IN TEQUILA'S LIFE SHE'D be hard put to sacrifice was being able to sleep late. One of the least fond memories of her childhood was having to rise early to get ready for school. It was no wonder she dropped out upon reaching the legal age of sixteen. By then she'd already discovered the loot to be made along certain city streets by simply impersonating a woman.

There was little in life that she enjoyed more than slipping into a slinky dress, strapping on high-heeled shoes, and making herself up. Going with some guy for 20 or 30 bucks in his parked car or under some steps—that was like finding a pot of gold.

She reached over to switch on the radio and checked the time on the digital clock. She didn't have to be at the theatre till 7p.m. Theatre? It was really a basement in a building off the Bowery. But there was a common (an apt description) dressing room and real theatrical lighting. And lately a lot of the uptown crowd was coming in regularly to see the shows.

Tequila liked to get to the theatre a little early and take time with her make-up and wardrobe. Those other silly queens usually rushed in at half-hour and hastily painted themselves up; that was not Tequila's style. No, she felt herself more akin to a professional like Joan Crawford. In fact, it was Joan who in many ways had been the inspiration for Tequila's life.

It was the flickering images of Joan's masterpiece *Mildred Pierce* that first raised Tequila's consciousness; here was a character whose drive and ambition she could identify with. Certainly there was no other cinematic memory from childhood that remained so vivid—except perhaps Dorothy Dandridge in *Carmen*

Jones, but that wasn't quite the same. He saw *Mildred Pierce* on the *Late Show* in the 1950's and somehow knew there was a very special relationship between himself and that incredible face on the screen.

Hooking on the streets had taught him a lot. (Wasn't it rumored Joan had turned a few tricks before her career took off?) Playing the roles and scenes the different johns demanded had given him numerous opportunities to hone his impersonation. When he was younger he did not feel threatened by the girl inside him who struggled for domination. She easily won, and it was only now when he was a little older that he could see within himself two distinct people. In recognizing his male gender he accepted the uncontrollable need of his psyche to manifest itself as a woman.

Tequila began the laborious preparations for the show. It was moments like this when she truly missed Chicken. She had a couple of days' growth of beard to remove, and since she was out of depilatory, she improvised with hot candle wax. After the wax cooled and hardened she carefully, painfully, peeled it away. Chicken had always stood by, holding the mirror and telling her when she missed some.

Tequila studied her nude body in the full-length mirror. There was no mistaking how exquisitely formed were the limbs; and with the right padding, the curves of the pectorals suggested abundant cleavage. Perhaps the shoulders were a bit broad—but Joan had paved the way ages ago; it was nothing to fret about.

She carefully packed her tote bag with the makeup accessories, and other incidentals she would need. Since it was just a Wednesday night she dressed simply in torcadors and a halter top. Chances were they'd be going to The Bar for drinks afterwards. The only reason Tequila went was so she could be seen and maybe meet somebody who could do something for her. It was always so much more fun to have Chicken along. He was the perfect escort. And couldn't those queens get jealous. Always wanting to know what's going on between them. How that used to make her laugh!

The phone rang. It was Manny, a john held over from her street days who called to say hello now and then. He wanted to come over later. "Sure," she told him. "But make it late. After two." He said he'd see her then, and she hung up.

If it weren't for a few faithful numbers like Manny, Tequila imagined she would have seen some tough times. For a while, when she was about twenty, she thought she'd try and go straight—well, get a straight job, anyway. She soon found out there wasn't too much available without job skills besides serving food and washing dishes. She gave that notion up quick. Luckily she hadn't heeded an impulse to get rid of her wardrobe.

Tequila fished around for some change. She didn't feel like walking and was hoping to scratch enough together to take a cab across town. It only took a couple of bucks for the ride to the theatre, and she was fifty cents short. Sure enough, in the bowl on top of the refrigerator she found a five balled up with some market receipts. Chicken would have had a cab standing at the curb when she came down. She walked to the corner, and there was a cab waiting for the light. She jumped right in and gave the driver the address. You'd have thought she had said "The Waldorf" by the grandness of her tone.

It had been almost two years since she hooked up with some queens who asked her to be in a show they were doing in a loft on Avenue A. At first Tequila had turned them down flat, but then she thought about it and realized it was just the kind of thing she could get into. After all, she was pretty good as far as her drag was concerned, and her nightclub act could sure use the polishing. Even Joan was once a hoofer named Lucille LeSueur. In the beginning she found it hard to catch on to "acting," and she was self-conscious about every move. The director was patient. He didn't have much choice. The script called for sixteen chorines, and with his budget he took what he could get. There weren't so many drags around then. Of course it's different now. Everybody's doing drag full-time, she moaned disdainfully.

About the third production the theatre started getting critical notices, and Tequila's parts kept getting bigger. At first she didn't understand what the reviewers meant when they touted her "flawless comic delivery" and "ribald sense of the absurd," but she sure knew how to get a laugh, even though most of the time the lines she had to say weren't very funny. She gave the dullest dialogue just the right twist—vocally or with a physical jerk—and it would send the house into hysterics. They would scream for more when the curtain closed.

Once in a while a playwright would complain that Tequila's "theatrics" were obscuring his meaning, but the director, who also owned the theatre and produced, would hear none of it. Tequila's good notices and the subsequent activity at the box office made him reluctant to worry about the playwright's deflated ego. The director was getting too used to things that had been unheard of when they first opened—like steak dinners.

Tequila lit a cigarette and stared blankly out the cab window. Her thoughts were full of the evening performance. She ran through her cues, secretly relishing each of the bits of business that were sure to stop the show. Tequila had to laugh. Here she was joking with a hundred people every performance instead of some stupid john from New Jersey who won't even take his socks off.

12

ANGUS WAS CONFUSED BY HIS VISIT TO THE police precinct. He'd expected his information to assist in the investigation, but instead they practically tossed him out on his can. He knew he wasn't crazy, that's for sure—but he was confronting a reality alien to his own.

He happened to pass a subway entrance, and on the spur of the moment decided to take the train back up to the motor inn. It was just as well. When he opened his wallet he found he was short of cash, and he had to dig in his pocket for change to purchase a token. He didn't have much of a wait on the grimy platform. A line of ancient subway cars rumbled into the station. He pushed his way into a crowded car packed with homebound commuters. It was hot and stifling, and no one spoke over the roaring engines. The riders stared vacantly into newspapers or out into nowhere with dull, tired expressions lining their faces.

Suddenly the train came to an abrupt halt. It was stalled between stations, and the delay seemed interminable in the suffocating heat. A few passengers complained about the wait; then they lapsed back into sullen silence. There was only the sound of the whirling fans that did little more than stir the air and the asthmatic breathing of the guy standing next to him. A train going in the opposite direction on the next track crashed past. Finally his train got under way. Angus was tempted to get off at the next stop but stayed on and got out at the stop nearest the motor inn.

The desk cashed a check for him and he stopped by the coffee shop to get a sandwich and drink to go. Back up in his room he absently flicked on the T.V.

as he prepared to eat his meal. The television made a loud noise then brightened into focus. Angus hurriedly lowered the sound.

"And now on the local scene," boomed the newscaster. "Members of the City Council's General Welfare Committee met in closed session today. The committee's recommendation is seen as a key to the passage of controversial Intro 77, which would guarantee the civil rights of gays in city jobs and housing. Now here's an on-the-scene report with Jim Jacobs."

The picture switched to the facade of City Hall. The camera zoomed shakily in on two figures descending the stairs. It was obvious from his garb that one was a priest. Angus thought he recognized the other man. A microphone with the station's call letters emblazoned across it was pushed into the latter's face.

"Councilman Rhodes, will Intro 77 be introduced to the full Council tomorrow?" demanded the unseen reporter.

"It certainly will, Jim. And with a seven-to-one recommendation," obliged the councilman.

Angus remembered where he had seen him before. It was at the party Panda had taken him this week. He was the son of the hostess. He remembered his wife, too.

"Seven-to-one," repeated the interviewer. "Were you the holdout, Father Stiles?" he asked, quickly maneuvering the mike onto the cleric's chest. The priest was noticeably flustered. "I-I would rather think my vote was the only sensible one," he countered.

"And how do you think the bill will fare before the full Council, Mr. Rhodes?"

"There's no telling, Jim," Porter sparred. "But I'm certainly confident the Council will give the bill serious consideration. After all, this is a civil rights issue. We're talking about the legal rights of a minority in this city—a very visible minority." And before the reporter could get out another question, the councilman indicated with a nod and a wave of his hand that he had to be going.

"Thank you, councilman."

Porter smiled genially and walked out of the frame. Father Stiles was also about to leave.

"Have you got any predictions on how the vote will go tomorrow, Father Stiles?" reporter Jacobs was quick to ask.

"I'm a priest—not a prophet, young man!" the clergyman snapped testily, and then the camera switched to footage of the reporter doing a wrap-up.

Angus hadn't had any idea who Porter was when he met him at the party, but seeing him on T.V. now, he wondered about getting in touch with him. Obviously the councilman had no real idea what this gay thing was all about. Angus would probably be doing him a favor if he called him up and told him about the scene he'd discovered. And maybe this way he could get some action on Earl's case. *My god, what about Earl's rights?*

The phone rang. Angus turned down the sound on the T.V. and answered.

"Hello."

"Mr. Rivers?" came a vaguely accented voice.

"Speaking."

"This is Fritz Hilton—you remember? You came about your brother the other morning."

"Of course. Mr. Hilton. How are you doing?"

"Fine, thank you for asking. Listen, please, I can only talk a minute. I think I can help you."

"Yes?"

"You remember the friend of Chicken I mentioned. The no-good one."

"Snicker, you mean?"

"Yeah, that one. He's here."

"In your apartment?"

"No, no. I'm working. The steam bath. He checked in a while ago."

"What's the address, Mr. Hilton? I'm coming right over."

Fritz Hilton dictated the address of the Riviera Baths. "Don't ask for me," he cautioned. "Just check-in like a regular customer. I'm in the massage room near the pool." He hung up.

13

PANDA WAS ALONE IN THE PRIVATE STUDIO. He was snorting lines of a silvery white powder from a mirrored tray and sorting through stacks of photo contact sheets. The phone rang. It was the private line, so he answered.

"Daisy's!" he ad-libbed.

"Mr. Pee," came a familiar cadence.

"Not tonight, Cookie," Panda said, slightly irritated. "I've already got something arranged." He was about to hang up.

"Hold a minute," Cookie said. "Ain't got nothing for you tonight but some information."

"What kind?"

"The cheap kind!"

"You must be taking yours off the top."

"Wrong again. Look," he advised, "there was some dude in here today looking for *Chicken.*"

"What about him?"

"You know him?" Cookie seemed surprised. "Then you better tell him he's looking for trouble."

"He's the kid's brother."

"How'd he find me?"

"I'm looking for that answer myself." Panda put down the magnifying glass he was using to study the contacts and leaned back in his chair.

"What if he comes back?"'

"I'm not your gatekeeper—you take care of it!" Panda depressed the receiver and replaced the phone in the cradle. He reached for the wine carafe and refilled his crystal goblet. He pensively sipped the ruby red claret. He was thinking about Chicken. He was thinking about the first time he set eyes on the waif. It was in Tequila's dressing room in that tacky cabaret. He was so easy: so easy and so pretty.

Chicken had agreed to come back to the studio almost immediately. They talked a little, snorted a little, and then Panda had his way with Chicken right there on the carpet. He began undressing the passive teenager by pulling the ragged T-shirt over his limp arms and shoulders. He undid one sneaker and then the other, sniffing each before putting it down. Panda carefully undid the fly buttons and pulled the jeans free of Chicken's smooth, hairless hips and legs. He compulsively groped the soiled jockey shorts then worked them down around the boy's knees. He fingered the silky strands of pubic hair and brought his face close to sniff the musky boy scent.

The limp noodle cradled on the crescent of his fleshy testicles stirred and started swelling. Panda nuzzled the down-covered testicles and brushed his lips between the smooth inner thighs, licking the dewy moistness. With his face buried deep in the boy's groin, he lingered; then slowly raising the boy's legs over his head, he worked his tongue into the fetid crevice, nibbling hungrily.

Later they shot film: rolls and rolls of stills. Chicken was a natural. He loved having his picture taken and slipped from pose to pose with amazing alacrity. His range of moods was startling—from coquettish innocence to tough sensuality and various shades in between.

Panda pushed the chair away from the desk and got up. He steadied himself, walked over to the file room, and unlocked the door. He flicked on the lights and went in. There were rows of file cabinets along the walls, and a long narrow worktable down the middle. The room had a closed, not-opened-often-enough smell. He knew without having to think which drawers contained the prints he wanted. He crossed and pulled the first drawer open. The long drawer contained thick files of 8'-by-10' glossies. He quickly flipped through a few folders. Each held several copies of each shot. They were all pictures of Chicken taken at various times during the several months Panda had kept him around. The artist had hoped to offer them in mail-order sets, another of his flourishing enterprises, but now he planned to hold off and maybe do a book one day.

On an impulse he pulled out one or two of every pose and laid them end-to-end on the table. He slowly circled the table looking at each picture carefully, some as if for the first time. Chicken was photographed from every imaginable angle. Each black-and-white print attested to the magnificent proportions of the youth's hairless torso, trim legs and arms. His striking features were no less photogenic: the dreamy sparkle in his eyes; the sensual mouth—here playful, there pensive; the fringe of silky curls that photographed white.

Panda leaned heavily on the table and surveyed the field of glossies spread before him. The more he thought of Chicken the greater became his grief. He wept. Soon his body was shaking with a mighty out-pouring that overwhelmed him. He was a latter-day Michelangelo and this had been his David! He slumped across the table, and the pictures scattered every which way, some sailing to the floor. He didn't care. In that instant nothing mattered more than immersing himself in the memory of Chicken. He buried his head in his arms and sobbed.

14

THE RIVIERA BATHS WAS ONE OF THE OLDEST establishments of its kind in the city, and in its heyday, the best. The facility enjoyed a booming popularity during the 1960's, but the advent of more imaginative competitors precipitated its sharp decline. The straight clientele lost during the gay interim never returned, and now the baths catered to a seedier element, men who would just as easily plunk down their three dollars for a flophouse cot.

Angus paused to examine the facade. The building, except for a red neon sign over the entrance, was not unlike other brownstones lining the block. He climbed the well-tread steps up to the brightly lit reception area. There were two others in line ahead of him waiting to check in. Several towel-clad men lounging in easy chairs and at tables in the adjacent snack bar scrutinized him heavily. He steadfastly avoided meeting their penetrating glances and concentrated on the geometric patterns in the marble floor tiles. His turn came.

"One, please," Angus said.

"One what?" the cashier asked suspiciously.

"One admission."

"Room or locker?" the cashier pointed to a peeling sign over the cage that listed the price for each.

"Locker," Angus said, because it was cheaper. He took the money out of his wallet.

"Put your valuables in the envelope and sign the flap," the cashier instructed. Angus did so.

"Sammy will take you up." He struck the bell with his palm.

A burly black attendant sauntered over from one side of the cashier's box with a towel in hand. He picked up the key the cashier pushed toward him and gestured for Angus to follow. They went up a flight of steps and down a dimly lit corridor with cubicles lining either side. At the far end the attendant stopped and unlocked one of the doors. It opened into a small walk-in locker with a plank bench and clothing hooks. Lit by a bare low-wattage bulb, the cabinet was secured by screened meshing at the top.

The attendant made an elaborate presentation as he gave Angus the key and folded towel. "You need any extras," he winked, "Sammy will get 'em for you." His hand remained extended. Angus got the hint and dug into his pocket for a quarter tip.

"Thanks, boss," the attendant said flippantly and moved soundlessly down the corridor.

Angus pulled the door shut and started undressing. He had once visited a sauna during his haul in Germany and wasn't the least self-conscious about stripping. He arranged the skimpy towel about his middle. The key was on an elastic band that slipped around his wrist. He opened the door and stepped outside into the hall. Several adjacent doors were open, their occupants resting in full view. One man loitered, and two others slowly drifted by. Angus addressed the shorter: "Which way's the pool?"

"Down two flights!" replied the taller. "If you want some company after your swim, I'm in room 210," he added.

Angus smiled. He had no trouble finding the steps. He passed through the lobby on his way down. The "pool" wasn't much more than a glorified wading pond. Off the pool were several different kinds of hot baths. In an alcove marked "MASSAGE" he found Fritz Hilton.

The stout German was hard at work kneading the bulbous flesh of a customer on his table. He looked up and recognized Angus. With a wink and nod he indicated the nearby steam room. Angus winked back by way of thank you and padded over to the door.

Billows of escaping steam enveloped him. The vapor was so thick it was difficult to see more than a few feet in front of him. He moved cautiously, gradually getting his bearings. Along the far wall was a three-tiered bench; Angus could vaguely see the outlines of two figures seated at opposite ends of the upper tier.

Angus positioned himself on the lower tier and tried to make out the forms on either side of him.

The man on his right stood up and stretched. He moved with arthritic difficulty in getting down from the upper shelf. Once down, he began a series of stretching exercises that consisted mostly of swinging his arms and bending his torso. Clearly he was an elderly bather. Angus looked away, certain that the other form was the object of his search. He eased a little closer.

Snicker was caught up in private reverie. He found the steam and intense heat soothing; it helped when he had a lot on his mind. One time a john had brought him here instead of going to a hotel. Afterwards Snicker often suggested the place to others procuring his services that didn't have a place to go. Frequently he came by himself just for the steam. He had developed something of a sentimental attachment to the place lately; like Marlowe's cellar, it offered refuge.

"Hot enough for you?" came a voice through the fog.

Though prowling, even in the steam room, was common, Snicker usually paid no attention to anybody here.

"Hot enough?" repeated Angus, louder this time.

Snicker looked over, trying to make out the speaker. The hazy image was no one he recognized. "Just the way I like it," he answered. Out of the corner of his eye he gave the fellow another once-over to see if he was a potential john or just a number looking for a free roll.

"Cleans out the pores," Angus said to keep the conversation going. He moved closer.

"Yeah," Snicker muttered. Deciding that the number wasn't buying, he didn't want to give him any encouragement. He got up, moved down from the tier, and left the steam room. He'd had enough anyway.

Angus waited. He didn't want his pursuit to be too obvious. When he came out of the steam room, he spotted Snicker using one of the shower stalls. Angus took the next one over. Several customers displaying themselves on nearby marble benches openly watched the men bathing. Snicker took a long shower. He was vaguely conscious of admirers from several quarters, not unusual at the baths, so he ignored them. He stepped out of the shower and toweled off.

Angus had to get an in quickly without overplaying his hand. He finished showering and started drying himself. "Come, here a lot?" he asked, to get the conversation going again.

Snicker looked up. "Once in a while," he answered and deliberately turned away.

"What's your name?" Angus persisted.

"My name?" he questioned. "What'd'ya wanna know my name for?"

"Just being friendly, that's all."

"Joe," he said. "Call me Joe."

"Joe?" Angus repeated. He was wondering if the old man had made a mistake. "Joe?" he said again. "That's funny, I'd swear you looked like a guy I met once...named Snicker."

At the mention of his name the bather scrutinized Angus with a hard glance. The look indicated Angus was on the right track.

"Oh, yeah," 'Joe' said. "And where'd you meet this guy—Snicker?"

Angus didn't answer right away. "Snicker," he said finally. "I met him in a bar in The Village."

"What bar was that?"

"Cookie's," Angus said, then threw in for good measure, "Kid I used to know named Chicken introduced us."

The look of recognition on Snicker's face was unmistakable. "Well, I never heard of Cookie's, and I don't know no Chicken," he lied. Snicker wrapped the towel around his waist and started to leave.

"Hey, wait up," Angus called.

Snicker spun around. "Look, man, who are you? What do you want?" The words spat out like bullets.

"What're you getting uptight about?" Angus asked carefully. "I thought you might be able to tell me where Chicken's hanging out these days, that's all."

"I said I don't know any Chicken," he snarled. "Got it?"

"Nothing to get uptight about," Angus said calmly.

"Who's getting uptight? I just don't feel like being bugged tonight!" Snicker turned and walked a few steps. He looked around. Angus was right behind him.

"Don't follow me!" His tone was menacing.

"Who's following *you?*" Angus countered.

"Good," Snicker said and raced up the steps.

Angus tried to stay with him, but an attendant with two enormous sacks of laundry came between them. When Angus got to the lobby, Snicker was nowhere to be seen. He cursed himself for letting the snake give him the slip, and he began a floor-by-floor search.

Every floor seemed a maze of corridors and cubicles. Many of the room and walk-in locker doors were open, and men lounged about suggestively, making passes with their eyes and gestures. In the dormitory Angus passed carefully up and down the aisles, scrutinizing the occupant of every bed. More than one man approached and tried to grope him. He pushed the hands gently but firmly away. Soon he found himself back in the lobby. There was still no sign of Snicker. He posted himself in the coffee shop at a table that gave him a view of everybody's comings and goings. He ordered a cup of coffee and sipped it slowly.

An odd assortment of men checked in and out. Some wore business suits and carried attaché cases; others were casually dressed in denims and light cottons. One customer emerged from the street garbed completely in black leather with heavy motorcycle boots and a wide ring of keys on his hip that clanked as he walked.

Then Snicker appeared fully dressed descending the stairs. Angus pounced. "I still want to talk to you," he growled.

"Look, man," Snicker said very loudly so as to be overheard by anyone who wanted to listen. "I told you downstairs: I'm not interested. So stop bugging me!"

"You're going to give me some answers, Snicker." Angus's voice was low but firm.

"I keep telling you my name's Joe." Snicker got on line for the cashier's window. There was one other man ahead of him.

Angus couldn't take it any more. "I want to know what happened to Chicken!" he boomed furiously.

The clatter of dishes in the coffee shop ceased. Every eye was on them. The cashier completed the previous transaction, and Snicker stepped up to the window. "I don't know any Chicken," he said, and pushed the key through the grate. "Checking out."

"I say you do!" Angus was losing control.

"Keep it down, fellahs." It was a man in tie and shirtsleeves stepping from behind the door marked "PRIVATE."

Snicker saw his chance and took it. "Look, man," he said to Angus. "Maybe some other time. I got to split."

The cashier slid the envelope of checked valuables through the window opening. Snicker scooped it up and moved to the door.

Held in check by the surprise entrance of the manager, Angus stood by helplessly. Seeing Snicker about to make good his departure, Angus lunged after him and was in turn tackled by the manager.

"What's your problem, fellah?" the manager demanded, subduing Angus. The muscular attendant came over to lend a hand.

"I just want to talk to him," Angus explained as he struggled. The attendant gave his arm a twist.

"It sound to me like he doesn't want to talk to you—at least not tonight," the manager advised.

"So you better get back upstairs and try and change your luck." He paused to give his next words emphasis. "Or I'm going to throw you out."

A small crowd was collecting and Angus started getting paranoid.

"He's just trying to be friendly," Snicker volunteered. He was hoping to make that his exit line.

"Hey, wait a minute," Angus roared. It dawned on him that his behavior was being interpreted as sour grapes over a rejected pass. "I'm not trying to pick this guy up."

"Tell it to the Marines," chirped a high-pitched cutie, and a rumble of laughter erupted in the lobby.

Snicker laughed along as he coolly walked out the door. Watching the object of his suspicions slip so easily away compounded Angus's frustration and embarrassment.

"All right!" barked the manager. "Show's over, you can sit back down." He loosened his grip on Angus, and the attendant followed suit.

"I think you better get your stuff and check out, Mister. We're not looking for trouble around here."

The manager nodded to the attendant to accompany Angus. His humiliation was complete.

15

SNICKER PRACTICALLY RAN ACROSS TOWN. He used side streets and kept his head down. Fearful of attracting attention or being pursued, he frequently looked behind him. He had no real destination; he just kept moving. He had to lie low, but how was he going to do that with no money and no place to go? Marlowe's was out. The old man had started freaking out—he was sure the police were looking for them and couldn't be convinced otherwise. He told Snicker to get out and to never come back! And now Snicker's last sanctuary—the baths—had been invaded.

Snicker wondered about the guy at the baths. Who was he? He wasn't a cop. Cops don't come on like that. They cuff you and run you in if they think they've got something on you. Maybe he was a pal of Chicken's and *had* seen him with Chicken somewhere. That's the impression he gave. But Snicker had a pretty good memory, and he couldn't place the face for the life of him. There was no mistaking the man's eagerness to renew the acquaintance. For an instant Snicker thought it might have been smarter to play along, but then he decided it was better to get out of there the way he did. He trusted his instincts.

He was on the waterfront. He needed a fix but didn't have the bread to get one. He stood in the shadow of the old pier. Several figures darted in and out. He decided to take someone off. He slicked back his hair and arranged his privates so they were outlined beneath the thin fabric of his trousers. He went into the dark and silent pier. Spotting a lone figure go into a storage shed, he followed.

The space was black. He groped his way through the scattered debris and placed himself so that the pale shaft of light from the entry illuminated his body from the chest down. As his eyes grew accustomed to the darkness, he could make out his prospective victim on the opposite wall. Snicker thrust his hips forward and rubbed himself. The man stirred, drifting toward Snicker, who then retreated further into the shadows. The man brushed against him. Snicker stood perfectly still. The stranger cupped his hand to Snicker's groin and slowly massaged. Snicker put his hands on the man's buttocks and guided him closer, feeling the bulge of a billfold in the hip pocket. The man deftly unfastened Snickers fly. Snicker loosened the man's belt, unzipped his trousers, and pulled them down around his knees. He knelt and pretended to blow the score while his other hand reached around and removed the wallet. The take stuffed in his boot, Snicker briefly put the stranger's erect organ in his mouth, and gagged.

"That's a baby," the man moaned, pumping his thighs.

Snicker jumped up abruptly. The number got down to reciprocate. Snicker feigned excitement for a minute, then whispered hoarsely, "Somebody's coming! Let's get out of here." He pushed the trick away and closed up his pants. Snicker was out the door before the number got to his feet.

"Wait up!" the man called. Quickly fixing his clothes, he stumbled after Snicker. It didn't take him long to discover his wallet was missing. "Son-of-a-bitch!" he swore and quickened his pace.

Snicker looked back but not soon enough; the gay was right on top of him. He grabbed Snicker by the shoulder and swung him roughly around.

"All right, give it back!" he demanded. "I won't make a stink."

"What you talking about—get your hands off me!"

"Gimme back the wallet." The guy meant business.

"Get your hands off me!" Snicker pushed him away and started out.

"Fucking pickpocket!" the guy started shouting at the top of his lungs. He managed to get hold of Snicker again.

"Get away from me!" Snicker warned and spun around wielding a small steak knife he kept for emergencies; it flashed menacingly.

The knife changed the man's attitude. He backed off "Keep the money. Just gimme back the papers in the wallet."

"What the hell are you talking about?" Snicker sneered. "Keep following me and get hurt!" he threatened and started running.

Snicker got out of the area fast. When he was sure the guy had abandoned pursuit, he headed down to Eighth Street to look for a drug connection. He scored from a dealer under the arch in Washington Square Park, making the purchase with some of the cash in the wallet. Instinctively he returned to Marlowe's, gaining entry through the broken window in the yard. He hid himself in the crawlspace behind the furnace.

When he was sure the old man was sleeping, he lit the nub of a candle and went through the stolen billfold. It contained 14 more dollars and some identification. Snicker cursed the bastard for carrying so little money and no credit cards. He pocketed the cash and pitched the wallet into darkness.

He checked out his recent purchases: two glassine packets of white powder. Methodically he prepared a fix and shot up. In the enveloping euphoria all of his cares slipped away. There was a vacant gleam in his eye and a lopsided grin on his lips. He started nodding.

Was he a bad son-of-a-bitch or wasn't he? He'd got his act together before, and he was going to get it together again. All he had to do was sit tight…Who was that bastard at the baths anyway? That was no john! Chicken—he kept talking about Chicken…Chicken…Dumb turkey. I told him to wait. He was so messed up. Snicker laughed.

He remembered that first night on Third Avenue: it was freaking cold. The kid was strung out. He needed a hit and he needed it bad—but first he had to earn the bread to buy it. Snicker overheard Chicken refuse to haggle over the price with a john. Though he was desperate, Chicken turned him down rather than go low. Snicker admired the kid's heart and saddled over to lay a few good words on him. They'd seen each other around but never talked too much. Snicker offered to turn him on, and Chicken jumped at the chance. They went to Snicker's room in a flop hotel off Sixth Avenue.

Chicken was a mess. He'd been on the street about a week. He drifted between Times Square and the doorways along Third Avenue. The camaraderie that developed between the two hustlers was easy. It was based on their mutual attraction to drugs. Snicker had long ago given up any pretense of digging women and Chicken had never embraced such notions. The drugs had made the two youths fundamentally asexual. Snicker had been living on his own a lot longer; he knew his way around. Chicken was used to having somebody supply him with drugs, and Snicker needed somebody to take care of. They were made for each other.

16

IT WAS LIKE OLD TIMES: ALL EVENING A steady stream of activists converged on the GLP storefront. Many were new faces, mainly college kids home for summer recess. Banners and signs were painted and spread around the room to dry. A delegation from the Gay Tavern Owners Association passed out free beer to all takers. Several boisterous meetings were under way. There was no mistaking the air of impending celebration.

Stan watched the activity through the glass partition. He was talking on the phone in the office. "We sure appreciate the support but…" he kept beginning, but he couldn't seem to get any further. The sight in the room beyond certainly made him feel like his old self again. That, and his reconciliation with Joey. They'd just come back from an intimate dinner at one of their favorite restaurants, where Joey explained that nothing had changed between them, even if he had made it with the reverend a couple of times. "Chalk it up to experience!" he gaily explained. Stan was doubly glad he hadn't made a scene.

Tyler came into the office. Stan threw him a get-me-out-of-this look. "Then we'll see you in the morning, Travis. That's right, City Hall Park, 8 a.m…. Bye." Stan hung up and settled in the chair with a sigh of relief.

"What's that all about?" Tyler asked.

"Welcome Home."

"What?"

"Welcome Home. It's a Vietnam vets organization. That was Travis, their president. He says they're coming to the rally tomorrow." Stan seemed a little puzzled.

"Hey, that's great. What'd'ya look so unhappy about?"

"Rufus, from the Black People's Coalition, told him to call." Stan seemed a little uncertain. "I just hope these guys remember what they're going to be rallying for."

"Well, if they show up at City Hall tomorrow that's what they're there for. Anyway, I think aligning with black militants and Vietnam vets can only help our credibility as a movement. They're already established."

Tyler was feeling very positive about everything. Still utmost in his thoughts was his visit to the newspaper. Shriner had said he would show up at City Hall tomorrow to freelance a piece about them. What more could Tyler ask for? Shriner even mentioned using him as the focus of the article. Already Tyler was picturing how the story would read.

Nicky could see Tyler and Stan talking in the office. He was still in a bit of a snit after being stood up that afternoon. He wanted to know where Tyler had gone and he was only half buying that lunch-with-the-newspaper-reporter alibi. Then to top matters, when he stopped by the apartment to feed the cat, Meow was nowhere to be found. He wondered how she got out and rued her return. He figured the bitch would get herself knocked up and he'd end up playing nursemaid to a litter of kittens.

Tyler came out of the office and was introducing himself to some of the newcomers. Nicky saw a chance for one more night alone with Tyler diminishing rapidly. Maybe he should play Tyler's game and get friendly. Who knows, he might hit it off with some one, and when you got right down to it, all he really wanted was to get laid anyway.

"You feel better?" Tyler asked playfully.

Nicky was somewhat startled. He hadn't seen Tyler coming over. He looked up with a bitchy smile. "Gay, gay, gay!" he managed. There was an unpleasant taste in his mouth, and he wanted something to chew on. "You got any gum?"

Tyler shrugged incredulously. "No. See you later," he said. He caught up with Rev. Tunney-Brown, who was sharing the top of a scarlet sleeping bag with two college juniors from Connecticut. They sat enraptured as he meticulously detailed his future travel plans.

Derek and his gaggle of cronies swept into the storefront a little before midnight. All were dressed in various stages of drag, Derek a standout in red satin hot pants, orange Lurex knee socks, and a white ruffled Carmen Miranda blouse. He fluttered about, kissing cheeks and greeting people, at the same time never straying too far from his entourage of transvestites and slack-jawed studs.

Tyler made no attempt to mask his contempt. He managed to give Derek an icy glare more than once. "Flaming queen" was simply not the best image for so-called "leaders of the movement" to project; he was sure of that. One of the major obstacles to the passage of Intro 77 was the controversial "cross-dressing" clause. Many opponents admitted they would support the bill if the stipulation were removed. What it boiled down to was that Derek was deliberately flaunting the point.

Tyler had pondered Derek's election and knew it had a lot to do with some underhanded campaign maneuvers. He made sure there was a big turnout of his supporters for the crucial election meeting then sat back as they voted him into office. These thoughts had passed through Tyler's mind before, but he had never considered doing anything about it. Tonight was different. Tyler was very caught up in the Movement and feeling very protective of its progress.

When Derek felt he had put in enough of an appearance to remind everybody he was still GLP chairperson, he signaled his retinue that it was time to leave. They made their usual conspicuous exit. "See you scouts in the morning," Derek called to no one in particular. He knew there were quite a few glad to see that he wasn't planning to stick around all night. But that didn't bother him one bit. Spending the night on that concrete floor in a sleeping bag was not the least bit appealing. He and his party had other plans for the remainder of the evening.

While making their way through the narrow streets of the West Village, they passed around and quickly swallowed some "uppers." Their destination was one of the after-hours clubs in the wholesale meat district near the waterfront. The lookout at The Hook recognized them immediately and opened the door. He collected the dollar cover charge and wished them a good evening. They boarded a freight elevator that very slowly carried them to the third floor. As the door opened, they were greeted by a loud blast of funky dance music.

Derek threw up his hands and screamed in ecstasy as he boogied on in. It was like they were playing that song just for his entrance. The dance floor was empty and Derek wasted no time taking center stage and putting on a show. He shimmied and strutted; moaned and squealed and hummed along with the record. Derek was in his element.

The D.J. waved to Derek as he segued into a slower pulsating number. Derek's mood changed with the music. He was more aware of the harsh bluish glow the black lights gave the dingy loft. He moved to the sidelines and several queens rushed over to dish the latest. Derek cracked a few jokes then sailed into the back room. It was dark, but there was no mistaking the presence of several partially nude bodies in heated embrace. He glided flirtatiously close to one couple and got a whiff of popper. He felt a hand caress his buttock. It was too early to get into anything he decided, and he tipped out to the bar and ordered a Scotch.

While he was waiting for his drink, he noticed the guy standing next to him. Their eyes touched and Derek threw the man a long sideward glance, all the while gyrating his hips, snapping his fingers, and bobbing his shoulders to the beat. Derek reached into the band of his Lurex socks and retrieved a joint wrapped in tinfoil. He lit the reefer with some matches off the bar. He and the stranger never stopped looking into each other's eyes. Derek made a whole number out of taking a toke, then boogied over to pass his new friend the joint. The man took a drag and started dancing along. Derek smiled, his *fun* smile—he was ready to dance all night.

17

ANGUS HAD NO RECOLLECTION OF LEAVING the bathhouse. Certainly he had dressed and retrieved his belongings from the cashier. There must have been stares and muffled comments. If so, the memory was completely repressed. And yet the feelings he had: the sense of inadequacy and futility, were all too present and familiar. The last time these feelings had surfaced was in a girl bar in Da Nang.

It was in the back room, in one of the curtained cubicles, with all around him the sounds of men grunting and groaning, the whispered incantations of copulation. The girl he was with was carefully undressing. She couldn't have been more than 16, yet her body had the full ripeness of a woman. He had wanted her out in the front, but as she passively straddled his hips, he couldn't get into it. He closed his eyes and tried to remember how much he wanted it and how he was going to kick himself later for not taking her. It didn't work; she just didn't turn him on any more. He gently pushed her off, reached for the bills he had tucked in his watchband, and paid her. She kissed his fingertips and took the money. While he dressed, she sat impassively on the bed. He stroked the top of her head and left. He walked, walked all the way back to camp, a journey doubly treacherous at night. He ambled along unaware of danger, just as he walked now through the silent canyons of Manhattan.

He found himself in the West 40's, approaching Times Square. He was assaulted by a myriad of converging images—the brightly lit theatre marquees, flashily dressed couples out for a night on the town, rumpled men darting into porno shops, riders gawking from passing cars, kibitzing knots of patrolmen, despondent derelicts, drug pushers, hustlers, the crazies.

He imagined Chicken walking this street, lingering in doorways offering himself. Suddenly it didn't seem so horrible; a kind of numbness was setting in. Maybe that cop was right—his pursuing Chicken's past had been a way to expunge the feelings of guilt he harbored. Knowing the events that led to Earl's death would not bring him back.

But didn't he owe Earl something?

He impulsively turned toward Third Avenue. He walked fast and easily discovered the corners he was looking for. Young boys and muscular men casually posed singly and in pairs. Some stood in doorways, others at the curb, and still more waited on side-streets as big expensive cars slowly rolled by, frequently stopping, to whisk one, sometimes two, away. They could have been a bunch of kids hanging out; only up close they exuded a hard, street-wise toughness. Angus wanted to talk to one of them, but he didn't know how to begin. One kid caught his eye and gave him a mischievous smile. Angus returned it. The kid strolled over. He was Hispanic and maybe 18.

"Going out tonight?" he asked. He wore a red T-shirt and tight white trousers that left nothing about his body up to the imagination.

"Maybe later," Angus said. "What're you up to?"

"The usual," the kid shrugged wearily. He had a couple of missing teeth and a scar or two on his face. "I'm trying to get by just like everybody else. You live around here?"

"No, no, I'm just visiting.

The kid seemed to like that. He brightened and became more animated. "You staying in a hotel?"

"Yeah."

"Which one? Somebody once took me to the Americana. You staying there?"

"Nah, just a motel over near the river. Nothing fancy."

"Well, you got a place," he said, even though he seemed a little disappointed. "So you going out tonight or what?"

That was the second time he used the phrase and now Angus recognized its meaning. Sometimes he was amazed at how slowly he caught on.

"What've you got in mind?" Angus asked. There was hollowness to his tone.

"Player's choice," the boy smiled. "What d'ya dig?"

Angus tensed. What this was all about came crashing down on him. He resisted an urge to take a swing at the boy and another to hug him.

"Hey, what's the matter, man?" the kid asked. "You look like you've seen a ghost."

"I have," Angus said and started walking.

The kid shrugged and looked around to see if anybody else was lonely.

THURSDAY

MAD JESSE PEERED OVER THE EDGE OF HIS perch. The vantage point gave him a bird's-eye view of the storeroom. A lone figure loitered below unaware he was being observed. Unwilling to give away his hiding place, Jesse rolled noiselessly back into his nest of soiled rags and newspapers. Patiently he waited for the intruder to leave. He guessed it to be around 7 in the morning, but the only sure way of telling was to see the sun. The sounds of the faggots coming and going last night had kept him awake, and it had seemed like a long time before he dozed off. Sometimes it was hard to ignore the nonstop carnality that went on below, the prowling footsteps, the sighs of pleasure and strident moans that punctuated the nighttime stillness.

The crib provided him with a haven. It had been suspended along the rafters of the narrower wall for some long-forgotten purpose. Unless you made a point of looking up, it was hardly noticeable. The ledge not only gave him a formidable view, but with a bit of sharp metal and a great deal of industry he had managed to scratch out through the rotting timber and rusting metal of the facade a peephole that gave him a miniature panorama of the cobblestone street and highway girders. Best of all, the arrangement made him and his belongings inaccessible to the bold wharf rats that sometimes riffled his bundles while he slept. This was his second season on the old pier. Last year he had shared the shelter with rodents and sea gulls, and an occasional mate who had a bottle to pass. When he returned this spring, the gaping holes in the loading doors told him that things had changed, that his private resort had been permanently invaded.

He peeped gingerly over the edge. Another had joined the intruder and once more Mad Jesse was an unwilling and undetected witness to sodomy. How many scenes of unbridled passion or rejection had he observed or overheard? What else? Last night he'd seen a man robbed at knifepoint; the week before, two men dragging a corpse. He made no value judgments; he only resented the disruption of his otherwise serene consciousness.

He looked again. The intruders were gone, and he seized the opportunity to get down. He gathered up the rags of his bed and stuffed them into plastic bags that held his other possessions. He dropped them over the side then swung himself down, using grips conveniently bolted to the wall for that purpose. Upright, he stooped, and in the plain light of day his face resembled a gargoyle's. He was a humpless Quasimodo, with spindly muscular arms too long for his squat torso. A shawl of matted black hair that draped down his shoulders and back fringed his bald pate. It had been years since more than a hard rain had cleansed it.

He gathered up his bags and moved into one of the storerooms whose windows and frames had been gutted. Unimpeded sunlight flooded every cranny. After relieving himself in a corner, he stripped to the waist, carefully hanging the layers of shirts and pullovers on nail heads randomly hammered into the exposed beams. His bare upper torso was trim and sinewy. He began pacing, swinging his arms furiously and grunting to himself, absorbed in turbulent reveries.

2

THE POLICE HELICOPTER HOVERED BRIEFLY in the sky over City Hall. The post-Colonial building with its marble pilasters, arched windows, and graceful portico, set in the center of Gotham's equivalent of a village green, was a charming anachronism—an 18th century chateau that remained undisturbed while all around an overgrown forest of skyscrapers and bridge spans loomed. The gilded statue of Lady Justice atop the hall's central clock tower glistened in the bright morning sunlight.

Within her prospect, waves of arriving gays milled about a speaker's platform erected at the far end of the green. An irregular corral of police barriers ribboned its periphery. Scores of uniformed officers were standing by, and more waited out of sight in buses parked on a side street. On the roof of a nearby office building, walkie-talkie-toting detectives surveyed the area and reported to another unit stationed on the other side of the park. Seasoned veterans, the cops watched with bemused disinterest as the gays and their supporters put the finishing touches on lavender and white streamers that artfully trimmed the stage, chairs and lectern.

The colorful assortment of long hairs frolicked and joked among themselves, occasionally spraying police or passersby with gay-power slogans. Others lounged on park benches or leaned defiantly against the barricades. A few stripped to the waist and stretched out on the grass to sun. Office-bound workers streaming from the subway kiosk were none too happy about running an obstacle course instead of taking their usual shortcut through the park. Tardy employees rushing past and casual strollers alike saw the flamboyant collection of activists and wondered what was going on. After reading the placards and banners, the passersby signaled indignant recognition, then followed with a shrug of dismissal, never breaking pace. A demented heckler shouted epithets and made obscene gestures but kept his distance. Ignoring him, Stan and Tyler beamed like proud papas at the impressive turnout. Their group was already several hundred strong, and more were coming all the time and from every direction.

"Doesn't anybody work for a living?" Tyler joked.

"Let's get a line going, some chanting and singing," Stan suggested. "We might as well let those guys in City Hall know we're out here." He clapped his hands excitedly.

Tyler didn't know what the hell he was doing, but with Stan and Joey's assistance he started a picket line that practically encircled the park.

"WHAT DO WE WANT?" Stan shouted.

"GAY RIGHTS!" came the refrain of hundreds of voices in unison.

"WHEN DO WE WANT IT?"

"NOW!" they thundered. Then in quick staccato, "GAY GAY HERE TO STAY! NEVER NEVER GO AWAY!"

Three late-model sedans pulled up. From the back seat of the first, an Olds 88, emerged a strapping bronze-skinned dude sporting a great Afro hairdo. His eyes shaded, he wore a purple dashiki and carried an exotically carved cane. On either side he was flanked by two amply proportioned sisters swathed in striking African-style gowns and several aides uniformed in green fatigues and black berets. Stan was the first to notice their arrival. He recognized Minister of Information Rufus Graves from his picture in the news and hurried over to introduce himself.

"Rufus?" he said with a certain familiarity. "I'm Stan Freed. Glad you could make it." He extended a hand to shake. Rufus eyed the outstretched palm suspiciously and instead of taking it, raised his juju stick and gave Stan a mysterious blessing.

Suddenly there was a terrible honking of car horns, shouting, and police whistles. A beat-up old school bus cut jerkily through traffic and came screeching up to the curb. The psychedelically painted exterior was prepared with slogans—VETS NEED BENEFITS, OUT OF VIETNAM NOW! MAKE LOVE NOT WAR. The battered doors belched open, and out spilled a motley crew.

Some were in partial military uniforms, others wore civilian clothes, a few had long hair.

The last out was a vet in a wheelchair who was lifted from the bus by two aides. The demeanor of the seated figure suggested an enthroned monarch. He had luxuriant red-blond hair, a full beard, and penetrating green eyes. His Mexican-style poncho was encrusted with medals and buttons espousing various causes. He puffed smugly on the stub of a thick stogie. Once on the ground, he activated the forward switch on his chair, and with the others following or running interference, he whisked off toward the knot of militants and gays.

"Hey, Rufus, baby!" he called when he spotted his old pal. He rolled up with his hand out, palm up. "How you doing?"

Rufus slapped him five. "Taking care, Travis. T-a-k-i-n-g care!" he said and slapped him five more.

"You got the low-down yet? Who's putting this thing together?"

"How'd'ya do, Travis?" spoke up Stan.

"Travis, this is Stan Freed. He's coordinator of…of the um…uhhh," Rufus stumbled.

"Gay Liberation Party," prompted one of the sisters with a stage whisper.

"Right, baby. Coordinator of the Gay Liberating Party."

"Oh, yeah, Stan," Travis recalled. "We talked last night."

"That's right," Stan said, and introduced Tyler, Joey and some of the others standing around.

"So, you work out the speaking order yet?" Travis got right to the point. "When am I up—first?"

"No—I am!" Rufus returned smoothly, then said to Stan, "If that's all right with you, my man? I've got another speaking commitment today." He smiled sweetly. "Now, who'd you say was covering?"

Meanwhile, the vets unrolled their sleeping bags and passed out beer, their interest momentarily aroused by the circling pickets. Rufus's dragoons fanned out to make a security check. They poked around the platform, and two began removing the huge gay activist symbol and were about to replace it with their own flag.

"Hey!" shouted Tyler, witnessing the maneuver and rushing over followed by Joey. "What're you guys doing? That's our stuff."

"Yeah, but we got to take it down for a few minutes," one said.

"Beat it, kid if you don't wanna get hurt," the other advised. He looked pretty mean.

Stan saw what was going on and came over with Rufus hot on his heels.

"The stage is off limits until we finish setting up," Stan diplomatically told the guerrillas leering down at him. "Your flag can go up next to ours if you like."

"You gotta understand," Rufus began tentatively, "when I agreed to speak here today…."

"You called us, Rufus."

"We did? Anyway, I can't have my presence misconstrued as an endorsement. I was merely planning to welcome you to 'the struggle'."

"You were?"

"Yeah—and later we can work something out. I wouldn't be surprised if one day our two causes converge on some common ground."

"Well, until then," reasoned Tyler succinctly, "our flag stays and yours goes."

Rufus viewed the upstart darkly.

"Break it up, you guys. Break it up!" warned Travis, zooming full throttle into the grouping and practically throwing Rufus off balance. "Two TV crews just pulled up—so everybody cool it!"

Heads and necks craned to see which way the media were coming. Everybody recognized Jim Jacobs. He was chatting with what's-his-name from the network news on the other station. The journalists approached the rebels while their crews got the equipment set up.

"How ya doing, Rufus?" Jim asked with a lilt of surprise in his voice. "I didn't expect to see you here today."

"I'm doing just fine, Jim. How's that fine lady of yours?" Rufus was basking in the glow of recognition.

"She's just great, thanks. Now, don't tell me you guys are joining forces?"

There was an awkward silence.

Rufus looked at Travis, Travis looked to Stan, and Stan gave Jim Jacobs an enigmatic wink.

3

THE TELEPHONE WAS RINGING. ALICE ignored it then remembered that Annie had the day off. Reluctantly she picked up.

"Hello."

"Good morning, Alice. Trust you're well. Let me speak to my son." Her mother-in-law was precise and business-like.

"Good morning," Alice managed. "Porter's still dressing. How are you today, Mother?" The last word stuck in her throat.

"Dandy, thank you!" There was no mistaking the sarcasm in her tone. "Have you seen the morning paper?"

"Not yet. What's in it?" She was afraid to ask.

"Skip Karlson's column. How dare she write items like that! Tell Porter I'm on the phone." Priscilla Rhodes's irritation was markedly increasing.

Knowing better than to step into the eye of a storm, Alice said, "Hold on, Mother," and did as she was told.

"Porter," she called, opening the door to his dressing room. He was still in the shower. "Porter!" she called over the rushing water, "Your mother's on the phone."

"So early," he moaned.

"There's something in the paper. She's upset."

"I've got soap in my hair. Tell her I'll have to call her back."

"All right," Alice said, none too happily, and pulled the door shut. Back on the phone: "Mother, he's still in the shower."

"Does he know yet?" the older woman demanded.

"Know what, Mother?" She managed to keep the edge off her voice. "You said something about Skip Karlson's column."

"Where does that woman get off writing such things?" Priscilla wailed.

"Writing what, Mother? Read it to me; I haven't seen the papers yet. Annie's off today," she apologized.

Priscilla put on her reading glasses and picked up her copy of the paper. "Skip Karlson's Big Apple," she read. "There's a picture of Skip set into the outline of an apple—does that make her a worm?" She quickly skimmed until she came to the paragraph headed "City Hall Hustle" in bold caps.

"'Hearsay: The cute frosh councilman with the gorgeous stride is doing some of his own empire-building. Mr. All-American Candidate has literally stepped into the Gay Rights controversy, feet first. At least that's what Porter Rhodes told a troop of activists he addressed on their own turf the other eve. Maybe he's got bigger plans than Congress and is stretching for every vote. He sure has mine—but let's hope he shares his secrets with us soon!' There! And she's run an old prep-school picture of him in tennis whites."

Alice couldn't see what her mother-in-law was so upset about. If anything, the column was an endorsement. But she dare not share the thought with Priscilla.

"Well?" Priscilla demanded after a deliberate silence.

Alice didn't know what to say.

"I see!" Priscilla snapped, sensing Alice's lack of sympathy with her point of view. "Have Porter call me the instant he can. Good-bye." She hung up.

Bewildered by the exchange, Alice went out to the service hall to retrieve the morning paper. She reread the item. Porter came out of the dressing room.

"What's up?" he asked peevishly.

Alice looked at him helplessly, not knowing where to begin. In exasperation she chucked the paper at him. "Read it yourself!" Suddenly she was very angry, and though it really had nothing to do with Porter, she directed her anger at him.

First things first, Porter decided, so before he did or said anything rash, he picked up the paper and looked for whatever he was supposed to find.

"Skip Karlson's column," Alice managed. "Under the paragraph titled 'City Hall Hustle'."

Porter read the column, and when he was done, he chuckled. "At least she *spelled* my name right. And hey, I looked pretty good in prep school. I wonder who gave her that picture."

Alice was not in a joking mood. "Do you know what your mother put me through over that innocuous item? Huh? Do you have any idea?" Alice was now extremely agitated.

"I'll call her when I get downtown. Now don't you let this get you upset too." He pulled Alice off the bed and into his arms. "We've got three whole days by the sea to look forward to," he affectionately reminded her.

Alice couldn't look into Porter's eyes. She was beginning to dread the weekend. Last night had been such a disappointment. Was the weekend going to be the same?

4

MR. LINDEN SELECTED BRAHMS GERMAN *Requiem* and put it on the turntable. He turned up the speakers in the Heavenly Rest slumber room and went in to check the sound.

The Rivers boy had received few floral tributes and Mr. Linden found the chamber irritatingly bare. He was hoping to use some of the basket arrangements from today's 10 o'clock to brighten things up. He paced the room to get a feeling and to make sure every touch was just so. Yes, he decided after listening a few moments, the music encouraged the requisite mood for the solemn occasion.

He paused to examine the deceased. The mother had selected a casket in the medium price range, an unornamented oak-veneered box with simple brass colored fittings, a good choice for the money. Of course he was not too pleased with the clothing she'd brought over. He'd have preferred a less jarring hue than the olive-green suit, though the color did set the boy's golden tresses off rather nicely.

As he moved past the window, he noticed mourners for the 10 o'clock already gathering at the curb. He drew back the curtain to take a quick head count, fearing that even with extra chairs he wouldn't be able to manage the turnout for Mrs. Douglas: her husband was a local contractor. Then he saw the boy's mother pass unacknowledged through the crowd and turn up the drive.

He spun around and crossed the room, giving it one more deliberate going over with his eyes. Everything was ready! He closed the door leading to the control booth—the former butler's pantry—and opened the double sliding doors that let into the front hall. He couldn't help but appreciating how well the layout of the gracious old house suited its current use.

As he came into the foyer, Mrs. Rivers was stepping in. Obviously she'd had a sleepless night. There were dark circles under her eyes and a slightly dissipated quality in her expression, probably more from trying not to cry than actual outbursts.

"Good morning, Mrs. Rivers," Mr. Linden greeted sweetly. "Everything is ready."

Mrs. Rivers barely acknowledged the lanky funeral director. She allowed herself to be shown into the Heavenly Rest slumber room. She walked directly to the casket, crossed herself, and knelt down.

Mr. Linden was touched by her pious manner, but he couldn't help feeling that her outfit, though black and relatively simple, was a poor choice for the mother of the deceased. He would have found something less flouncy and more tailored even if it were just a plain dark skirt and blouse—a hundred times more appropriate than the dated cocktail dress she was wearing. Even her black scarf was tied too much like a babushka and did nothing to flatter the oval of the woman's poorly made-up but attractive face. He smiled pleasantly and noiselessly left the room.

In the front hall he encountered two teenaged girls, both very developed physically though they couldn't have been any more than 18. Dressed casually in blue jeans and revealing halter-tops, they wandered about, a little uncertain.

"May I help you?" Mr. Linden's voice rang out, as one girl was about to step into the chapel.

"Oh!" she gasped and abruptly turned. "You scared me," she confided breathlessly. Her fright probably had more to do with the setting than his approach.

"We're...we're," the other stuttered, not quite knowing how to put what she was about to say. "We're here to see Earl...Earl Rivers. We used to go to school with him, and the paper said he was here."

"Of course," Mr. Linden smiled. "Young Mr. Rivers is right this way," he said with a flourish of hand that directed them into the room he had just left.

The girls thanked him with nervous giggles.

Their arrival made him wonder if he would need the larger chapel for the funeral Saturday. He was expecting just a family turnout, and there was nothing the mother had said that suggested more. Of course, he could double-book the chapel so that an early and late service were easily accommodated. Moving things around though would mean staff overtime.

If business kept up, he was definitely going to have to consider expansion. There was an adjacent property facing on the next street, a main thoroughfare. He could build a spanking new facility designed to his own specifications and live in the old house. He toyed with the prospect of restoring the Victorian mansion to its former glory. The thought was intoxicating and, oddly, he started thinking about his father. Inwardly he laughed. Did he really care enough about the old man to want him to see what a success he'd made of the family business? Ten years ago nothing of the sort would have crossed either of their minds.

Mr. Linden decided he'd give that contractor Douglas a call—in a week or so, of course—just to get the specifics on undertaking such a project. The price could be high, what with the cost of building materials going up all the time, but in the long run a lot cheaper the sooner things got underway.

The mortician paused in front of the full-length mirror. He was wearing a three-piece gray suit with charcoal tie and highly buffed black shoes. He fluffed up the points of his pocket-handkerchief and adjusted the length of his shirt cuffs. Several visitors were coming through the door. He turned to greet them; delicately inquiring which party they had come to mourn. And in a flash, just as he reached to open the chapel doors, he enjoyed the sensual memory of a recent escapade: the tongue bathing of a satin-skinned Hispanic man on his recent trip to the city.

5

MARLOWE BREAKFASTED ON BLACK INSTANT coffee and a pair of greasy pork chops left over from last night's meal. He got right to his chores: sweeping down the sidewalk, bringing in the trashcans, mopping out the vestibule and first-floor hall. But busy as he was, something didn't feel right. It was just beyond his mind's grasp, not quite something he should remember as much as something he should know. Then it came to him when the old tom Samson brushed up against his leg: *Snicker had come back!*

He trained the beam of light from his flashlight into the narrow crawlspace behind the furnace. Snicker was back there all right, sound asleep on the soiled mattress. His mouth open, limbs askew, it looked as if he'd crumbled rather than consciously gone to bed. Marlowe could also make out the junkie's paraphernalia spread out on a nearby crate. The old man searched the floor of the furnace room until he found what he was looking for: a wrench that he used to make adjustments on the boiler. He concealed the length of metal behind his thigh.

"Get up, you bastard" he cried, and kicked Snicker's dangling foot.

The intruder awakened instantly and threw his guard up. Crouching warily on the far comer of the mattress, he rubbed the sleep from his eyes.

"What're you doing here?" Marlowe demanded. "I told you to stay away."

"Screw you!" Snicker hissed. The bright light was making his eyes blink, and he couldn't get his mind going. "I ain't had nowhere else to go!" he blurted.

"Take a trip. Get out of the city like I told you. Use your thumb." Marlowe was beyond compassion. He had to look out for himself. He revealed the wrench he was holding and played the beam of light on it. "Get your things," he said hoarsely.

Snicker could fight the old man, take him, though he might get a few scratches for his trouble, but definitely take him if he wanted to. Somehow it was easier to scurry around for his belongings.

"I'll split," he said, because once the old man had been his friend, and he didn't have the heart to hurt him.

Marlowe kept his distance as Snicker emerged from behind the boiler.

"Stake me fare to the coast?" the boy asked.

"Can't do it!" Marlowe said quickly.

"How about a few bucks anyway?" the boy pressed. Pride was too expensive.

Marlowe eyed the addict with open disgust. He clicked off the flashlight and stuck it in the loop of his coveralls. He reached into his pocket and separated a single bill from several folded together.

"Here," he spat, and squeezing the paper money into a ball, threw it at Snicker's feet.

Snicker scooped the money up, automatically checking the denomination.

"Thanks," he said and pocketed the twenty.

"You know the way," Marlowe said, waving the tool.

Snicker picked up his things and took one last look around, as if he'd forgotten something. The dim light of a single naked bulb and the roughly hewn stone foundation made the cellar seem more ominous than he'd remembered. Other than the living room couch at his sister's, it was the only place where he'd lived for any length of time. He pushed a clump of matted hair out of his eyes and started out.

Marlowe followed. When he reached the side door, Snicker paused and faced the old man. He knew it was for keeps this time, and he wanted to say something appropriate. No words came. Finally, he pulled the door open, and the tom skittered inside. Snicker threw the old man a parting glance and stepped into the alley, letting the door slam loudly behind him.

The cat eased himself slowly between Marlowe's feet and rubbed the length of his body against either ankle. The old man reached down to stroke his pet. He thought: This here cat's the only one worth a damn—'cept Chicken.

6

ANGUS ROLLED OUT OF BED WHEN THE phone rang taking the receiver to the floor with him.

"Hello," he barked.

"Angus, honey?" came his mother's anguished voice.

"Ma?" he answered. "You all right?"

"What's the matter, baby?"

"I'm fine, I'm fine: just waking up."

"Your car giving you trouble again?"

"No, no, it's working good."

"What's keeping you then? I thought you'd be back by now." She started sobbing. "I can't do it by myself, I just can't."

"Come on, Ma," he soothed. "Don't start crying." He felt utterly helpless.

"Your Pa won't come out of his room. He says he's going to stay there until the funeral's over."

"You know he don't mean it, Ma. He'll come out."

"The arrangements are set," she said, her tone softening. "I stopped by early at Mr. Linden's. He made everything real nice. You'll see."

"That's good, Ma," Angus said, and a deafening pause followed.

"What's keeping you so long?" she asked.

"Just a lot of bureaucratic mumbo-jumbo," he lied. "Nothing for you to worry about."

"The service is Saturday, son," she said very evenly, with no trace of the earlier outburst. "Eleven o'clock. You be there, son. To help your mother."

"I will. I'll be there."

His mother broke the connection first. He felt bad about her calling. Maybe she thought he was staying away intentionally. There was no way to tell her about his discoveries; he barely understood them himself. Not only about Earl but also the world that he had moved in. He wondered how many other outsiders had ever taken as thorough a glimpse of this world or even knew it existed.

Angus sat up against the headboard of the bed. He was still a little sleepy, but he was determined to stay awake. He wondered about Sally and the boys. His mother hadn't said anything about them, so everything must be all right. He knew that he still loved Sally and that she would never completely accept his ways. Suddenly he had an urge to talk to her.

The phone seemed to ring forever. He wondered where the hell she was. As he was about to give up she answered.

"Hello," she gasped, out of breath.

"Hello," Angus said. "You all right, honey?"

"I was in the yard hanging laundry."

Her tone was much easier than it had been in a long time. "I'm still in New York," he told her. "Be home later or tomorrow."

"What's keeping you?"

"Tying up some loose ends. Earl led quite a life down here. I'll tell you all about it when I get back."

He wanted to tell her he loved her and that he wanted to come home, but the words didn't seem to come. "I was just calling to check on you and the boys."

"We're just fine."

Why didn't she say something? She knew why he was calling. Why wouldn't she help him?

"Honey, I got to go," she said after a long silence. "The boys are calling me."

"O.K., O.K.," he said. "You go see what they want."

Putting the phone down, Angus flipped onto the floor on all fours and started doing push-ups. The sheer physical effort was invigorating. He sprung up and down; up and down at a rapid clip until he reached his limit and couldn't pull his body up any more. He stayed completely still, breathing very heavily into the carpet, then rolled over onto his buttocks and did sit-ups. When he was done, he fell back, exhausted. His quick short breaths seemed to focus his thoughts as they kaleidoscoped through the images of the past few days.

And what had "playing detective" got him? Certainly there was no way to bring Earl back. Perhaps he would have been better off not knowing so much about his brother. He remembered passages in Earl's diary and considered for the first time that Chicken may have been irretrievable. Drugs and prostitution marked his life. Why wasn't he stronger? How could this have happened to him and others like him? Angus didn't have any answers, but he was convinced he must make one last attempt to confront his brother's past and settle all doubts for himself. He must find Snicker. He had no idea where to begin looking, but he would allow the remainder of the day before heading home.

After showering and dressing, Angus started packing. He came across the packet of gay-rights literature the guy in Sheridan Square had handed him the day before. There were a couple of political tracts and some old fliers announcing meetings and demonstrations. There was also a two-page sketch on the GLP Drop-In Center and how it was becoming a gathering place for runaways and street people. He wrote down the address and threw the material away. In the lobby he made checkout arrangements and went into the garage to pick up his car. Automatically he started driving downtown, toward The Village. Intuitively Angus knew that if he were ever to cross Snicker's path again, it would most likely happen on that particular chunk of Manhattan Island.

7

JOEY BACKED THE TRUCK UP TO THE platform. Two muscular dudes in matching club T-shirts gave him a hand unloading the extra chairs that Rufus demanded to accommodate his women and soldiers on the podium. Stan was making the concession in the hope of working out the differences on the speaking order. He convinced Rufus that the opening remarks were more appropriately spoken by Reverend Tunney-Brown in the form of a prayer. Rufus gave in when it was agreed he would go next. Travis would close.

"Like the keynote speaker," the Vietnam vet decided.

As the rostrum guests took their places, the demonstrators and curious passersby crushed in closer to the platform. Stan loped up to the microphone.

"Testing, one-two-three," he spoke into the crackling instrument and looked to Tyler, who was handling stage-managing chores.

"It's working!" Tyler sighed with relief. "You're all set."

Stan looked out into the crowd. He saw many friendly and familiar faces. "I'm the best they could come up with for an emcee," he joked. A cheer of appreciation rang out. "And I want to thank you for the beautiful sight of seeing you all here today!"

They vigorously applauded themselves. Several photographers snapped away. Stan suddenly realized that he was their subject. His days of anonymity were ended. He became very nervous, but continued, "To get things under way, I'm proud to introduce the guiding spirit of our movement, the Very Reverend Robert Tunney-Brown of the Los Angeles Municipal Congregation!" Stan led a polite patter of applause.

The grinning Reverend popped up from his seat and strode to the lectern. Simply garbed in a dark suit, clerical collar, and love beads, he nodded graciously to the assembly. "Thank you, Stan," he said with a perceptible drawl. "Let's have a hand for our grand emcee Stan Freed!"

When the applause died down, the Reverend grew serious. "I'm delighted to be here on this historical occasion. And I'd like to show my appreciation by sharing this meditation with you." He lowered his head piously and closed his eyes. In his evocation dedicated to the day's crucial vote, he declared, "No matter what the outcome, we must never lose Hope!" Many auditors bowed their heads, while others merely looked on with polite indifference. When the Reverend called "for Understanding and Fellowship," there were several loud gasps.

A smoke-gray Rolls Royce stenciled with peace symbols had glided up, and to everyone's amazement out stepped international superstar and political activist Cassandra Heathe on the arm of her latest jet-set romance, rock drummer Almond Joy.

"Amen," the Reverend concluded then opened his eyes to see what the commotion was all about. A radiant Cassandra, in feathers and shimmering silks, swept gushing and glittering through the worshiping crowd. A nervously smiling Almond and a husky Hindu bodyguard flanked her. Cassandra was rich, beautiful, and famous. Her father was a wealthy oil prince; her mother, a celebrated Hollywood actress. Movement groupie bar none, and a star in her own right, she was certain to get an Oscar for her latest film. As she was lifted onto the stage there was no mistaking whose show this was turning into. She and Rufus greeted each other like old comrades. She recognized Travis from the televised Senate hearings and paid her respects. And of course, she knew Reverend Tunney-Brown from the Coast.

"When did you get into town, darling?" he asked cattily as they affectionately bussed.

"I'm always in town!" she informed him mysteriously.

"I suppose the captivating Cassandra Heathe needs no introduction," the Reverend intoned over the sound system speakers.

There was frantic clapping and screaming. Cassandra took the cue. She leaned into the mike and in her famous syrupy voice said, "Thank you, thank you, thank you. You're all awfully sweet. Peace and Love." She made the V-sign with the fingers of both hands. "As I was saying to Almond Joy this very morning—you all know Almond Joy of the Sweet Licks, of course?"

The smiling drummer clasped his fists together over his head and waved champ-style to show his appreciation for the applause.

"I was saying, 'Almond, we have to make a statement, show our solidarity with the gay movement.' So we got into the car and down we came. On behalf of all my gay friends—and gay fans—that are trying to come out of the closet, I wish to say these words to you today. The *door* is open! You can come out any time you want."

The cameramen were having a field day. The vets were hooting and whistling, and Tyler had to discourage more than one excited fan from trying to get up on the stage.

"I want to wish each one of you your gay rights and may it go jolly well for you in the Council."

Somebody screamed for Almond to play his current hit single, but he mimed that he didn't have his band or skins with him.

"Good luck!" Cassandra signed off and turned to once more acknowledge her fellow activists. "Plane to catch," she cooed apologetically and allowed Almond to lead the way off the stage as she waved and blew kisses. Jim Jacobs tried to get an interview, but was quickly punted to one side by her frisky bodyguard. To get a better look for themselves, the police cleared a path to the Rolls. Throwing one last kiss, she and Almond disappeared into the Silver Cloud and drove off.

Black activist Rufus knew that Cassie was a tough act to follow. To scattered applause he approached the mike, and giving the black power fist salute, he greeted the crowd in Swahili.

8

ANGUS DROVE RIGHT UP TO THE GLP storefront and found it closed. There was a sign about a rally at City Hall, but figuring he had no reason to go down there, Angus bought a newspaper. When he saw the name of Councilman Porter Rhodes mentioned in one of the columns, he remembered the TV news footage. He suddenly decided to give Rhodes a call to tell him that all this gay stuff he was stirring up had prevented a proper investigation of Earl's case. Angus was hoping the Councilman might be sympathetic enough with his plight to help him make an impression with the authorities.

Angus got Porter's office number out of a directory and dialed.

Alice was glad it was Annie's day off because then she didn't have to worry about her looks—even though she hated like hell waiting on herself. The phone started ringing. Usually Alice ignored the office tie line, but when the service let it ring more than was bearable, she picked up.

"Helllooo," she slurred.

"Hello," came an uncertain male voice. "Is this Councilman Rhodes's office?"

"Yes it is," Alice said matter-of-factly. "He's down at City Hall; can I take a message?"

The woman's voice sounded familiar to Angus. "Is this Mrs. Rhodes?" he asked.

"Who's calling, please?"

Angus could tell by her tone that he was right. "Mrs. Rhodes, this is Angus Rivers. I met you at your mother-in-law's party the other night."

"I'm sorry, who?" she asked, wondering if she was going to regret answering the phone.

"Panda brought me to the party. I was the guy with dark hair."

"Yes, I remember," said Alice evenly. And she did. She remembered his big coarse hands and the hot way they felt when he pressed hers during introductions. She remembered the shape of his mouth and the little mustache that tickled his upper lip.

"Is there another number where I can reach your husband?"

"Today the Council is in session. I'm sure he won't be out of there until late, and then we're off for the weekend. Can he call you Monday?"

Angus liked her crisp formal manner. He'd bet she'd gone to one of those rich-girl schools.

"I'm trying to leave town myself, but I sure wish I could talk to him for a minute."

Alice volunteered that Porter was usually hard to reach at City Hall especially when the Council was in session. "I think they are taking some kind of a vote today. Is there something I can help you with?" she asked and for some reason found herself suddenly out of breath.

"I don't think so," Angus said. "Your husband's the one I've got to talk to *about this.*"

There was something about the way he emphasized the last two words that Alice took for a cue.

"Well," she groped. "Would you like to stop by for a drink anyway?" she found herself saying. "You sure sound like you could use one," she added nervously. What was coming over her? What was she doing? Did she really want to do this?

"I sure could use that drink," Angus said without hesitation. He'd been thinking about getting next to one of these classy broads for a long time. "What's the address?"

Alice told him to come over in about an hour and hung up. She slipped into the shower and made a concerted effort to pull herself together. She thought about Porter—but only for a moment. This wasn't the first time. Last spring she'd given herself to a telephone repairman working in the building.

She called down to the doorman and told him she was expecting a messenger and to send him right up, adding, "He may have to wait because the papers aren't quite ready."

Alice set up the bar and put on a stack of her favorite records. She slipped into a blue silk tent dress and brushed her hair loosely back from her forehead. She arranged herself on the settee and lit a cigarette. Taking a deep drag, Alice figured she was in for quite an afternoon. And just so she'd be sure to enjoy it, she fixed herself a stiff drink.

9

RUFUS'S ORATION WAS LONG AND ARTFULLY paced. He spoke fervently of "the Struggle," doomfully appraised the decline of "the ruling classes," and lauded "the surge of People Nationalism" that greeted him everywhere. His pronouncements were punctuated with the prophecy AFTER THE REVOLUTION! Or the judgment OFF THE PIG! His revival-tent gestures and well-modulated delivery whipped impressionable listeners into frenzied screams of POWER TO THE PEOPLE and OFF THE PIG!

The contingent of "pigs" on duty had originally viewed the gay gathering as some kind of a freak carnival, but now that attitude changed dramatically. Security around the gay rally was stepped up, and all goings and comings were strictly monitored. A gypsy cab pulled up to the barriers. Two cops approached from either side, "Where do you think you're going?" one officer grumbled at the pack of "faggots" crammed into the back seat.

"Officer," chimed Derek over the kind of flurry that ensues when four queens are counting change to pay one fare. "I'm scheduled to speak today. Is there a V.I.P. trailer?" Derek knew there wasn't supposed to be one, but he wanted to let the cops know who he was. "I'm Derek Wiggins, chairperson of the sponsoring organization." He was ever so gracious. One would have thought he'd be dog-tired after bumping the night away—but it's amazing what a snort or two of crystal will do to perk things up.

"Likewise I'm sure," the cop muttered then said to the driver, "You gotta get this hack out of here, buddy."

The cabbie couldn't be more pleased. "You betcha!" He counted the fistful of change while the back seat emptied.

"Are we expected to push through that mob to get to the stage?" inquired Derek, the first out. His "date" was close behind.

"You better talk to your friends," the cop suggested.

"Thank you!" Derek bettedavised. "Are we ready?" he called to his minions.

"Ever, darling, ever," chimed Lourdes, holding up the rear.

Tyler spotted Derek and his retinue advancing. His eyes searched the stage for Stan. Rufus had completed his speech and was acknowledging the reception with power salutes. Stan came up to the mike.

"Thank you, Rufus Graves, Minister of Information, the Black People's Coalition." There was more applause. "Rufus has other commitments," Stan explained, as the militants abruptly exited the platform en masse and headed for their waiting cars.

Derek and his pals wasted no time scrambling onto the rostrum to fill the vacated seats. Stan was none too pleased.

"And now we have a special treat. A musical interlude by the movement's favorite poet and songwriter, Bobbie Bishop, the Gay Balladeer."

Bobbie was all smiles and nods as he leaped onto the platform with his guitar slung over his shoulder. He gave the crowd an "Aw-shucks, howdy!" and chorded right into his first number, "Ain't Staying Home No More," a toe-tapping ditty of his own composition.

Stan eased over to confront Derek. Tyler closed in from the other side. Derek saw them coming and was ready. "This is *my* rally. And I'll sit where I please." Since it would be bad P.R. to have this conversation in front of an audience, Tyler suggested, "Let's go discuss this somewhere a little more private." He indicated the area behind the platform.

"What's to discuss?" whined Derek, who refused to budge. "When the Gay Balladeer closes his set, I'll show you whose rally this is. Right, Stan?" Derek turned a hard glare on the older man. It was meant to intimidate, but it didn't work.

"Sorry, Derek," Stan began firmly. "We talked about it last night, and we're pulling out of GLP. The name's all yours as far as me, Tyler, Joey, and a lot of the others are concerned."

Derek hadn't the vaguest idea of what he was talking about. The speed was making his thoughts race at an incredible pace. "You're damn right, its mine. I worked my tits off to get elected!"

"Yeah, that's it, all right, your tits!" Tyler agreed contemptuously. "What it comes down to Derek is we're sick of your camping queen mentality. When are you going to get real?"

Derek was unimpressed. "Please, I've had enough of your macho crap for one day." He turned to get the approbation of his associates, only to discover that Lourdes and the two new friends were nowhere in sight. Now where are they? He squinted into the crowd. His friends always seemed to disappear when he needed them most.

There were hoots and clapping as Bobbie finished his first number. He found the key for his next song and went right into it.

Derek was getting nervous with Stan and Tyler hanging over him. "Well, all I can say is: if this is a GLP-sponsored event, I'm in charge."

Stan was fed up. "All right," he snapped. "You get up there and tell the crowd that. When you're finished, I'll tell them we're through with you!"

Derek had never seen Stan's temper before, and he didn't like it one bit. "Who needs you? Who needs any of you?" Derek took the offensive. "The hell with GLP! The hell with you all! I'll form my own party. We'll call it…." he sputtered. "We'll call it…. Street Queens! Street Queens…United. S-Q-U!" He'll show them. "Who needs this rally? I'll have my own!"

Derek rose regally; if he had had a fur to throw over his shoulder, he would have done so. The speed had increased his paranoia, and he needed to go somewhere to collect himself. He stomped off the platform without another word.

Stan and Tyler, braced for a major confrontation, were pleasantly surprised. The Gay Balladeer's rendition of "There's a New Day A 'Coming" was highly appropriate.

10

SNICKER WAS NURSING HIS THIRD OR FOURTH cup of coffee at a luncheonette counter not far from the waterfront. At first the counterman had eyed him suspiciously and made him pay after every cup. After a while the Greek decided the scruffy hippie wasn't going to bother anyone or make trouble, so he let him sit there, and the intervals between cups grew longer.

Snicker had dropped by the GLP storefront earlier, but to his surprise it was closed, and a partially ripped-away sign said: RALLY AT CITY HALL. Snicker had been counting on hanging out there, just as he had during the cold winter months when he had no place else to go to keep warm. He got so mad he kicked the door and pulled the rest of the sign down. What a freak show that place used to be, he laughed. Every queen in the world must have passed through there at one time or another. Still, the old storefront was also the setting for fond memories, mostly because it was someplace to go when he didn't want to feel so alone.

Snicker locked himself in a stall in the men's room and was going to prepare a fix, but the Greek got suspicious and sent the dishwasher in to scrub the floor. Snicker dropped a "downer" instead and got back up to the counter to finish his coffee. He huddled at the far corner of the counter, wary of the sunlight that streamed through the plate glass window. He was a night person, and the daylight made him edgy. Like a somnambulist he preferred the soft edges that night lends to the landscape. Snicker put his sunglasses on, and he felt a little better.

How did this happen? he kept asking himself. How did he end up on the street with nothing? At least the last time he found himself on the street he had a partner: Chicken. It didn't seem so bad when you shared hard times with

somebody else. Chicken had understood. He was a night person too. He'd tag
along any where, and never asked a lot of stupid questions—there was this feeling of being together and knowing what the other is thinking without asking.
Snicker had never known anything like it before.

He recalled one night in particular, a night they had dropped acid and
tripped out on the abandoned pier. Running madly about, they made all sorts of
weird noises and siren sounds until every sissy in the place had been routed. For
a moment Snicker was warmed by the memory of the raucous fun time they had
had with the pier all to themselves…

What was he going on about? What made those times so great? Chicken was
just another kid! Some do their time faster than others—that's all…No! That
wasn't right. Chicken was his Main Man. They really got off on the same things.
Without Chicken to take him to the hospital he might've died of hepatitis in that
stinking hotel room on Eighth Avenue.

For an instant it seemed crystal clear to Snicker that his only alternative was
to go back to his sister's in Jersey. But maybe he ought to call her first. If he did
that she'd think up some reason for him not to come.…

No, going back to his sister's was out. He had to be some place private. He
wanted to crawl into bed in a dark room and shut out any sensory impressions
that might invade his thoughts and trigger his demons. He scooped out some
greasy dollar bills from his pocket and counted them. He had almost enough for
a room and a pack of cigarettes. But what about getting uptown? He was too
spaced out to walk or ride the subway. No, he had to take a cab. And what about
another fix? He had to lay his hands on more money.

11

BY THE TIME VIETNAM VET TRAVIS WOODS rolled his wheelchair up to the microphone to make a speech, word had spread through the crowd that the doors to City Hall were opening to admit spectators for the one o'clock Council session. Within minutes there was a long queue running from the barriers protecting the building's entrance and a cordon of anxious looking cops with nightsticks watching the line grow.

Joey and Nicky had gone ahead and were holding places near the front. Soon Tyler came over to join them. "Did your reporter friend make it?" Nicky asked Tyler. It was the first moment they had had together all day.

"Not yet," Tyler shrugged.

"Too bad!" Nicky acidly consoled.

A couple of cops walked past, telling them, "Two across!" Tyler discovered Derek out of nowhere easing into the line between him and Joey.

"Thanks for saving me a place," he said breathlessly. Derek was very spaced-out, and he looked it.

"Hey!" somebody farther down the line hooted. "Get out of there!"

Derek ignored him and calmly waited it out. When no one else spoke up, he figured it was time to thank his benefactors with a big smile. "You won't believe how hard it is to get a taxi," Derek said to no one in particular. He wanted to make small talk whether they did or not. He sure missed his friends. They knew how to laugh when he said something funny. He tried to see if he could see them anywhere; but the line looped around out of sight. The sun was high, and the sparse trees provided little shade. He absently fanned himself with the back of his hand and hummed the tunes he'd danced to the night before. He seemed to have completely forgotten the humiliating confrontation only moments earlier.

The cops watching the line made it pretty apparent by the sour expressions on their faces that they would sooner exterminate the lot and be done with it. A City Hall aide trotted out to confer with several of the police brass. The brass in turn gave orders to the men holding the line. A red-haired lieutenant used a green bullhorn to address the crowd: "We have just been informed by City Hall that seating in the spectator's gallery is limited to 50 seats. I repeat: 50 seats remain in the gallery."

The line was more than 200 deep, and there were loud expressions of disappointment: booing, hissing, and muffled obscenities. Those on the end of the line seemed to be more vocal.

"Now we will let you in one at a time." As the lieutenant said this, two cops opened the barrier slightly and flanked either side of the opening. A third motioned the gays through one at a time, making an audible head count. "One two three four," he droned.

Those in back pushed forward, and several took advantage of opportunities to jump ahead. There was elbowing and shoving, and harsh remarks passed. As each person feared he wouldn't get in because others were pushing ahead, the mob went wild. There was a surge and the barricades fell away. The lawmen were unprepared for the sea of bodies that engulfed them.

Those activists who got through before the police regained the upper hand broke into a dead run toward the entrance to City Hall. An ancient security officer saw them coming and made a vain attempt to get up the stairs and lock the doors. The protesters were too fast for him and he stood by helplessly as they rushed inside. Secretaries and aides lingering in the lobby joking with reporters about "all the excitement" were sent scurrying by the stampeding pack of gays. Once inside, the activists were unsure which way to go, and for an instant the men leading the group faltered. It turned into Tyler's golden moment.

"This way!" he yelled, knowing the direction from a previous Council meeting he'd attended. He broke through the confused ranks and dashed toward the circular marble steps in the center of the lobby. Close on his heels were the 50 or so men who had managed to get past the police and barricades.

Porter Rhodes was small-talking with Father Stiles on the landing when he heard the commotion below. He immediately crossed to the rail and was startled by the sight of scruffy protesters rushing up either curve of the double stair. He instinctively moved to the head of the steps and raised his arms, palms up, to stop them. "Hold on a minute!" he called. "Hold on!"

Many recognized Porter from the meeting the other night and stopped. A few others, concerned about the consequences of their act of defiance, saw Porter as a way of putting responsibility back into the hands of authority. But most were simply awed by the commanding presence he exhibited, as he stood poised in the rotunda with his long arms extended. "What's going on?" he demanded. The boxy suit accentuated his broad shoulders and narrow waist.

"The pigs are trying to keep us out of this meeting!" Tyler flared.

"Well, I think we can work this out before you fellows get into trouble," Porter said as he surveyed the two flanks of strong-looking gay activists.

"All right, you guys!" came a loud authoritative voice from below. "Get down here, and I mean get down here now!" The speaker sounded like a person who was used to having his orders obeyed.

Everyone froze. The activists were caught in limbo between Porter, who was trying to be accommodating, and the policemen, who'd like nothing more than to crack a few skulls.

"We've got the matter under control, officer," Porter called down in a distinct tone of dismissal. "I'm going to introduce these young men to Mr. Mulfreddy, the head usher."

"Oh, ya are, are ya?" the gruff-voiced cop called back. He didn't sound too happy.

"Not to worry, officer," Porter continued. "They've promised me that those who don't find seats in the gallery will leave. Haven't you, gentlemen?"

The activists quickly rang out their unanimous agreement.

"I'll assist Mr. Mulfreddy to make sure things go smoothly," Porter announced graciously, and without further ado stepped aside to show the protesters to the gallery steps. He knew the cops would back down because they knew who he was and who his father had been.

12

IN BED ALICE RHODES WAS A TIGRESS. SHE thrashed and screamed and begged for more. Angus was horny and very obliging. He didn't realize how badly scratched he was until he was getting into the shower and glimpsed his bloody shoulders in the mirror.

When he came back into the bedroom, Alice was another person. She had put on a housecoat and was nervously pacing, smoking a cigarette. Though she didn't say it, he got the feeling she wanted him to get the hell out—and quick. Once more Angus was obliging. He had got what he came for, so he got dressed and made polite small talk. Alice calmly warned him he shouldn't think she made a habit of this and there wouldn't be a next time. She thanked him and showed him out into the service hall.

The drive down Fifth Avenue was a nightmare of stop-and-go traffic and aggressive pedestrians. Angus welcomed the shady, narrow Village streets, and, discovering a parking space on a particularly charming block, he rested for a while. The row of immaculately restored brick houses caught his fancy. As much as he hated to admit it, even in New York City there were nice places to live. He found a gas station and while the tank was filling emptied his bladder. He started slowly driving up and down the streets of the far West Village. He was still determined to connect with Snicker and figured this to be as good a way as any other to begin his search.

His meanderings took him past The Cookie Box and down by the abandoned pier. In the late afternoon, when the trucking firms and meat wholesalers had closed for the day, he parked directly across from the pier and waited.

Soon he realized he'd picked a good spot. There was a steady trickle of single men going in and out of the pier. Some moved purposefully as if they had little time and couldn't dawdle. Others were more casual in their approach and would stroll along at a leisurely pace, then wander nonchalantly inside. Then there were some who would hang around out front for a long time before venturing in. And others would change their minds and not go inside at all. It seemed to Angus that more men were going in than coming out. And though it was apparent what must be going on inside, he couldn't actually visualize it. He tried to think of two men making love, and he recalled the image of two men he discovered kissing in a wooded area behind a highway rest stop. He had come upon them by accident, and in the brief moment before they sensed his presence, he had stared dumbstruck.

He had never really thought about what two men who were sexually attracted did to each other. Sure, he had heard smutty asides about "cock suckers" and "asshole pussy," but he could never quite picture what the words so graphically described. The thought of himself caressing another man was difficult to imagine. He closed his eyes and tried to trace back through his sense memory any instance when he'd been involved in homoerotic activity. In puberty there was the occasional circle jerk with his cousins or neighborhood playmates. The boys had never touched each other, and the whole procedure was more mechanical than erotic.

In high school there was an older guy in town some of his buddies used to visit. They tried to get Angus to come along once or twice, but he didn't have to because he and Sally were practically engaged and having at each other pretty regularly already.

Angus opened his eyes. He could feel someone watching him. He looked around and met the eyes of a stranger: an olive-skinned man dressed in tight chinos and red T-shirt with the short sleeves rolled tightly over his bulging biceps. He met Angus's glance unflinchingly, and with an insolent smile. Angus recognized the suggestive look and turned away. He didn't want to encourage overtures from the man. He was determined to wait it out rather than give-up his vantage parking space. The Latin didn't budge for a long time. He even crossed in front of the windshield to get Angus's attention. Angus steadfastly ignored him—but if he had taken a moment to look closer, he might have recognized the man.

Jose Romano a.k.a. Tequila Sunrise would have known that humpy number sitting behind the wheel of the Impala anywhere. When he'd called and came by the other night, he said he was Chicken's brother, and even then he didn't seem too interested in getting together. Jose gave him the hard cruise just to make sure he hadn't changed his mind. When Angus ignored him, it meant two things: he wasn't interested; and he hadn't recognized Tequila. Jose chuckled over his deception. It was the price he paid to get laid. The less he looked like what he wanted, the better his chances of getting it. He threw the occupant of the car one last surly look, then headed for the pier.

And in an alley not too far from the waterfront the orange tom Samson scents a confused Meow. Samson wastes no time initiating foreplay, and after the ritual hissing and sparring, he mounts her. Her wails of copulation pierce the stillness of the quiet townhouse gardens.

13

AN UNEASY CALM HUNG OVER THE CROWDED spectator's gallery as the City Council meeting got under way. The long rows of hard wooden benches were packed, and there were more people standing along the back wall. Uniformed police officers posted on either side of the entries monitored all comings and goings. The casually dressed gays easily outnumbered the lingering secretaries, City Hall aides, and curiosity-seekers that squeezed in wherever there was room. In the front row, two long-haired boys with their heads together and entwined in each other's arms looked about to kiss but didn't, and returned their gaze to the floor below.

City Council members have little difficulty in dispensing with routine matters when something urgent or controversial is pending on the day's agenda, and since it was such a day, the roll call and old business were conducted with brevity. What couldn't be immediately resolved was set aside, and in no time Porter found himself taking the floor to present his motion for Intro 77. The gallery perked up considerably. Several people applauded; there were hoots and screams. The Council President banged his gavel furiously as the chamber churned with excitement and expectation.

"Well, it's about time!" Derek groaned under his breath. He had arrived with the first wave of protesters but had foolishly abandoned his second-row seat to go to the bathroom. He was none too happy about standing along the rear wall with the rest of the overflow. He thanked his lucky stars he had another upper to pop to keep him going. He was speeding like a maniac, but tried to keep cool so as not to draw attention to himself. From time to time he couldn't resist the urge to make a campy wisecrack, and his remarks elicited stares from a gaggle of straight-looking file clerks and office boys. One of the guys was kind of cute—if you like the type—and Derek tried to catch his eye but to no avail. A couple of the others he caught staring at him. He returned the hostility with his "Fuck-you straights!" look: narrowing of the eyes, a pout, and a quick twist of the neck, chin high. Derek was waiting for one of them to say something. He was ready; he'd let them know fast who *the Diva* was!

Tyler soon established an easy rapport with one of the cops in charge of the door detail and was permitted to go back and forth, no questions asked. One set of officers treating him with deference set off a chain reaction, and many of the cops assumed he was one of the leaders. Tyler looked so much like the kind of guy they could relate to that the cops asked themselves how did a nice kid like that get involved in all of this crazy faggot stuff. The cops truly believed that one day Tyler would come to his senses, or they would never have been so nice.

Tyler pretended to be checking in with the demonstrators when he went outside, but he was really looking around for Shriner, the reporter from *The Record*. The reporter had promised to stop by and do a story, and Tyler was still hoping to give him an interview. At any rate, the sight of so many protesters sticking it out heartened Tyler, even though there was obviously no chance of their getting into the session. He enjoyed the role of spokesman and gladly told anyone who was willing to listen the details of what was happening inside. He even used his influence with the cops to get Stan through. Just as he and Stan came in, Jonah Kersh, another liberal from the Lower East Side, was seconding Porter's motion.

As discussion of the bill got underway, sides were distinctly drawn. There was a noticeable partisanship smoldering. Council members who had pretended to have an open mind on the matter until now found themselves sorting out their allegiances and weighing the most politically beneficial move. Others knew how they must vote because their conscience wouldn't let them do otherwise. And no one was surprised by the heated arguments that broke out.

Councilwoman Pegeen Fitzpatrick was most strident in her disapproval of the bill. "We are opening the very gates of Sodom," she prophesied. Her eyeglasses, suspended on a silver chain around her neck, were like miniature headlights bobbing atop her stiffly corseted breasts. A representative of the Firefighters Benevolent League was given the floor, and he added more fuel to the controversy. "The men in my department along with other city employees would like to go on record as firmly opposed to the passing of Intro 77," he summed up.

There was scattered applause on the floor and boos and catcalls from the gallery. One Levi-clad number jumped to his feet and yelled, "I taught in the public schools for ten years, and I was damn good too!"

Repeated strikes of the gavel resounded through the hall. "Have that man put out," the presiding officer commanded. "The Council will suffer no more outbreaks from the gallery!" The police moved in, and the offending gay was escorted out without a scuffle.

There was a motion to go right to a vote. Father Stiles challenged it: "Before we take a vote, I would like to raise a whole aspect of this controversy that has not been touched upon." He paused for effect then continued, "Not only does it concern our able firefighters'! He nodded benignly toward the League representative "but our teachers and policemen. Namely, the problem of cross-dressing."

A hushed rumble rippled through the gallery.

"Certainly there is no doubt that unwitting exceptions have opened up the ranks of these city employees to so-called 'closet gays,'" the good father emphasized. "But what would happen if all restrictions were lifted? Why, only moments ago I saw a man coming out of the ladies' room! In my opinion, before the passage of Intro 77 can be considered at all, a rider must be added to the bill specifically excepting cross-dressing and other flagrant types."

This suggestion put Derek over the edge. He'd been quietly fuming to himself since Father Stiles began his discourse on cross-dressers, only sharing a hoarse whisper now and then with anyone who cared to listen. But now Father Stiles was addressing him directly, and he had to answer.

"I beg to differ," Derek boomed in stentorian tones that carried clear to the dais and brought the session to a startled halt. Every head on the chamber floor turned toward the gallery. Before the cops could get within reach, Derek continued, "My name is Derek Wiggins. I'm chairperson of the Gay Liberation Party. I would like permission to address the Council." It wasn't quite Kate Hepburn in Cukor's "Pat and Mike" but close.

Tyler's eyes found Stan's; the two friends shared a look of absolute horror.

"Remove that person!" roared the indignant Council president, pointing the gavel accusingly then pounding furiously with it.

All hell broke loose. Derek attempted to escape. He clacked down the gallery steps and pushed his way into a row. Several brave aides grabbed him and held on until the cops got there.

"This is brutal and outrageous," Derek screamed. "I know my rights, and I'll sue this damn city if it's the last thing I do." Derek's voice trailed off as the gallery doors swung closed behind him and his burly escorts.

"One more outburst, and I'll close the gallery!" the president warned testily.

The floor reopened to discussion, but the heat had gone out of the issue. The gallery had grown progressively subdued since Derek's departure. A motion for a roll call vote passed. Tyler speculated that the vote would be unfavorable, and the look on Stan's face said he shared the hunch. As the secretary called each councilor by name, a tense quiet pervaded the chamber. It was measured by the secretary's abrasive pronunciation of surnames and abetted by the increasing margin of negative votes.

Tyler's thoughts began to drift, and his eyes were drawn to the portentous ceiling murals depicting "New York Receiving the Tribute of the Nations." Soon he was admiring the other fine decorative appointments that enhanced the chamber. There was rich oak paneling and crafted mahogany furnishings. Enormous oil portraits of the city's founding fathers dominated the walls. It was a room steeped in history, and he wondered about the kinds of men who had sat on that very dais through the years.

"Helena," intoned the secretary.

The recently indicted councilman from Staten Island pulled his enormous bulk from behind the desk. "No," he declared and dropped heavily into the chair.

"Hernandez."

"No," the meticulously groomed Latin barked.

"Klein."

"No," the gangly attorney moaned emphatically.

"Peterson."

"No!" boomed the funeral director-turned-politician.

"Rhebas."

"Yes!" the retired lady schoolteacher from Brooklyn begged to differ.

Except for the women who have joined their ranks in modem times, many of today's City Fathers are probably much like their predecessors of the last 200 years: sons of aristocrats and well-to-do merchants, or self-made men of immigrant ancestry kicking about in shiny patent leather shoes and crisp custom-tailored suits. Certainly that very portrait of George Washington hanging high on the chamber wall had looked down as benignly on countless other Council sessions.

Tyler read the phrase "Equal and exact justice to all men whatever state of persuasion" inscribed on one of the wall panels and couldn't help smiling at the irony of Jefferson's words.

When the final vote tally was read, numbness descended upon the gallery. Optimism had been high for the passage of Intro 77, and no one wanted to believe the bill had been defeated. They had lost by a mere seven votes, yet it might have been a hundred for all the comfort a near miss gave them. The Council moved to adjourn. As the activists trickled into the corridor and down the stairs, Stan wondered aloud, "What next?"

"We're going to keep fighting," Tyler said resolutely. He gave Stan's shoulder a reassuring squeeze.

As they emerged from City Hall, their supporters greeted them with a loud roar. Word of defeat had already reached their ranks, but they were still a hundred strong, crowded behind N.Y.P.D.-marked barricades, yelling their heads off and waving clenched fists. A spontaneous chant erupted, "WE'LL BE BACK! WE'LL BE BACK!" The sight exhilarated Tyler. Overcome with emotion, he moved into the crowd with his arms outstretched, randomly hugging and kissing his cheering brothers and sisters. He wanted to say something, to say how good their reception made him feel and how today's setback had only strengthened the Cause but the words did not come.

A shimmering band of orange light on the western horizon marked the approach of twilight. A calm settled on the demonstrators as boxes of candles were distributed. The first taper was lit. It was used to light another, and the two each lit one more. The flame was passed to the next four, then eight, and so on until every candle was softly flickering. Tyler hugged Stan as the two men led the procession out of the park. Joey caught up with them and took Stan's hand; they beamed lovingly at one another. Tyler was touched by their display of devotion but shrugged off the sentiment. Behind them, the other candle bearers had fallen into step as they moved away from City Hall onto Broadway. Departing Council members and City Hall staffers paused beneath the portico as the gays marched by. Few spoke, and those who did, spoke in hushed whispers.

The police had rerouted traffic to open a lane for the marchers. A slow moving police car led the way, and at intervals mounted officers flanked the line. The quietly moving demonstrators, their sad faces illuminated by the flame's warm glow, were an impressive spectacle marching up the canyons of Manhattan. Many were visibly shaken; others held tightly to friends and lovers. Here and there a face chiseled with marked determination strode pass. Two muscular men held a banner aloft that read GAY PRIDE NOW AND FOREVER. Disgruntled motorists honked their horns and spat ugly epithets.

Tyler was oblivious to everything but his thoughts.

The struggle ahead was crystal clear. His spirits lifted as an inner voice urged him to further action. He needed a plan, and before the night was over, he'd have one, for sure.

"Tyler! Hey, Tyler. Tyler!"

Someone was calling his name. He turned to see who it was. It was Shriner on the sidewalk walking abreast of the marchers.

"Hey, sorry I'm late," he apologized. "But look," he winked. "I got a photographer."

And just as he said the word—a camera flashed.

14

DEREK COOLED DOWN CONSIDERABLY DURING his confrontation with the City Hall pigs. They dragged him into a windowless room and threatened to charge him on numerous counts of assault and disorderly conduct. There were moments when he was sure he was going to end up spending the night in jail, but when the Council session ended, the cops escorted him out of the building with a warning that next time he wouldn't get off so easy. As he was leaving, Derek saw his former "pals" getting ready for the candlelight march, but he was not going to have any more to do with those *macho* queens. Like he told Stan, he was going to form his own organization. That way he could run things just the way he wanted. He was tired of putting things together and having somebody else steal the glory.

Derek found a subway and rode the train into The Village. He wondered where the hell Lourdes and the rest of his crowd had disappeared to just when he needed them. He checked out Washington Square Park and Christopher Street, two of the usual places they could be found. Unsuccessful, he walked over to the waterfront. Sometimes Lourdes and his buddies hung out on the pier because no one hassled them over there. Bingo! As he approached, he could see Lourdes, Freddy, Nickels, and several of the others sitting out front on the loading dock, camping it up. Nickels saw him coming and signaled Lourdes.

"Well, well, well," laughed Lourdes, spinning around. "Miss Gay Liberation! How'd you make out?"

"Where'd you guys go? Left me to deal with those Boy Scouts all by myself."

"Oh, honey, I couldn't take it another second. Did you see all that hot ass? You'd think with all those humpy numbers there I'd pick me up a piece! Nothing. Who needs those stuck-up sons of bitches?"

"You said it!" Derek agreed. His anger with his friends for leaving him subsided. "Anyway, you know what I told them we were going to do? Form our own organization. How do you like 'Street Queens United'? S-Q-U: SQ-U!" he cackled.

"As long as it don't cost me nothing it sounds fine. I'll be social director," Lourdes winked.

"Yeah, and I'll be the warlord," piped Nickels. Freddy slapped him five, and so did some of the others.

"Honey," Derek said disdainfully. "This isn't a street gang—were revolutionaries! Queers in dresses! We're going to have out own newspaper. We'll show them what this gay revolution is all about."

All the while they were talking, Lourdes was keeping an eye peeled on the traffic in and out of the abandoned pier. He was still planning to get laid before the night was out, but so far he had not seen anyone go in who struck his fancy. He noticed the guy sitting in a car across the street. Now *he* looked like the kind of man Lourdes liked to be handled by. There was no rush. Lourdes knew they all ended up going inside sooner or later. He'd wait.

15

THE CANDLELIGHT MARCH WOUND UP Broadway and across Bleecker Street to the GLP storefront. Stan unlocked the door. To his dismay the lights weren't working. He wasn't surprised. Apparently the light company had finally gained access to the cellar to cut them off. He suspected the landlord had a hand in that. The loss of electricity was an additional blow after the day's major setback.

The disappointed gays, their numbers dwindling, filed in, relighting candle stubs and looking for places to sit. Many had been going since dawn, and the strain and exhaustion were taking a toll on their lowered spirits. Stan lit two kerosene lamps he kept for emergencies and found a flashlight.

"Stan, you're always ready," Tyler said with admiration for his friend's resourcefulness.

In the lamp's glow Stan looked beat. He'd been on his feet most of the day, and his bad leg was hurting. "I think one of us better get up and say something," he shrugged.

"I'll do it," Tyler said. He picked up the portable bullhorn and jumped on a table. Stan directed the flashlight on him.

Tyler banged his foot to get their attention. "I'd like to share some thoughts with you," he said, not sure how to begin.

Some of the group was feeling surly and not easily calmed.

"I'm sick of speeches—let's boogey!" a voice declared emphatically. Several others hooted loud agreement with whistles and catcalls. They needed some way to release all their pent-up frustration.

Tyler raised his eyebrows in exaggerated surprise. He had been undecided about how to start but now found his pin. "Great idea!" he boomed. "Let's boogey." He threw up his hands and gyrated his hips to an imagined beat. The crowd loved it, and a few started clapping in time to his movements.

"I've got a glorious idea!" Tyler declared. "We'll turn the abandoned pier into a giant disco! What'dya say?" There was a roar of approval, laughter, and scattered applause.

Tyler began to describe meticulously the magnificent dance palace that would flourish at the water's edge. He spoke of the incredible sound system, the light shows, and always two disc jockeys for continuous music. The crowd ate it up. Tyler was the focal point of the waves of positive energy they were generating. A feeling of euphoria enveloped his body. He raised his arms and stilled the listeners. He spoke slowly at first, but gradually the words began to flow as if a rich vein had been tapped. Impressions, idea, dreams commingled into affecting oration. There were times he stumbled over a word because an image wasn't clear in his mind—but the pauses were dramatic, and the crowd hung suspended in anticipation.

The experience was exhilarating, and when he was done, Tyler couldn't remember a thing he had said. But that was all right—Shriner, using a Penlite, got practically every word down. There was affectionate cheering and applause. But not everybody was impressed.

"So what do we do until this fantasy comes true?" some spoilsport challenged loud and clear.

"Leave the pier to the muggers and pickpockets!" another suggested sarcastically.

"Yeah!" came a third indignant activist a few feet away. "Somebody got ripped off again last night."

"Last night?" Tyler asked, echoing the curiosity of others.

"At knife point!" continued the speaker with a hint of titillation in his tone. Then he added matter-of-factly, "Some strung out junkie did it."

"That scene at the pier is what's giving faggots a bad name!" someone admonished.

"Converting the piers for community use will clean the area up in no time," Tyler asserted.

"Convert what? Honey, maybe you weren't at City Hall today. I was. They don't even want to give us our rights," someone tried to burst the bubble. "Why will they give us the piers?"

The stinging words of some invisible person in the dark were like a slap in the face. Tyler interpreted this as a personal attack, and he saw his prestige slipping. He had to get back the good vibes at all costs. "We'll close the pier ourselves," he said firmly.

"Close the pier!" a strident voice echoed.

The cry spread like a contagion. "CLOSE THE PIER! CLOSE THE PIER!" everyone started shouting.

"Close the pier!" Tyler repeated emphatically. Once more he was the focus of the crowd's energies: the force was overwhelming. "What the hell are we sitting in the dark for?" he found himself saying. "Let's go liberate the pier—NOW!" He jumped down from the table. He felt compelled to take action. The crowd's enthusiasm was a narcotic on his good judgment; being center stage made him bolder. "Our Movement was born in the streets!" he raved, running toward the door. The others wasted no time following.

"CLOSE THE PIER! CLOSE THE PIER!" they shouted, fanning out into the narrow Village streets. The marauding gays stopped traffic and sent pedestrians scurrying. Their ranks swelled as they swept down Christopher Street. Soon a small army of gay guerrillas marched toward the waterfront.

16

WHEN IT WAS DARK ENOUGH, SNICKER FOUND his way to the pier. He was very spaced out and not sure how he was managing to stay on his feet, but he did, and he kept moving. There were a lot more people around than he cared to see but he went inside anyway and found a resting place on some pilings. After waiting what seemed like a long time, he saw the silhouette of a man enter. It was immediately apparent from the way the guy stood looking around and moving cautiously about that he didn't know which way to go. Snicker figured they were made for each other.

Keeping in the shadows, he edged closer to get a better look at the score. His foot kicked a bit of metal; rolling away, it made a tinkling sound. The guy spun around and strained his eyes in the direction of the sound. Snicker could not be sure if he'd been spotted, so decided to play it casual. He slowly strolled into full view and walked into a nearby shed, hoping to lure the number inside behind him.

Through a broken window Snicker could see that the score had taken the bait and followed. At the threshold the man lingered. The interior was pitch black.

Snicker coughed. When that didn't work, he shuffled his feet against the littered planking. Finally, the score stepped in and stood to one side of the door in complete shadow.

Snicker decided it was now his move, so he began drifting toward the score. He placed himself within arm's reach. He tried to look into the man's face for some feedback, but it was too dark. Snicker hesitated. He wanted the number to touch him first. It would be easier to pick his pocket if the guy was occupied with trying to put the make on him. If Snicker made the first pass, there was always a chance the guy would back off because he was a tease or just not interested or uncertain. Or simply being very cautious.

They seemed to be standing in this position interminably, and Snicker could make out no more of the stranger than before. The man stood perfectly still. His breathing was inaudible. It was driving Snicker crazy. A myriad of suppositions flashed through his mind: Maybe he's a cop? Nah, probably just his first time. So what's he waiting for? I'm here! I'm available! Go ahead! Go for it. You can touch me…yeah, touch me all you want…

Snicker's desperation got the better of him. He impulsively threw caution aside and reached to grope the score. Unexpectedly the man put his hand over Snicker's and closed on it a tight, steely grip. Snicker tried to pull away but the man's hold was firm. Momentarily Snicker froze in a spasm of panic; then he started struggling wildly. Vainly he grappled with the victim-turned-assailant until the man maneuvered Snicker into a headlock.

"What do you want? What do you want?" Snicker begged as he squirmed to free himself.

The score increased the pressure around Snicker's neck. "Calm down," the man said evenly. "I just want you to tell me something."

"You ain't got to break my neck," Snicker pleaded. He strained to break the man's hold. "What'dya want?" he asked plaintively.

"What do you know about Chicken?" Angus asked.

"Chicken?" Snicker echoed. Now he knew who this sucker was. Snicker marveled at the unlucky coincidence. "Chicken," he said again. "I don't see him anymore."

"Nobody does—he's dead. You give him the overdose?"

"Give him what? I ain't give him nothing! Look," Snicker said, assuming a reasonable tone. "Are you 'The Man' or what?"

"That's right!" Angus said, deciding to play the part. "You give me some answers, and I won't take you in."

"You're hurting my neck. Let go. I'll talk to you, tell you whatever you want."

Angus didn't trust the bastard, but he loosened the hold more in deference to his own comfort. "All right, what happened to Chicken?"

Snicker made a big deal out of rubbing his neck and pulling himself together.

"All right, let's have it," Angus growled.

"I'll tell you this much about Chicken: he never listened to me or anybody else."

"You dump him?"

"Hey, man, what'dya you talking about?" Snicker was frightened. How much does this guy know, he wondered? "You gotta understand," he started explaining. "I told him to be careful. He never heard me...."

The night of the overdose Snicker was acting as the go-between in a big drug deal and had managed to skim about a spoon of almost pure heroin off the top for himself. The sight of so much high-grade snow mesmerized Chicken. Snicker left him alone with the heroin. Maybe he shouldn't have, but it would have broken the kid's heart not to leave it and show he didn't trust him. As he returned, Chicken was depressing a syringe pinned to the curve of his bent arm.

"He swore it was only a little taste, but the minute he said that he tumbled over. I tried to catch him. I pulled the spike out of his arm. I kept him walking…"

When that didn't work, he yelled for Marlowe. The old man was no help. He freaked out when it was apparent that Chicken was dead. "We were at a friend's place. I had to get him out of there."

Snicker sobered Marlowe up with coffee, and in the pre-dawn they carried the body out to the street propped up between them like a passed-out drunk. After laying the corpse in the back seat of Marlowe's old Chevy, they looked around to see if anyone was watching, then threw a paint-stained drop cloth over the body. Marlowe wanted to dump the corpse in the river, but Snicker didn't have the heart to do that.

"We brought him over here, and when the coast was clear we carried him upstairs." His voice trailed off.

Angus had let his guard down as he pictured what Snicker was telling him. Seeing that it was now or never, Snicker tried to make a break for it. Angus tripped him, and they fell struggling to the debris-strewn floor.

"Lemme alone! Lemme alone!" Snicker wailed like a cornered alley cat. He managed to break away from Angus and get to the knife in his boot.

"Stay back, motherfucker!" he screamed. "I'll cut you!"

"Gimme that knife," Angus demanded, trying to call his bluff.

"Where's your piece, copper?" Snicker laughed. "You ain't no cop," he opined. He moved closer, cutting the air threateningly. Angus held his ground.

"Gimme your wallet!" Snicker demanded smugly.

There was no telling how long Lourdes and the others had been standing in the doorway listening. When Angus saw them there and saw that Snicker's back was to them, he regained complete assurance. "You sure that's what you want?" he toyed. "I think you're looking for more trouble. What'dya say, fellahs?"

Snicker thought it was the old trick and just smiled.

Lourdes gave a command by snapping his fingers. Nickels and Freddy moved in on the knife-wielding Snicker and effortlessly overpowered him. Freddy grabbed his arms and Nickels took the knife.

"I'm sure glad you guys came along," Angus sighed, trying to size up the rescue party.

"You are very welcome," Lourdes allowed graciously. "Maybe there's some way you'd like to show your appreciation."

"Sure, sure," Angus said, knowing full well what was implied, but pretending he didn't. "Could you give me a hand, I want to get this guy outside."

"What's the rush?" Lourdes hissed. He lit a match, and holding it a few inches from Angus's forehead, slowly lowered the flame along the length of his body. "You're cute," he said appraisingly and blew out the match. "Why don't we step over there for a little privacy," he whispered and boldly groped Angus.

Angus caught the hand in his own and firmly pushed it away. Lourdes jerked his hand free with a throaty laugh and sang languidly, "What ever Lola wants, Lola gets," and took a slow mambo turn. Nickels and Freddy laughed.

Suddenly the night was filled with a low rumbling that was growing louder. At first it didn't sound human, but as the uproar drew closer, shouting voices were discernible, then the thumping of hundreds of feet running in all directions.

17

MAD JESSE WAS DRIFTING OFF TO SLEEP when he became conscious of shouting voices. At first they were far away, and the urge to sleep was stronger. But the clamor was getting closer and louder, and he couldn't shut it out. He opened his eyes and listened. The words were garbled. He crawled into the corner of his littered crib and pulled the rags out of the peephole. The fist-size opening gave him a limited view of the street. There were several figures scurrying about. More joined them, and soon it seemed like hundreds were streaming into the pier. Jesse didn't know what to make of it. The uncertainty made him fearful.

Angus was as confused as the others by the "CLOSE THE PIER!" chant that reverberated all around them. Snicker saw the confusion as a chance to escape and kicked free of his captors. He dived through the broken window and rolled over onto his feet.

Seeing Snicker make a run for it, Angus pushed Lourdes out of the way and followed. Lourdes tried to grab him, but when he failed, he let him go. Angus gingerly climbed over the jagged shards of glass in the window frame. He spotted Snicker running deeper into the pier and began pursuit.

Snicker saw a group of activists coming toward him and veered to avoid them. "Hey!" Angus shouted. "Grab that guy!"

"Everybody out of the pier!" Tyler commanded through the bullhorn. "We're liberating the pier for the community."

Angus ran up to Tyler and Stan. "Look, that guy tried to rob me—he's got a knife," he breathlessly explained, pointing at a swiftly retreating Snicker. "Could you guys help me catch him?"

"You bet!" Stan piped and motioned for the others to join in the chase.

"Thief! Thief!" Tyler bellowed into the bullhorn.

Snicker disappeared through a waterside opening. When Angus and the others reached the portal, they discovered a narrow ledge running along the pier's periphery. A form was visible gingerly making its way up ahead. Angus followed, and the activists stayed right behind him.

Stan's gimpy leg gave on him, and he lost his balance, falling, arms flailing, into the dark oily water. "Christ!" Stan yelped as he paddled around helplessly. "I don't think I can make it by myself. Not with this damn leg anyway."

Angus slipped out of his shoes and shirt and dived in after him. He pulled Stan over to the pilings and lifted him high enough for Tyler and the others to grab hold of his arms and hoist him back onto the ledge. Two others helped Angus. Stan coughed and spat out some water, but he was beaming with immense relief.

"You O.K.?" Angus asked.

"It's great being alive," Stan assured him. "But it looks like we lost that mugger."

"Not to worry," Tyler said. "I'll go tell the others. We'll give this place a thorough search." He was practically gloating at the prospect. They helped Stan inside the pier, and Tyler dashed out to enlist the others. Assent spread quickly through the rallying gays.

"Another mugging!"

"He's still inside!"

"Let's get him!"

Chanting and singing, they dispersed into the pier.

Snicker had hidden himself beneath a rotting storage deck and could hear the activists converging all around him. He was short of breath and sweating profusely. One vigilante came close to finding him when he peered diligently into the cracks and knotholes of Snicker's hideout. He appeared to be looking right into Snicker's eyes, but the overwhelming blackness made the fugitive hard to see. When the vigilante moved on, Snicker tried to change hiding places. He scurried from under some planking and crouching on all fours, scrambled across an open stretch when....

"There he IS" a spotter called like a tripped alarm.

Snicker sprang to his feet and started running. For a split second it looked as if he was cornered, but he flashed on another way out and turned toward an ancient fire ladder bolted to a far wall. The ladder connected to a catwalk leading onto the roof. Chicken had discovered it when he and Snicker were horsing around.

Meanwhile, the squad searching the warren of cubicles and storerooms came upon a cavernous closet. To see inside, one man lit the candle stub he retained from the march. In the quivering yellow light they espied a grotesque gnome who seemed ready to pounce. The bedraggled monster let out a hideous belch and batted its arms. In the panic that seized the activists the candle was tossed. It rolled into a pile of greasy rags and debris that easily ignited.

Mad Jesse pushed unchallenged past the terrified gays. His tenure in the barren pier had expired. He went to collect his belongings.

As the bizarre aberration walked away, the gays quickly recovered. They tried to stomp out the spreading flames, but the structure was old and the dry wood burned like kindling. The best they could do was run for help.

Snicker reached the far wall and began frantically ascending the rickety ladder. Angus and Tyler were among the first to spot him, and without a moment's hesitation they started up behind him. Several more men began the climb, but their combined weight was more than the old ladder could hold. Two rusting bolts near the top pulled out enough to send a deathly jerk along the ladder's length. The bottom man lost his grip and fell the short drop. Angus and Tyler held tight; the rest turned back. Snicker made it safely to the catwalk.

"FIRE! FIRE!" warned scattered cries below.

Angus first then Tyler scrambled onto the catwalk as Snicker disappeared through an opening to the roof. Angus threw a fleeting glance below and saw the gays stampeding the exits. Tyler and he eased themselves onto the roof. A transparent quarter moon shined in the eastern sky.

Angus leaned in close to Tyler and whispered, "You look left, and I'll look right," referring to either side of the sloping roof. The two men edged slowly along the peak, scanning the badly weathered surfaces.

18

THE RAGING FLAMES CONSUMED THE ROTTED timbers like match-sticks. Billowing cones of black smoke darkened the night sky, sending shivers through those who had safely managed to get clear of the burning inferno.

Fear traumatized Mad Jesse. He stood rooted, uncertain, wondering wistful-ly if this was a dream and he would soon awaken. His numbness subsided when the smoke and crackling made the danger evident. He tightened his grip on the shopping bags and fled. The dense smoke made breathing difficult. He ran to an open hatch and leaned out, gasping for air. The awesome drop to the inky waters below sent him reeling backwards. He reached the stairs. His throat was burning and his eyes smarting as he stumbled down the steps, clinging fiercely to his belongings. As he turned the landing, a wall of fire crashed down behind him. Sparks and fiery missiles shot everywhere. Jesse's shopping bags were smoldering, and he beat them against each other, but they burned faster so he dropped them. The heat intensified, and he turned to see how close it was. There was a searing pain at the base at his back, and he reached around to discover his ratty mane aflame. He beat and tore at the burning hair with his bare hands until his fingers were raw and blistering.

Running out of the pier, the human incendiary raced blindly toward the horrified crowd gathered beneath the highway. One man screamed as the burn-ing derelict fell just short of him and began rolling violently against the cobble-stones. A quick thinking officer in an arriving patrol car rushed over with a rub-ber raincoat to smother the flames.

Snicker pressed his face flat against the roof. He was short of breath, and his heart was pounding. He cupped his hand to his mouth to muffle the panting and raised his head to peer across the black vista. He sighted the two figures stalking him. A blast of sirens ripped the stillness. Snicker gouged loose a chunk of roof shingle. As a diversionary tactic he tossed it beyond his pursuers. It made a thump then slid off splashing into the river.

His adversaries fell for the ruse and crossed to the other slope to investigate. Snicker scampered back over his tracks. Angus heard him and gave chase, with Tyler close behind. Snicker got to the hatch and disappeared. When Angus reached the opening, a tongue of flame lashed out at him, and thick smoke started pouring out. He jumped out of the way.

Suddenly there was an agonizing scream and a loud thud. Snicker had taken a misstep and lost his balance. His body, neck broken, lay below in a lifeless heap.

"This way!" Tyler shouted. He knew another way down.

The two men began a desperate race to the far end of the pier, a distance roughly equal to a city block. The roof was badly damaged, and a portion gave way the moment they were safely pass. Behind them the fire was burning in all its glory, giving the sky a garish incandescence.

This had to be the weirdest moment in Tyler's life. He could very possibly die right now, and he didn't even know who this guy was.

"What the heck's your name?" he asked, keeping stride.

Angus laughed and told him. He was amused by the absurdity of the question and touched by the sentiment it conveyed: "Angus."

"I'm Tyler. Pleased to meet ya!"

Introductions had been no sooner made than they reached a fire ladder that brought them down on the river end of the wharf. Several gravel barges were moored. They untied the lines to one berthed downstream and hopped aboard. The barge pulled away from the pilings and was swept along by the water currents. As they hoped, the boat banked into the side of the next pier south, and the two men jumped clear.

Stopping to rest and reflect they were soon enthralled by the splendid devastation taking place across the channel.

19

THE SPECTACLE OF THE BURNING PIER COULD be seen for miles on both sides of the harbor. As sections of the roof collapsed into the fiery abyss, a dazzling display of fireworks sparked the sky. Traffic on the West Side Highway was detoured, and the street below was chocked with stalled cars and onlookers. Two engine companies answered the alarm. Firefighting apparatus was maneuvered into position and hoses clamped to hydrants. Gigantic lassos of white water lashed the unyielding flames.

"I keep telling you there are three people—that I know of—inside," Stan pleaded, keeping pace with a pair of fire marshals overseeing the operation.

"And I keep telling you," countered the more harassed of the two. "The fireboats are on their way. They'll pick up your friends on the river side."

Shriner was close by Stan's heels, taking notes. He couldn't believe how well the story was turning out! He had been hoping to keep it an exclusive, but TV news crews and a photographer from the *other* tabloid had showed up after hearing bulletins on their police band.

"How long you know Tyler?" Shriner got in edgewise.

Giving up on the marshals, Stan responded, "A little over a year, I guess. He's from someplace out west."

Joey let out with an ear-splitting yelp. "Tyler's safe! Tyler's safe!" He bellowed.

His worries alleviated, Stan dashed off in the direction of the hubbub. Ditto Shriner.

The two survivors were dirty and disheveled but not without a certain rugged glamour. They were flabbergasted when the gathering well-wishers hoisted them up on their shoulders and conveyed them through the throng like returning heroes. Angus was smiling and trying to look thankful, but inside he was seething. He wanted to be grateful to the strangers for the concern they were showing, yet he really wanted to get the hell out of there. In his mind all he had done was run for his life. On the other hand, Tyler was a born crowd pleaser. He called out heartily when he saw a familiar face and discreetly gave the rolling cameras his best profile.

No sooner were they set atop a parked car then Shriner made his presence known to Angus. "Say, aren't you the kid's brother—Chicken?" he managed to ask before the excited mob pushed him out of the way.

The TV reporter with his magic wand mike was more successful. "How'd you manage to get out of there?" he fired off.

"We caught a raft," Angus growled under his breath.

"What were you guys doing in there in the first place?" he insinuated.

"We were chasing a knife-wielding mugger!" Tyler spoke up for both of them. "We would've had him too if it wasn't for the fire."

"He took a bad fall from the roof," Angus added to set the record straight. "I doubt he made it out of there."

Shriner was back. "How ya doing, Angus?"

That was it. Angus had had enough. "Stay lucky, Tyler," he told his new friend and crawled off the car.

"Hey, wait!" Shriner pushed after him. "What're you doing here?" All sorts of conclusions raced through his fertile mind.

"You got the story *once!*" Angus flared and pushed the reporter out of the way.

Shriner was learning how to take a hint. No story was worth a punch in the mouth. Screw him. Tyler was the better interview anyway.

Tyler didn't realize for some time that Angus had left. He became absorbed in a rambling and dramatic re-creation of their near miss with fiery death. He turned to Angus for corroboration on a point and discovered his fellow survivor was gone. "Well," he grinned sheepishly into the camera. "Believe me, that old roof was giving way practically under our feet."

Nicky edged in closer. He hoped that Tyler would see him and call him over.

Tyler's mood turned reflective. With the panorama of the burning pier as a backdrop, and the camera rolling, he waxed on about "the growing visibility of gay life in this country," and how "our fight is only beginning." He philosophized, "You know, I see this fire as some kind of a symbol. Let's face it, what was going down on that pier reflected very negatively on this community. But the fire, you might say, is giving us a chance to 'clean up our act,' to make the lifestyle more viable. And like the legendary phoenix, we are going to rise from the ashes." And he almost believed it.

Nicky was sure Tyler had seen him standing there. Then the truth sank in: things between them were over. Nicky soon rationalized that it was for the best, and when you got right down to it, Tyler wasn't *that* hot. Casually he wandered off. He was tired and wanted to go home; and he should probably do something about looking for Meow. But first, he might as well take a look around—just to see who might be interested.

20

STAN SAW ANGUS LEAVING AND FOLLOWED him. A short way from the crowd Stan caught up. "Where you running to?" he asked.

Angus turned around and recognized Stan. The sight of the old veteran limping over with painful determination made Angus's defenses evaporate. "What's there to hang around for?" he retorted, backtracking to meet Stan halfway.

"You did a helluva nice thing back there—don't you want any of the glory?"

"I was promised that once before. And I'm still waiting to collect."

"You saved my life, and I don't even know your name. Did I even thank you properly?"

"The name's Angus. No thanks necessary. I'd expect the same if it happened to me. How'd you hurt your leg?"

"Piece of shrapnel I picked up in Korea. You a vet too?"

"Aye, aye, sir." Angus lackadaisically mustered to attention and saluted.

Stan could tell that Angus was straight. "How'd you end up on the pier?" he asked softly.

"The kid they found here last week, he was my brother. The guy that tried to take *me* off, he was the last person to see him alive; the last piece in a crazy jig-saw puzzle. And I'm no better off than I was the day I came down here and started putting the pieces of my brother's life together. If you let it, this town just swallows you whole!"

"Gulp!" Stan ad-libbed for added effect.

"Gone—without a trace. So I'm getting out of here."

"Well, thanks for passing through. You've touched one grateful soul who wishes you nothing but safe passage—whatever that means for you."

Angus smiled. He was moved by the older man's simple and direct affection and wished he himself could be more open. He was conscious of never letting his tender feelings show and he found himself envying Stan. So much of his life was tied to emotions he didn't understand.

"I don't mean anything by it," Stan began, "but I just got this uncontrollable urge to hug you," and he impulsively wrapped his arms around Angus and gave him a paternal squeeze.

Angus tensed up, but then his thoughts took the weirdest turn. The sensation of being held triggered a long dormant memory. He recalled his own father, and it struck him as odd that the only shared moment he could remember was not a very fond one. It was before Earl was born and just he and Dada were sitting together on the front steps. Something happened, Angus couldn't remember exactly what, but it made him very happy. It could have been something his father said or did, because Angus's response was to wildly clasp his hands about Dada's neck and kiss him on the face. It was the kind of thing his mother would do to him.

He remembered Dada pushing him away roughly explaining, "You're a big boy now. Men don't do that!" Angus wanted desperately to please his father, and there was never cause for Dada to mention it again. His father was afraid or unable to express feelings, and his imprint had come to pervade Angus's relationships. Angus thought of his own youngsters and how they were growing up, out of his life. He couldn't even tell his wife he loved her.

Whatever Chicken's misfortunes, he had left behind a legacy of people who cared about him. The only villain was circumstance. While issues beyond his control had taken Angus halfway around the world to war, a more insidious battle on the home front had claimed his brother. And his death had touched Angus more deeply than Earl would ever know. Stan could feel Angus trembling.

The two strangers parted. Stan hobbled back toward the blazing skeleton, and Angus got into his car. He backed up a side street and drove north until he found an entrance to the elevated highway. As he eased into lane, the orange glow illuminating the sky was framed in his rear view mirror. Finally, Angus stopped looking back.

By daybreak a light rain was falling. Steamy vapors rose over the smoldering heap of twisted metal and charred pilings of the ravaged pier.

THE END

AUTHOR'S AFTERWORD

The depiction of children in crisis in Western literature goes back at least as far as Charles Dickens. His heart-wrenching tales of orphaned or abandoned youths in Nineteenth Century England during the Industrial Revolution later found expression in the redeeming tales of American author Horatio Alger. This writer's stories of poor homeless boys who end up achieving prosperous and successful lives—the American Dream—had an inspirational influence on early Twentieth Century values.

But the phenomenon of "wild" children on the streets of such Western urban centers as London, Paris, Berlin and New York has not gone away and by the 1970's as their legions grew they were being called throwaways: disposable youngsters who for whatever reason have severed ties with their biological families before the legal age of consent.

I was living in New York's East Village at the height of the counter-culture when I got the idea for writing *A Brother's Touch*. The area was (and still is) a magnet for teenagers: runaways, throwaways: kids either pushed out by their families or those who simple found living conditions at home no longer tolerable. The majority comes out of working class backgrounds marked by divorce, violence and economic uncertainty. They are poorly educated, unprepared to care for themselves, and without direction. They are easy prey for predators but they quickly learn to live by their wits on the city's sometime mean and unforgiving streets.

In the East Village were several homegrown storefront outreach centers, even a Catholic priest who turned his apartment into a refuge that eventually grew into an international organization. But even so, many youngsters still fall through the cracks and end up in the half world of drugs and promiscuity, quickly learning that the most valuable thing they have is their bodies and vulnerability.

I observed the progress of several youths: the first days of their arrival as they made their presence known on St. Marks Place. Soon they'd be panhandling, looking for places to crash, abusing drugs and drink—doing whatever it took to forget their pain and survive. I wanted to tell their story and tell it in such a way that when it was placed within the context of larger society, it could be better understood and the impact greater.

A Brother's Touch was written and originally published before the full impact of the AIDS crisis was to change human sexual behavior forever especially in the gay community. The novel is set in a time when safe sex was not an issue, the hedonistic 1970's. The epidemic soon became another pitfall for poorly educated teenagers and young adults.

Early on the book was labeled a gay novel because I choose to set the story in that particular milieu. But I never meant to limit my readership and always hoped to reach as broad an audience as possible. And in the years since its first publication I've been gratified by the number of different and diverse reading lists it has made—from gay studies programs and GBLT support groups to recommendations for young adult readers.

In the years since publication there have been numerous television programs and international films that have tackled the subject. But even with the increased awareness of the phenomenon, the kids keep coming, and society remains pretty much unprepared to help them.

There are of course many success stories of young men and women who beat the odds, survived their street experience and went on to make productive lives. And though many may have surmounted the damage, they continue to live with the scars of that early experience.

A Brother's Touch has been out of print for a score of years but I still receive the occasional letter of inquiry or appreciation so I though it was time to release a Twentieth Anniversary edition, making it available to a new generation of readers. I hope you have enjoyed the book and feel free to share with me any thoughts or feelings the story has provoked.

Owen Levy
New York City, 2001
(Email: Owlwriter16@aol.com)

ABOUT THE AUTHOR

OWEN LEVY is a fellow of the Helene Wurlitzer Foundation in Taos New Mexico, and the Edwin MacDowell Colony in Peterborough New Hampshire, where the Lila and DeWitt Wallace Readers Digest Foundation endowed his residency. A native New Yorker, his fiction, reviews, interviews and articles have appeared in numerous publications. For many years he was a Berlin, Germany-based cultural correspondent.

0-595-22674-4

Printed in the United States
86878LV00013B/78/A